The Thirteenth Disciple

A Requiem for America

Thomas Kirkwood

The Thirteenth Disciple

Before moving to Amazon, Thomas Kirkwood was published by Macmillan, Collier Macmillan (Europe), Donald I. Fine (an imprint of Penguin), Signet (an imprint of NAL), Brilliance (audio), and Stjerne-Spenning (Europe).

***

This novel is a work of fiction. Names, characters, places, and incidents either are the product of the author's imagination or are used fictitiously, and any resemblance to actual persons, living or dead, events, or locales is entirely coincidental.

ISBN-13: 978-1523770243

ISBN-10: 1523770244

For Christina Sostegni

"Whoever fights monsters should see to it that in the process he does not become a monster. And if you gaze long enough into an abyss, the abyss will gaze back into you."

Friedrich Nietzsche

"History is a compilation of events that cannot happen."

Thomas Kirkwood

PART I

CHAPTER ONE

In winter, Colorado County Road 734 ends abruptly at a snow wall thrown up by the plows. A faded yellow sign clattering in the wind reads "Road Not Maintained beyond This Point."

Tim Kelly parked in the small plowed area beside Lisa's Jeep. He got out, stretched and took in the lonely sweep of Colorado's Elk Range. The azure sky of morning had become a gray dome. A major snowstorm was predicted, but clouds hadn't yet blanketed the high peaks. He had plenty of time to make it to John Welton's cabin.

Still, he needed to keep up a fast pace. He'd been late getting out of Aspen. Knowing how punctual he was, Lisa might start imagining bad things.

His heart beat a little faster as he buckled the waist band on his pack and stepped into his cross-country skis. Ten miles up the Slate River Valley from Crested Butte, he was going to enjoy a rare taste of what he once took for granted – privacy.

He poled over the crusty snow and stomped through the drifts at the edge of the parking area. Soon he was gliding along in Lisa's tracks, propelled by a rush of freedom he hadn't felt in years. The burning in his thighs and arms quickly vanished as he settled into a steady rhythm.

The valley narrowed beneath a darkening sky, the wooded slopes to either side grew steep. He could see where avalanches, some recent, had crashed through the pines.

Kelly knew the mountains well from his boyhood in the Northern Rockies – the deceptive calm and serene vistas, the sudden raw violence of Nature that seemed to come out of nowhere. Lisa, though an accomplished skier, had no experience dealing with this type of extreme weather, especially not in the wilderness miles from the nearest outpost.

He'd checked the latest report on snow conditions before agreeing to let her go in ahead of him. Avalanche advisories had been lifted for now

9

and the storm wouldn't hit until later. She had a window of opportunity; she had convinced him she'd be okay. And, like she said, it was important for them to avoid even the slightest chance of being seen together. Lucky, he thought, that winter had come so early this year.

He had planned to take a 15 minute rest at the halfway point, but a brisk head wind came up, slowing his progress and piling drifts across Lisa's tracks. He wasn't worried about getting lost. The valley led like a giant chute directly to the cabin. If he veered off course, he would find himself on a steep, pine-covered slope. Even in darkness, Welton's place would not elude him.

Good thing. This was to be a very special weekend, a tryst that would have taken place months earlier if it wasn't for the image he had to project and protect. Now, at long last, he could drop his guard. Tim Kelly, the nation's second-most-watched cable TV host, passed up his rest stop for the sake of lust.

Now, as darkness fell, the overcast sagged around the base of the peaks. Ragged, luminous seams in the clouds rushed southward, draining away the last pale afternoon light.

Snow began to fall. Icy ground blizzards stung his face and pelted his Gortex parka. But he was all right, he had not cramped up, he'd gotten a second wind. He was in decent physical shape from his daily workouts at the network gym. But it was his need to make this time with Lisa special that carried him beyond the limits of his 46-year-old body.

He was close now, having passed the final landmark on Welton's map – a rotten heap of timbers from an abandoned mineshaft. He told himself to enjoy the sensation he'd been longing for, the sensation of being completely alone. Easier said than done: his incessant worry about deadlines and interviews stalked him through the immensity of the stormy night.

He supposed he'd spent too many years in the limelight, too many years under the daily pressure to perform. An adoring public and a hypercritical group of network executives . . . Free at last, he whispered to himself, free at last. Yet Tim Kelly felt as he always did, felt as if he was being watched.

***

The man turned off Washington Gulch Road and gunned the raised truck up a steep, icy path. Even with his snowmobile trailer in tow, the four-wheel drive with studs was unstoppable. Hell of a machine, this new diesel. The guy beside him better not bang up his truck while he had it. He'd also better be waiting where he was supposed to be after the job.

10

Bouncing and plowing through the drifts, the truck devoured the final stretch of path. He parked behind a craggy rock formation where his rig could not be seen from the road. The two guys unloaded the snowmobile. Then the passenger got in the driver's side and drove the truck away.

Night was closing in and the snow kept coming down harder. It wasn't deep yet, maybe five or six inches. He didn't need his snowshoes to walk to the observation point, but he would sure as hell need them before morning.

He crouched on the promontory that offered the best view of the turnaround at the end of Washington Gulch Road. Focusing his field glasses, he could make out three trucks, all of them hitched to snowmobile trailers.

He was anxious to get going, but he knew the police came by in the evening to make sure no one was lost on Anthracite Mesa. He would have to wait until he confirmed that all of the snowmobilers had made it back to their rides before he moved.

When the cops finally showed up around seven, the night had become a howling vortex of wind and snow. There was one truck still in the parking area, one goddamn truck. A cop jotted down its license number. His buddy walked over to the police Bronco to use the radio.

The man felt a flash of rage. He had too much at stake to have his plans wrecked by some big city idiot who'd gotten his ass lost in a blizzard.

He needn't have worried. A faint circle of light appeared on the mesa, bobbing through veils of blowing snow. The cops' headlights weren't giving him much of a view, so he tried out the high-tech night vision goggles he'd brought along.

He watched a big-inch Arctic Cat burst out of the soup. Its middle-aged driver clawed at his frozen beard and shook hands with the cops. The cops lectured him for a while, one of them gesticulating like he was seriously pissed. Then they helped the dumb bastard get his machine onto his trailer. Both vehicles drove off, leaving him alone with the night, the blizzard, and the prospect of a serious score.

***

"I don't remember when I've felt better," Kelly said, pulling off his cross-country boots. "I was beginning to worry we'd never make this happen."

He heard the cork on the champagne bottle pop. Lisa came close and put her arms around his neck.

The fire crackled in the stone hearth. The storm hammered noisily at

11

the north wall but couldn't get in, making the cabin seem even cozier.

Kelly wanted their first time to be on the heavy rug in front of the fire. The image of Lisa's blonde hair touched by the golden light, the thought of her cries mingling with those of the wind, made him forget his other life. He finally started to relax. She was everything he desired: young, brilliant, beautiful, willing.

She handed him a glass of champagne. They toasted.

"I'm afraid, Tim," she whispered.

"Afraid? You live in Manhattan and you're afraid of *this*?"

She curled up beside him on the sofa. "Not of being here, silly. It's your cell. I know it's going to ring. Remember that night in Bangor we thought we'd finally managed? You've never been out of Bernie's reach. Not once since I've known you. I can feel it, Tim. He's going to try to find you."

He brushed a kiss across her lips, nothing more. He wanted to drag out every delicious moment of anticipation.

"You can stop being afraid." Kelly laughed. "I left the phone in Bernie's suite. If he's a big enough prick to call me, it'll ring in his upstairs bath. And even if I had glued the thing to my ear, it wouldn't matter. There's no coverage out here."

She suppressed a grin, playfully put a hand over her mouth. "Tim, coverage or not you shouldn't have left it at his place. He doesn't appreciate pranks, and we both know the network's policy on being incommunicado. Bernie's going to be CEO of the entire group soon and –"

"And?"

"And," she whispered, "I'm glad you did it."

They laughed. "Listen," Kelly said, "if I get fired we'll come back here and live happily for the rest of our lives."

A shadow passed over her face. "We won't, Tim, and you shouldn't joke about it. I know how much you love your kids. You'll never leave Beth. I've accepted that."

"You're –"

"It's all right. I want us to be glad for what we have. We're talking too much. We can talk in New York. Come. Hold me."

***

As a master tracker and genius of improvisation, the man had at first objected to using a military GPS SPS device. It was, he supposed, a matter of professional pride. He always got where he was going and always got back, whether he was in the jungles of Columbia, the deserts of Iraq, or the mountains of Afghanistan. He'd carried out dozens of missions in every possible condition and, after his retirement from the Army, even led rich doctors who'd become climbers up K2. The area around Crested Butte was a joke.

But tonight he had to admit he was glad for the help, glad that he and his professional pride had been overruled. Now that visibility had dropped to 50 feet *with* night vision, he could let GPS technology do his long-range navigation while he kept his eyes peeled for drop-offs, avalanche chutes and trees.

He inched ahead, the sound of his muffled engine scarcely audible in the storm. He kept his speed down, which wasn't his way of doing things, and forced himself to be extra cautious. As they had stressed, you didn't get Tim Kelly delivered to you on a platter every day.

Well, these guys didn't need to worry. He'd do what they said, but even if he'd taken on the mission as a challenge and not a paid job, he wouldn't have blown it. He was the real thing, a trained professional with an uncanny instinct for sensing and avoiding danger. However he snuck up, fast or slow, Kelly wasn't going anywhere tonight.

***

She was stretched out beneath an afghan, sleeping peacefully. Her hair was tousled, her lips slightly parted. The embers in the fireplace cast a rosy glow across her cheeks. Kelly had never seen a more beautiful woman. In his case that was saying something.

He propped himself on an elbow and poured what was left of the champagne. He thought about getting up and putting another log on the hearth, but his legs were weak. Instead he rolled over, kissed her hair, slid a hand beneath the afghan and ran his fingers across her belly and thighs. She moaned and reached for him. This time he was going to make it last until morning – and hope morning never came.

***

When he reached the coordinates programmed into his system, the man parked his snowmobile beside a tree. The cabin was supposed to be a quarter mile away on a predetermined compass heading. He strapped on his snowshoes, slid an ax out of the mounting brackets on the side of the snowmobile and patted the 9mm. Glock in the breast holder under his parka.

The wind howled and the snow fell in blinding sheets. He walked as fast as he could in the unwieldy snowshoes, checking his compass every few steps with a tiny flashlight. He wasn't more than several yards from bumping into the log wall of the cabin when he saw light. It was coming from a window frozen halfway up. He peeked inside. A man and woman were stretched out under a blanket in front of the fireplace. An empty bottle of champagne and bent iron poker stood on the stonework. No gun in sight. These kinds of people probably didn't believe in guns, so there was a good chance they were unarmed. Shaking his head, he took off his snowshoes.

***

They were snuggling happily beneath the afghan laughing about who had the energy to fix dinner when a deafening crash sounded at the front door. Lisa screamed and leaped to her feet. A second and third crash shook the cabin.

Kelly threw her the afghan and grabbed the poker. He was on his haunches reaching for his clothes when the fourth crash sprang the lock. The door flew open, driven wildly by the gale. Shards of splintered wood swirled and skittered around like debris from a tornado. The door banged against the inside wall, bounced back as if it would close, then blew open again, propelled by an icy blast of wind and snow.

"It's a bear," Kelly shouted. "Shut yourself in the john!" He jammed the poker in the red hot coals.

Lisa tried to scream but nothing came out. A man wearing a down parka and stocking cap stepped into the room with an ax, propped it in the corner and smiled. His snow-caked beard was brittle and cracked like porcelain. His face blazed red from the cold. But he did nothing to hide himself, nothing that would prevent them from recognizing him if they got out alive.

Kelly started for the poker.

"It's not hot enough yet," the man said calmly. "Don't waste your energy."

Kelly nodded and left the poker where it was. The intruder, he thought, was at least talking. Maybe there was hope. Just keep him talking, don't make him mad.

"Lisa, it's okay. He obviously needs shelter. He probably didn't know there was anyone in here. Look, whoever you are, would you please shut what's left of the door. We'll make you a hot tea."

"I don't believe it," the man said, still smiling. "You're a nice guy, just like you come off on TV. None of that lame shit. You know, I really liked the guy. Got my ass tricked. That usually doesn't happen. But the image is everything for you media people and you're good at seeming to

14

be someone you're not. Good to find out sometimes the image is the real thing.

The intruder sounded intelligent enough. He'd put his ax down and told Kelly not to upset the situation by grabbing a hot poker. They were going to be okay. "Lisa . . . Lisa, would you mind heating up some water."

"Don't bother, miss. I've got a thermos outside, double-insulated. I'm actually real sorry about this, especially seeing that Kelly's not a fake but a decent sort of guy. But some things just gotta go down. This is one of 'em."

"Care to be more specific?"

"I'm afraid I've gotta kill both of you before I leave. So don't get your hopes up if I hang out a few minutes."

Lisa seemed paralyzed. She stood where she was beside Kelly, staring at the stranger but unable to talk. He needed her to talk, needed her to add some charm or softness or something to the mix, anything that would win them more time. But a quick glance at her told him he was on his own.

"Look, you could at least explain to us why you're here."

"To meet a famous guy. No, actually that's not it. We're talkin money. Sorry, real sorry, but I need to get this done now. Wanna kiss the lady a last time? I would. She's plenty hot."

"If it's for money, be reasonable. However much you're getting, I can give you more. A phone call when this storm ends and it's done. Transferred wherever you say. Then you leave without doing something you'll get caught for and spending the rest of your life in prison. Sounds like a smart decision to me."

"Yeah, right. And if you don't die tonight, they'll kill me. I'll take my chances."

Kelly swallowed his panic and forced himself to stare the man in the face. "I want you leave my companion out of this. This is between you and me – and the people who sent you."

"True enough," the man said. He drew a pistol from his breast holster and turned it over in his hands as if reflecting on whether he should use it.

So much for the plan Kelly had been trying to put together. The ax wasn't his only weapon. He gestured for Lisa to leave the room, but she stood there clutching her afghan like a child with her favorite blanket.

"Lisa, go up to the loft while he and I come to an arrangement."

"Just a minute, buddy," the man said, "It's not *entirely* between you and me yet, not with her up in the loft. We'll have to change that." He raised his pistol and matter-of-factly shot Lisa in the forehead. She

15

dropped to the floor with a sickening thud. *"Now* it's between you and me. Not that it makes any difference."

A fresh blast of wind-driven snow blew into the cabin.

Kelly cried out and rushed to Lisa, leaving the poker in the coals. While he held her lifeless body, the man strolled over to the hearth. He tapped the poker with his gun.

"You were hoping to use this on me?" he said. "Sorry to disappoint."

Kelly buried his face in Lisa's blood-soaked hair and wept. He had no more illusions. From the corner of his eye, he saw the gun being trained on his head. He didn't move, didn't flinch. He couldn't do much about the tabloids and the cruel way his wife would learn about Lisa. He couldn't do much about the damage his dying this way would do to his reputation among the millions who admired him.

About all he *could* do was accept death with dignity, staring right into the muzzle. Slowly he brought his head around. He wanted to ask the stranger one more thing before he died. He wanted to ask, but the man pulled the trigger before he got the chance.

***

Take anything of value. Then burn the place down like they'd told him to do. Get good and warm while he raked the coals from the fireplace onto the floor and made sure the blaze had taken hold in some of the main beams. Pitch the Glock, which they'd somehow managed to register in Kelly's name, into the growing conflagration. A fight, a fire – that's what the investigators would conclude if they got that far. Otherwise they'd chalk it up as another backcountry burglary. It was a good plan with no loopholes he could see. It was also the biggest haul of his life. He would have been a fool to pass it up.

The storm had gotten worse when he got back to his snowmobile. But it sure as hell wasn't dark anymore with that cabin fire roaring like an exploding ammo dump a hundred yards away. He put the ax into its mountings, climbed aboard and started the engine. Wiping the snow off his night vision goggles, he dialed the coordinates into the GPS device that would take him back to his truck. Everything set. Before dawn he'd be ready to begin his new life.

***

Once he came out of the long narrow canyon onto the mesa, he hit the gas. No obstacles out here, nothing like speed to express his exhilaration. He'd used machines a lot like this civilian beaut during his military days. No doubt he could hold it at redline plus a thousand in top gear. What a feeling to do it now. He was still accelerating, still high, still feeling the rush, when he flew over the edge of the gorge at a speed his gauges couldn't register.

CHAPTER TWO

"I want you to go up there," Aunt Lilly said. "Find an honest contractor, keep an eye out for the usual scams and stay until you have the permits in hand. Beau, listen to me. They're not bluffing this time."

"Why don't we just call, Aunt Lilly? They must have a Better Business Bureau or something. It's not a good time for me to leave."

"Beau, darling, you'll enjoy a change of scenery and a challenge. You haven't been out of Louisiana for a long time. You're depressed. All you do is mope around."

"Mope around? I'm trying to figure out the rest of my life. You call that moping around?"

"I do when it goes on for eight months." Aunt Lilly put on another coat of lipstick. Her gold bracelets jangled when she powdered her cheeks. A stranger might have thought she was about to storm out of the room in frustration. But Beau knew better. She had raised him since he was ten and not once had he seen her go anywhere until she got her way.

"Well, dear," Aunt Lilly conceded, "even if moping is the wrong word, you know what I mean. If you don't get on with something soon, you'll still be figuring out what you want to do with your life when they lay you to rest."

"A pleasant thought."

"Beau, I don't mean to be contrary, but you've got to do something that makes use of your talents."

"I'm helping Fletcher build houses."

"You're also thirty years old and a former football star at Ole Miss – with a Masters in Journalism from Vanderbilt, in case you've forgotten. I don't think part-time carpentry makes use of your talents. Getting the permits will. And who knows? You might just figure out your future in the process."

"I wouldn't bet on it."

Lilly ignored him. "Beau, we've been able to lead a privileged life because of my painted ladies, which will someday be yours, someday soon. They need attention now and I'm too old to give it. That leaves you."

"What in God's name are you talking about?"

"I want you in Aspen to oversee their restoration. As I told you, they've been condemned by the city."

"You want me in Aspen *when*?"

"This week."

"Aunt Lilly! It's winter up there! What's the rush? You make a fortune off skiers every year even if the places are falling apart and the management company is stealing you blind. I'll go this spring. You have my word."

"Sorry, dear. We have to start now or we won't finish by the deadline. A lot of the work listed in the order addresses the interiors. A crew can work inside even if it's ten below. I've also heard of builders up North who work *outside* all winter. The management company is just going to have to move the people they've already booked."

"I'm not buying it, Aunt Lilly. We've been given condemnation deadlines as far back as I can remember. There are other obvious reasons you want me to freeze my ass off."

"There aren't. The difference this time is that there are buyers waiting in the wings for the city to seize our ladies. If that happens, our compensation will be next to nothing. Then the city will sell what it's stolen from us to a party that is both willing and financially able to renovate. You need to trust me on this, Beau. I've already had Edgar go over their order. It's valid, and he believes it would stand up in court. So we're about to lose properties worth millions if they aren't brought up to the Historical Society's standards by March 31st – and the larger part of that loss will ultimately be yours."

Beau walked over to the window and looked out on Lake Providence. What was his problem, anyway? Aunt Lilly might be right. A trip to some faraway place might be exactly what he needed. And even if it wasn't, he had a duty to contribute to the family business that had given him so much.

He felt happy to have come to a decision that would end the tiff on a positive note. For all the arguing between him and his aunt, there wasn't a person in the universe he loved more. He hoped she knew. "Okay," he said, hugging her gently. "Okay, I'll do it."

"Don't mess up my hair," Aunt Lilly said. "I just had it done this morning."

"Did you hear me?"

"Of course I heard you, darling. I knew you wouldn't let me down. And it's not like there's nothing in this for you. Beau Wellington the Third, if you succeed you will be a wealthy man. I've had the deeds to the houses put in your name. Dorothy Mae and the Crones will think you struck oil."

"But Aunt Lilly, you can't just give me –"

"We'll talk about it at supper. Run along now. Take your truck over to Johnny's and tell him to make sure it's ready for the trip. I'll have Shanella press your things and pack your bags. I'd like you to leave in the morning."

***

So much land, so little to see. Beau pulled into a truck stop somewhere in the middle of Kansas and went inside for coffee. He didn't know how the truckers he joined at the counter stayed awake. In the South, where he'd always lived, there were trees and lakes and other stuff to keep you halfway alert. If you got sleepy, you turned off the Interstate and drove on two-lanes. Something always jolted you out of your daze. Maybe it would be a possum and her babies waddling across the pavement, or a drunk with one headlight coming at you head-on down the wrong side. Maybe it would be a shanty church so close to the road worshippers had to watch where they stepped to avoid a premature trip to the promised land, or an antebellum plantation home rising out of the ground fog like a ghost from the past. You didn't need to drink bad coffee till you pissed your pants to keep from slumping over at the wheel.

He thought for a moment about staying in this forlorn place for the night, but swarms of fat black flies in the fluorescent lights, paper napkins stuck to the greasy counter and truckers who didn't seem too friendly made him think again. He paid, wandered out into the mild night, filled his tank, slapped himself and did a few stretches.

Warm, he thought, slamming his door shut. How the hell could it be warm in early December this far up north? He'd read about Fall blizzards closing I-70 and had actually seen one in Denver on Monday Night Football. But there wasn't any storm within a million miles of here, just a clear night and dead fields stretching as far as the eye could see. Sometimes the fields were flat as a table top; sometimes they undulated in mile-long mounds, but they never stopped glowing in the pale light from the stars.

He didn't like it here. Something about Kansas was spooky, especially after the sun went down. It was supposed to get dark but it didn't. Nothing ever changed, not the light, not the landscape, not the road. A sign drifted through the beam of his headlights: Denver 390 miles. Those wagon trains of settlers that crossed this land long ago had it good. No truck stops where the big guys inside greeted anyone who talked different with a scowl; no signs that lied about distance.

He switched off the country music crackling through his radio. Thoughts and memories replaced the static as the night wore on. He really didn't have a clue how he was supposed to get the permits Aunt Lilly had sent him to get. But at least she'd given him a name at some sort of historical society. She didn't know any more about the problem than he did, just that their painted ladies were going to be seized if he didn't do whatever the city or state or feds wanted done by the end of March. He drifted onto the shoulder, swerved to miss a bridge abutment, switched the radio on, listened to more country whining, switched the thing off again and vowed to pay more attention to driving. But his mind had a will of its own and quickly got hold of his thoughts.

Their so-called painted ladies. Four Victorian houses near the Aspen town center. How strange, he mused, that almost half of his aunt's considerable income came from those places, places that no one still alive in the Wellington family had ever set eyes on. How strange that they'd been owned by a Southern lady from Louisiana who'd probably never seen snow – and now were his. He hadn't even learned of their existence until after the passing of his grandmother, Belle.

He was a teenager then, playing tailback on the high-school football team and trying to get laid. Victorian houses were about the last thing on his mind. His grandmother's life was another matter, or would soon become one. She had lived until he was sixteen. Everyone liked Belle, but with him it was different. He'd always had a special place for her in his heart.

About the only time she was strict was when she gave orders to the kitchen help on how to serve the fried chicken and mustard greens. Sometimes, when she was having bridge parties, he'd peek into her parlor with all the antiques and flowered sofas. She'd see him and invite him to come inside and greet the ladies he'd known all his life. He couldn't do it because the moist cloud of perfume made him gag. He never told her this, and she never scolded him for disobeying her and disappearing down the hall. In the kitchen before the parties were mounds of whipped cream he

21

wasn't allowed to stick his finger in. But he did anyway, sometimes twice. When Belle caught him, she shook her head, took two silver spoons out of the drawer, gave him another taste with one while she repaired the damage with the other.

He was trying to remember how the whipped cream had tasted as a kid when he drifted onto the shoulder again. That made him pay attention to the road . . . but not for long. There was something about those endless glowing fields that made him feel tired, almost drugged. They put him in some kind of a trance that opened the long-sealed vault of his memory.

When Belle died unexpectedly, the whole family came to the funeral, from Yazoo City across the river, and from faraway places like Dallas and Atlanta. Everyone cried in church, and he had even shed a tear. But the sadness lifted in time for a catered lunch at Belle's home. When they'd had their fill of all the fabulous dishes, when the plates and platters had been cleared to make way for dessert, Beau started to nod off. Aunt Lilly revived him with a lightning-quick whack of the butter-knife to his knuckles.

He realized he was nodding off at the wheel again – without Aunt Lilly to keep him awake. He'd better pull over and take a short nap or he might never get out of this place.

***

He didn't know how long he had been sleeping when the flashing lights of a police car woke him and he found himself blinking out the side window into the face of a beefy cop.

"Get out."

"Okay. Just a second." Beau reached across to open the glove compartment for the registration he assumed he'd need.

The cop pulled his revolver. "I said GET OUT. Don't touch that glove box."

A second cop was behind the lead guy now, hand on his holster.

Beau opened the door and stood unsteadily while the two men looked him over in silence. Better to keep quiet, he decided, than try to say something friendly that might backfire in this strange land.

A couple of giant semis thundered by, whipping him with wind and gravel. "Walk that line," the first cop ordered.

"I am not drunk."

"Yeah, right. Maybe you got a trunkful of weed. Bring me the breathalyzer, Aimes."

An unpleasant hour of explanation passed before Beau was moving

22

again. He wanted to reflect on what had just happened, but the memories of his youth wouldn't let him. His mind returned of its own accord to the funeral dinner, and he listened as if he were there to groaning chairs, chatter from the kitchen and softly humming ceiling fans. Then the stories of Belle's life began. And what stories they were! His very proper grandmother hadn't been so proper after all. After her husband died, she'd left her kids with friends and taken off on a road trip with a married man! She'd gone out West with him, gotten as far as Aspen, a ghost town he swore would become a fancy ski resort one day, bought some properties for a song and came home alone on the train.

He checked that he was in the middle of the right lane, glanced in his rearview mirror for cops and returned to his reverie . . .

"You can't blame her," Dr. Provine said. "She'd come down from Memphis on a riverboat when she was sixteen. She was already a real beauty, I'm told, and she looked marrying age. That must have been true. In her first month in Lake Providence, she got proposed to seven times."

"But just one of those proposals was worth anything," Mattie Palmer said.

"You don't know that, Mattie," objected Dr. Provine. "She rejected my Dad and, if you ask me, she would have been better off accepting. But she *was* a little young. She was still climbing trees and playing hide-and-seek. When she gave Dad the thumbs down, she told him men and marriage didn't interest her and never would."

"But she must've got married," Beau said, now a full-fledged member of the conversation. "If she hadn't . . . well, if she hadn't my Mom and Aunt Lilly wouldn't have been born and I wouldn't be sitting here . . . isn't that right, Doctor?"

"Yes, son. Of course it is."

Aunt Lilly pushed her lemon chiffon cake aside. "Stop your sniggering, Essie Pringle. I want one thing understood by all of you. Nothing scandalous happened. Belle's Dad left Memphis for a quiet life in the country because of his health and his bad luck in business. Belle worried about him all the time. So what did she do? She married a man twice her age, hoping to earn the family some money and respect. It was the good Christian thing to do.

"Before John Edward passed away, he gave her four children. That's how we *all* got here. But the little girl in Belle never went away, not even when she was thirty. On the day her husband died, no one could find her. She was in her treehouse in the big oak out back. She loved her kids, I know that, but I guess she hated the work involved. It wasn't a problem. John Edward had increased the help by six in his will. They were all mothers to us.

"When she met this Carl person, she'd been widowed for a long time. She fell in love with him and expected to marry him. When she took her *scandalous* trip with him to the Rockies, she went to look at a few investment opportunities Carl swore by. Well, the car trip must not have gone so well because she came home alone. But the man evidently wasn't a total loser. She made those investments. We've never seen them but we've been living off them ever since."

***

The sun was coming up behind him as he drove. He was getting close to Denver now, so close he could make out the towering white peaks in the distance. He was about to stop for gas when he noticed something really odd. Several of the cars coming toward him had snow on them. He turned off the Interstate, ate a big breakfast and asked the guy next to him how it could be sixty degrees when all that snow was on the cars. He found out about the big storm in the mountains and decided to get snow tires before heading up there. And he learned something else, something he wished wasn't true. Tim Kelly, his favorite cable newsman, had died in that storm.

CHAPTER THREE

From his corner suite on the 12th floor, FBI Special Agent Randall Connor looked out on the gray December morning. New York at its best. Wet garbage festered on the sidewalk, frenzied honking pierced the hotel's soundproofing, wind gusts blasted the wall-to-wall windows with a frigid mix of rain and sleet. He stood naked before the entire city, feeling at once smaller and more powerful than he was. It was an oddly pleasant sensation he hoped would linger.

Was any of this improper? Not that he cared but his ex-wife, Betty, would have. He squeezed his 260 pound torso into a terry-cloth hotel robe to escape her reproachful stare; or, rather, the stare he imagined. Connor had been seriously in love only once his entire life. Not with his ex but with a fugitive from the women's prison near Sing Sing named Kristýna Sondheim. Yet it was Betty's eye that traveled across canyons of time and space to make sure he felt her loathing. Why this was so he had no idea, but the fact that it happened nudged him closer to a belief in the subconscious. It also improved his relations with the Bureau's shrinks.

Well, he thought, enough about weather, garbage, noise and the semi-occult. He wasn't here to look back but to tackle a future assignment Washington considered of critical importance. He hoped he was up to the job, hoped the unpleasant beginning of his stay wasn't an omen of things to come.

Randall Connor was Deputy Director of the Los Angeles Field Office. Yesterday, his flight to New York in one of the Bureau's jets, with a three-hour time change and two stops for refueling, had not arrived until after dark. Exhausted but starving Connor immediately dialed up room service. Twenty minutes later someone rang him back to tell him the kitchen had been unable to fry his fish. He tried to explain with a little humor that growing up in Memphis you never developed a taste for anything that wasn't fried . . . especially fish. Too late.

He was still conversing with the receiver when his dinner arrived. The fish, some bizarre species he had never seen, was half raw with its head still on.

"Take this thing away," he ordered. "It belongs in the lobby aquarium."

While the room service girl gawked at him in disbelief, he checked off the items he wanted for his early breakfast. "And make sure the coffee is Maxwell House. Understand? Casa de Maxwell."

The girl, who looked Puerto Rican, spoke perfect English. "Sir, I'm afraid this establishment does not serve 'Casa de Maxwell.'"

Connor stuffed the ten-dollar bill he had readied for a tip back into his wallet and turned away. He waited for the door to close before unleashing a torrent of invective. The anger management course he had been required to take seemed to be working. Until now, anyway.

***

The short ride to the New York Field Office at 26 Federal Plaza might have offered Connor a chance to think about how he wanted to approach the Director; instead he slept. Arriving on the third floor, he was escorted without a moment's wait to conference room 21. At a stout mahogany table, rising to greet him, was Kenneth Hatcher, one of the few FBI people he got on well with.

The two men shook hands, and Connor uttered a few uncharacteristically friendly words. It had been a long time since he had seen his colleague: the end of the Sondheim affair, to be exact.

Connor, who had packed on 30 pounds in the interim, hoped he wasn't the only one in the room to show signs of aging. But Hatch, to his irritation, looked as he always did. Something was wrong with the man. He never put on weight, never lost hair, never changed his tasteful but conservative dress, never even tried another brand or color of shoes. Connor doubted he had been born in a birthday suit. He had probably entered this world wearing silver wire-rimmed glasses, a white shirt and a light blue tie.

"Jesus, Hatch, have you discovered the source of eternal sameness?"

"I take care of myself, Randall. You should too."

"I started my diet last night."

"Good to hear, *amico*."

Hatch might be indestructibly normal, thought Connor, but he was also a top-notch agent. He had a quality sorely lacking in the Bureau: heart.

26

When they worked together, Mr. Normal provided an effective counter-weight to his partner's mercurial mood swings. And that exotic characteristic of his, heart, always seemed front and center when most needed. Now was such a time, and Hatch did not disappoint.

The Field Offices on both coasts had switched to Starbucks or some other undrinkable Yuppie brew. Hatch knew Connor's preferences from years together in the field; he also knew his partner's black moods when those preferences were not met – and his partner knew that he knew.

But who could say for sure, Connor mused, if the miracle he had just noticed was a product of Hatch's self-interest in which heart played no role? That thought nipped itself in the bud when he realized he didn't give a rat's ass. Salvation lurked in the can of coarsely ground Maxwell House on the drink table, a one pound monument that moved him more than the *Pietà*.

"You know, Hatch," he said, "it's the little things that tell you who your friends are. Screw all the fancy words. You've just saved my morning."

"Our morning," Hatch corrected.

When the two men sat, Connor sipped gratefully at the first real coffee he had had since leaving L. A.

"So, tell me, what is it Forsythe has planned for us?"

"No idea," Hatch said.

"Okay, I understand you can't share what you've been told with a security risk like me. But still – it's a little annoying."

Hatch laughed. "Randall, I honestly don't have a clue. You know Forsythe likes secrets, especially when they serve no purpose."

"I wouldn't believe just anyone, especially not a guy who sounds like he's been silenced. In fact, I don't know if I'd believe *anyone* besides you; and I might not believe you either."

"Well, Randall, thank you for the profiling. The whole thing doesn't matter anyway. What I have been promised, and what I happen to believe, is that we'll be brought up to snuff this morning. Given the lack of progress I've made on the Keenan case, I wouldn't be surprised if the Director is recreating the team responsible for his promotion, the Sondheim team."

"You and me in charge, no bureaucratic meddling?"

"That's my gut feeling. By the way, that Sondheim woman, Kristýna. She was a real catch – and not just as a fugitive. I see why you were so invested in getting her released. How's it going? Are you still living with her?"

"No," Connor said with a mix of irritation, anger and pain. "She and her kid went back to Europe when the furor over her prison break died down. We weren't living together in that sense anyway. She had her own apartment in my cabin, and I was seldom there. We didn't see much of each other."

"Less than you would have liked?"

"Could be, Hatch. But now she's gone and I'm still standing. Story over. We're done talking about her."

"Understood, Randall. I'd feel the same way."

"I doubt it."

Connor poured himself another mug of Maxwell House. "What about Forsythe? What the hell is he doing in New York? The Director's office is in D.C."

"I'd be speculating."

"Then speculate."

"He doesn't like Assistant Director Barnes. Coming here gives him a chance to put his authority on display. But let's cut him a little slack, at least until we know what he wants. You're the one who schooled me in the art of administrative massage. Amazing how well it works when protocol and funding limits are involved."

***

Connor was pouring himself a third mug of coffee when FBI Director Jason Forsythe strode into the room. He seemed impressed with himself, a common trait of those who rise to the top through politicking rather than performance. Just eight months into the job, this agency head had conveniently forgotten that he owed his success to the work of others. He had become a creature of Washington. Fortunately, he was a smart and intuitive creature.

After a round of handshakes, Forsythe began as he always did. "Look, guys, the Bureau's under big pressure from D.C. It's not the usual posturing this time. It's for real. You probably know about Glenn Bay, that British reporter who said on BBC America, and I quote: "In the U.S., it would appear that school shootings have replaced baseball as the national pastime." That really pissed off the President. He was in my office the next morning, all but accusing the Bureau of incompetence."

"Maybe he's right."

"Look, Randall, we don't need to joke about this. We're not incompetent but we're starting to look that way. Five major events this Fall, and we haven't been able to solve one of them. Count them off. The Mall of

America, blown up in September. Forty-one kids massacred at Shady Grove Elementary in October. The Keenan murder in November. And already in December Kelly, which we've now classified as a murder, and another school shooting. You're here, Randall, because you're the best and I have to start showing results. Otherwise my ass is out of a job. Let's begin with Sean Keenan's murder."

"So it's a personal matter? We're tasked with keeping you employed."

"Of course not. Sorry if I made it sound that way. We're all under the gun, you two included."

"You mention Keenan as your November murder," Connor said. "The papers say it was a suicide."

"It was, it is – as far as the press and public know. Randall, Keenan was strangled while he was on the phone. A video of the entire episode was left poorly hidden near the crime scene. It was, in other words, intended to be found. The NYPD missed it the first time through, thank God. We didn't."

"What did it show?" Connor asked.

"Fill him in, Kenneth. You've seen the thing a hundred times."

"Gladly, Jason. It begins with ten seconds of footage shot by someone standing behind him and to the left. Keenan has his pants around his ankles, a cell phone in one hand and his dick in the other. We see a noose made out of an extension cord being lowered to just above his head – no hands in our picture, just the cord."

"Phone sex?" Connor groaned. "The guy could afford to fly in an entire brothel from Paris and he whacks off to a Verizon symphony. You're telling me Keenan's not an American hero, just another sicko! This is going to kick my view of humanity to the bottom of the basement stairs."

"Not possible," Hatch said. "you're already there."

"Okay, I'm already there. But I can still conduct an objective investigation. Keenan might have pressured a female employee at Freedom News, as I'm sure you've surmised."

"We have. In fact, that was where the boys began."

"What about the woman's voice? Do we have anything from her side of the conversation?"

"Yep. The whole thing. Whoever did this was kind enough to hack into her phone and recreate the two-way conversation on the tape."

"Unfortunately," Forsythe intervened, "the people are technically sophisticated. The female voice they gifted us was altered enough to confound our matching software. So here we sit with a crystal clear video of

29

the most-watched anchor in the nation caught in a less than flattering situation . . . then murdered and . . . "

"And it's worse," Hatch said, filling the void left by Forsythe's pause. "We all know how Keenan makes a big deal out of his military service. On TV he presents himself as a tough guy. This goes well with his hard-line agenda. But he squealed like a pig being castrated when he realized what was happening. Every once in a while the cord seems to have been intentionally loosened. Each time Keenan begged for his life. He never attempted to fight back. Not once."

Connor shook his head. "So you're saying the courageous bastard who wants the US to show some spine is a wimp? He had me fooled."

Hatch said, "He had tens of millions of Americans fooled. They looked to him for reassurance that their feelings were justified, reassurance that the nation's problems could be solved with a different style of leadership."

"So what happened to the extension cord?"

"The killers hung him from an exposed ceiling beam with it, lending credibility to the suicide finding – and saving us the bother of having to stage anything."

"Why would we stage anything? The press will find out at some point every detail you told me and more. Why don't we just tell the truth and get it over with?"

"The NSA," Hatch said matter-of-factly. "With the terror court's blessing, they've ordered all details kept secret – and that order has been extended to us. If the truth were to become known, it would have dangerous national security repercussions."

"National security repercussions!" Connor boomed. "I don't think so. Those pricks at Fort Meade liked Keenan's support for anything done in the name of national security, constitutional or not."

"It's more complicated than that," Forsythe explained. "They're understandably worried about the reaction Joe Six Pack if he finds out his country's hardline anti-terrorism guru was a wuss. They say it could mean an erosion of support for a dozen indispensable government programs."

"That doesn't make sense. How do you lose popular support for programs the public doesn't know exist?"

"Randall, now's not the time for cynicism. The American people are already confused by political gridlock at the very time that domestic violence is spreading like the plague. Our government seems to be entirely incapable of action."

"What's new?"

"Nothing on the government end, but the violence has a new texture. You will have gathered that from the video left at Keenan's. Anyway, we received a threatening letter from Libya yesterday. 'Just one more celebrity killing before we move onto bigger things. Your country can't defend itself.' So I'm with the NSA on suppressing news of Keenan, especially now. Also, we'll need to hide any findings that indicate Kelly's murder might be linked to the same perps. Think about it, gentlemen. If there really is a third celebrity killing, and if the public knows as much as we do, we won't only confuse them further. We'll scare the hell out of them. Where that leads is anyone's guess. We could find ourselves drawn into another war – which might be the exact objective of the people behind this."

"Jason, respectfully," Connor said. "It's not our job to formulate hypotheses on how the public might react. The Bureau solves crimes. Let's solve the Keenan murder first and see where we stand. It's probable that Kelly's case is unrelated and there will be no 'third murder.' A letter claiming responsibility for violent acts and predicting others is old hat. It could have come from anyone."

"Basically I agree," Forsythe said. "However, we're going to continue to keep the results of our investigations secret. Those are orders. And what I didn't make clear earlier is that they are not from me or any other agency but from the top. With that understanding, I think Randall is right. We need to figure out first what happened to Keenan." Forsythe stood. "We'll reconvene here at two."

***

"So, Hatch, where's the present investigation going?"

"Nowhere."

"Impossible." Connor slapped the table in frustration. "We're not talking about murder at a rural estate. This murder took place in the middle of town in a luxury apartment building full of the rich and famous. This means doormen were present round-the-clock, armed guards were on duty all night – and the best electronic security systems money can buy were no doubt installed and functioning."

"Randall," Hatch said politely, "I've been working on this for the last three weeks. I think you trust my ability. I promise you there are no leads."

Connor's color was high. "No disrespect, Hatch, but that's gonna change when I get in there."

Forsythe spoke softly, as if he dreaded Connor's response. "You're not going there. You're being assigned to the Kelly murder. You too, Hatch. Assistant Director Barnes assures me he has what's needed to go to the next level in New York. At this point we're of course looking for solutions. But we're also interested in what the two cases have in common. If we find something, it could fill in the blanks. You'll be working with the Keenan team on evidence of commonality. For your cooperation to be successful, you needed the information contained in today's briefing. I understand this is going to be another tough case to crack, but it won't be as tough as Sondheim . . .

"By the way, Randall, are you still living with that woman?"

CHAPTER FOUR

"**I**'m afraid I can't arrange that," said H. L. Gibbons.

"Oh, come on," Beau pleaded. "I almost killed myself getting up here. I *own* the places. I'll take the risks."

"You don't know the risks. You don't even know where the homes are, which – if you don't mind my saying – is a disgrace."

"Listen, ma'am, we didn't get the city's letter until last week and I've only owned the homes since Tuesday. I think you should cut me a break."

"Young man, it's been *seventy years* since an owner or anyone related to an owner of what you call your painted ladies has bothered to drop in and check on them. I'm glad you're finally here. Nonetheless – "

"You're glad I'm here!" interrupted Beau. "In that case, let's start over. I don't know how we got off on the wrong foot. If it was my fault, I apologize. Now, please. We're going to be working together for the next four months. It will be a whole lot easier if we're on good terms."

"Four months? You're not here to fight the condemnation order?"

"Not on your life. I'm here to have the places restored, and restored exactly as the Historical Society wants them. Like I said, my ladies have only been mine for a few days. My aunt wanted me to have them. So now I've got them and I want to do right by you all."

"Nellie, are you still here?" H. L. called through an open door.

"Yep, still here. What's up?"

Beau thought he detected a vestigial Southern accent beneath the Yankee talk. He tried to catch H. L.'s attention so he could scribble a question about the girl's provenance on a note pad, but H. L. was still looking in the direction of the door. "Would you mind bringing the Scotch and a couple of glasses out here. You drink Scotch, don't you, Mr. Wellington?"

"Yes ma'am. "

"Right away, Ms. Gibbons," sounded the voice from the other room.

33

This time he was sure. The girl, whoever she was, had to be from his corner of the universe. Her accent wasn't pure but it was definitely there, buried beneath some northern urban dialect. He felt a little less alone.

"On second thought," H. L. called back. "I'll come out there myself. The doctor wants me up and about every hour. It's been almost three."

Her attention came back to Beau as she struggled to stand. "Is neat all right?"

"Excuse me?"

"Neat. Without ice."

"Sure. I've just never heard – "

No use trying to chat. She had already limped out of view. People up here always seemed to be in a hurry, even people who could hardly walk.

The Historical Society's main office had been moved to a temporary location on the third floor of a downtown office building. He gazed out a window and shuddered. It wasn't even five o'clock, but the deep blue sky and resplendent white mountains of midday had disappeared. Black peaks loomed against a cold phosphorescent twilight. Skiers were already heading for the bars. They looked like a parade of gray shadows cloaked in the steam of a hundred breaths. He had always loved this time of day in Louisiana, even in winter. Not here. It gave him a chill, and deposited a vague, inexplicable foreboding in his gut.

"Neat." Now he knew how to order his drinks. Ice was the last thing he wanted to see until he was home again.

***

Harriet Leigh Gibbons had been head of the Aspen Historical Society for as long as anyone could remember. Back in the Seventies she married Johnston Leigh, a local artist, and took his family name in place of her own. When he died a few years later, Harriet Leigh officially reclaimed her maiden name but hung on to Leigh as a middle name, hoping this symbolic gesture would help immortalize what she and Johnston had shared. She soon realized that this, like most ideas conceived in grief, had been a mistake. She didn't like double first names, which she said reminded her of the South. "Hattie Leigh" she found particularly revolting. She might have gone with Harriet Leigh-Gibbons but she didn't like hyphenated last names, which she thought pretentious. She didn't like Harriet Gibbons, her maiden name, either. It reminded her of her unpleasant years as a single women. And she didn't like Harriet Leigh, her former married name, which reminded her that she was single again and likely to remain so.

In fact, there wasn't much besides homes and buildings on the National Register of Historic Places than Harriet Leigh Gibbons *did* like. Her name dilemma ended when a developer-friendly governor, whom she hated, scribbled a hurried note to her during a whistle-stop political appearance in Aspen. "Dear H. L." it began, and that was all she knew about the note because she didn't read any further. For some reason, though, she found H. L. a perfect representation of who she really was and immediately began signing her correspondence with the first two initials of her most recent name.

By now the Harriet and Leigh had long been forgotten. H. L. Gibbons, at age 73, was a legend to all and hero to some: she knew enough to spot the Aspen properties that might make it onto the National Register, enjoyed the respect and connections in D.C. that allowed her to assert herself, and thus managed to preserve what she could of old Aspen. And there wasn't a person on earth who called her anything but H. L.

Beau didn't have a clue about any of this the day he met her. Small wonder he added her to what he would later call his "national register of unpleasant persons," a list that had been growing by leaps and bounds since he crossed the border into Kansas. Southern charm wasn't going to get him anywhere with this woman.

***

She put the bottle and glasses down hard and held onto the conference table for support before she tried to sit. Beau went around the small table to help her, unable to suppress the impulse left by a lifetime of Aunt Lilly's etiquette drills. To his surprise H. L. thanked him.

"Back surgery," she explained. "I'm still supposed to be in bed."

He poured them each an inch of Scotch. H. L. relieved him of the bottle and tripled the amount. "Medicine," she said. "Theirs doesn't work." She downed a healthy swallow, then tipped her glass toward Beau.

"Now, young man, I want you to listen to me. If you're serious about bringing your painted ladies up to federal, state, county, city and Historical Society standards, we will not only have a civil relationship but a pleasant and productive one. The town's booked to the last room, as you can see. The carriage house of your Emma Claire, which you wanted to stay in, has no heat and no plumbing. The city nixed the idea of the place being inhabited for those reasons and others. There's only one possibility: the Paepcke suite at The Little Nell."

"Nell? Wasn't that what you called your assistant?"

"Nellie. If I'm not mistaken we were discussing something else."

Beau longed to ask about the girl's mix of accents but decided wisely to hold his tongue. H. L. had come back into the conference room a changed woman. He wanted it to stay like that. "Nellie, okay. I thought I heard Nell. So what about this Pepsi suite?"

"Paepcke. The name is synonymous with the birth of postwar Aspen. It was practically a ghost town after the war, but the Paepckes of Chicago, along with the Tenth Mountain Division, brought it back to life. Learn the history of this town, Mr. Wellington, and you'll get on better with the ladies, both those painted and those not."

"I will. I promise. So what about this suite? You make it sound pretty special."

"The only thing special is the price."

"You telephoned for me?"

"I did."

"That was really nice."

She filled both their glasses. "You might not think so when you hear the rate."

"Hey, don't worry about it. I'm glad just to have a place. We've got a big restoration budget. It includes my lodging, at least until I can get into my own carriage house."

"The rate is eleven hundred bucks – discounted."

"For the week or the month?"

"For tonight, Mr. Wellington. Nellie's on better terms with the city inspector than I am. I'll make sure she finds out everything he wants done before he lets you move in. Be here early tomorrow morning and we'll go to work."

***

Around nine that evening Beau headed out for a tour of the city, thinking it might be a good idea to know where his painted ladies were. He hadn't made it to First and Main when snow began to fall. A gust of wind took off with his city guide. To hell with it, he thought, ducking into the Hotel Jerome's J-Bar.

He sat among revelers of all types, oblivious to their talk of powder, first runs and film stars, and ordered a double Scotch – neat. It was then that he heard it, the mystery voice from the Historical Society. But it was different this time. She was speaking to *him*, tending bar, taking his order.

"And what particular Scotch would that be?"

"Excuse me?"

"You know, Lapfroaig, Glenmorangerie, McCallan. Our clients usually have even more specific preferences, such as age, year – "

"Oh, come on. You're a Southern girl at heart. You know Scotch is just Scotch."

"Excuse me? I'm from San Francisco."

"Maybe now you are. Where did you move there from?"

"Ashville, nine years ago, Mr. Beau Wellington."

"I suppose H. L. told you why I'm in Aspen?"

"Yes. Listen, it's seventy degrees in here. Give me your things and I'll hang them up."

"Hey, thanks." Beau took off the stocking cap and parka he had bought in Denver, shed his outer layer of Norwegian sweaters and apologized to the people he had bumped. "Nellie, right? I believe that's what H. L. called the invisible presence next door."

"Nellie Vaughn," she said, momentarily disappearing behind the mountain of clothes he'd handed her. I'll have Peter bring your Scotch, but I'll be back. I've got to a make a quick call. I promised one of the locals I'd let him know when and if an owner of the condemned properties came to town. He should be back at his ranch by now."

"But I'm not selling. I made that clear this afternoon."

"Please, just talk to him. I promised him you would because . . . well, because I didn't know you and I assumed the condemnation letter would be ignored. The previous letters were."

"I know. But I'm a new owner and I plan to do things differently."

"I'm glad about that, I really am. But it's going to be very embarrassing for me if you don't meet with this man. I'll make it easy. Let me arrange a private conference room so you can see him right here in the Jerome. Please, Beau."

"When would this happen?"

"Tonight, if he can make it. Starting tomorrow, you're going to be swarmed by hordes of buttoned-down L. A. developer types. Whatever General Shiller has in mind, he wants to run it past you before you see anyone else."

"General Shiller. The guy everyone thinks will run for President?"

"Yes, exactly. Maybe that will give you some idea of my predicament."

"Well, my social calendar for this evening isn't entirely booked. But you realize I'm going to have to disappoint him. I'm sure it won't be a joyride."

"I know. I'm sorry. But it's not a problem if you turn him down. All I promised was a meeting."

"All right, then. Let's get it over with."

She touched his forearm and looked him in the eye. "You don't know how much I appreciate this. I owe you one."

"Which I intend to collect."

CHAPTER FIVE

Beside them was a linen-bedecked table adorned with flowers, a selection of wines and spirits, an ice bucket and embroidered napkins. Antique silver chafing dishes lined the side bar. In the hearth crackled a fragrant wood fire, aspen logs for all he knew. Nellie had gone to a lot of trouble to make things special for the meeting. She knew it wouldn't come to anything, even if the guy was going to be President. But one thing was clear: she had set a formal table correctly in a place north of the Mason-Dixon line. Aunt Lilly was wrong. Certain people up here had a proper sense of etiquette. Whether those people were limited to transplants from the South, he couldn't say.

"Do you know who I am?" Shiller asked, smiling as he dropped a cube of ice into each glass.

"Of course I do. Everyone does. But, General, excuse me. I'd like mine neat."

"I'm sorry. I should have asked."

"It's just that I'm not used to the cold. Ice makes me think I'm freezing to death, even when there's a fire in the room."

"I guess we'll have to toughen you up, Mr. Wellington. That can wait. What I've come to discuss cannot. Shall we sit?"

"Sure."

Beau took the glass Shiller handed him, happy to see that the absence of ice in his new pour hadn't lowered the level of Scotch. The General, in spite of his charm and cheerful demeanor, didn't seem like the kind of person you'd want to disappoint. He understood better now why Nellie had wanted to keep her promise.

The General was watching him intently, as though the moment was important. His eyes were as gray as the Gulf in winter . . . and unreadable. "How did you hear of me?"

"How could I not have? I read the *Vicksburg Post* every day, and we

39

get the Sunday *Picayune* from New Orleans. Everyone seems to believe you might jump into the presidential race. Besides, I never missed Tim Kelly's nightly news show. You were always being discussed as a possible candidate. I guess you'll have to do without his coverage now. I heard what happened to him."

Shiller shook his head. "Incomprehensible, really. He was by all standards a good man, whether or not you agreed with his politics. I didn't know people in your part of the woods watched liberals."

"We don't. I mean, not usually. I did because I liked the guests he had on. But I know what you're saying. When I heard someone coming I always switched channels. The instinct for survival is strong."

Shiller laughed and sucked down a couple of oysters. "I haven't said more than ten words in public on the subject of my running for President, none of them conclusive. But those words have spread like wildfire. You know what that means, Mr. Wellington?"

"I think so. Not for sure, but I think so."

"Let me remove any doubt. It means the country wants someone at the helm who can deal with the problems we face – real problems, big problems. Kelly's murder is just one example of the disintegration of the America we once knew and loved. More specifically, it means a majority of the electorate finds me the person who, as President, would offer the best hope of national salvation. I hope you agree with that majority. I need your help."

"My help? I don't even vote."

"Nonetheless, you may soon find yourself part of a national political upheaval. You see, the Kelly affair and my need for your painted ladies are not unrelated."

"I'm sorry, General Shiller, but you've lost me there. What does Kelly have to do with the painted ladies?"

"Nothing. His death, however, convinced me the time to act has come."

"To act?"

"To run for President. You will, I trust, not mention that I have come to a final decision until I have made my announcement – regardless of the outcome of tonight's meeting."

"I will not mention it. Just that you're still considering. That's what the newspapers and TV are all saying."

"Good."

"But, General, we've gotten sidetracked. What about Tim Kelly?

How did his murder convince you to run."

"Mr. Wellington, his death wasn't only a murder; it was part of a sophisticated attempt to destabilize America. God might be indifferent to our fate, but I am not."

"Okay. It makes sense. But leaving all the decision stuff aside I still don't see what Kelly has to do with my properties."

Shiller stood and paced. He stopped at the bar to pour himself a glass of ice water. "Of course you don't see the connection. I haven't divulged it yet. Allow me to do that now. Mr. Wellington, Kelly's murder was, for me, the straw that broke the camel's back. I saw clearly what I had struggled not to see: my moral obligation to grasp and shape to our advantage what has become a historic opportunity.

"So, you are asking yourself, what does this mean in practical terms? I'll tell you. I am going to hold a press conference next month that will make clear my intentions. First on the agenda will be securing the nomination of the Republican Party. I am going to need decent lodging for Senators, Congressmen, military brass, agency heads, elite members of the Washington press corps, state and local politicians and, perhaps, international leaders. If circumstances permit, I will insist they come to me – a first step in the change I plan to bring to the American political process.

"I wouldn't have the slightest interest in your properties if I was planning a traditional campaign. But I'm not. Most political business will be conducted from here; most everyone interested in working on my election will come to me. Unless, of course, you make that impossible."

Beau said, "I think I'm starting to get the picture. You want to buy the painted ladies."

"I do not. I've been told by Ms. Vaughn at the Historical Society that you're here to restore, not to sell – and that you're firm in this regard. This dovetails perfectly with my needs."

"You're losing me again. What are your needs?"

Shiller lit a pipe and took his seat at the table. In the soft light Beau could see that he had been an extremely handsome man. Actually, he still was. He must have been around sixty, with a strong chin, gray hair, thinning a little but combed back in a way that made him look like a rich executive. Then there was that steel-gray aspect – sometimes warm, sometimes inscrutable – around which his appearance seemed built. No fat on him either. His sports coat was tailored for broad shoulders and a thin waist, and the neck protruding from his open collar gave you the idea he was in perfect physical condition. He was tall, 6'3" give or take, but

41

his imposing physical presence wasn't what stood out. It was, rather, a sense of confidence and authority that his smile – whether warm or cold – did nothing to change. Nor did his sense of confidence translate into an aura of superiority: he was a man of unorthodox but pervasive charm.

Shiller refreshed their drinks, stood in front of the fireplace and cleared his throat.

"Mr. Wellington, I've looked into the condemnation papers and I've studied what must be done to secure the necessary permits for your properties. It's a lot, yes. But your homes, properly restored, will be perfect for bringing the campaign to me in all seasons of the year, even when Aspen is completely booked. I won't need the properties forever, just until my inauguration. So, here's my offer: I'm willing to pay the full cost of their restoration in exchange for a twelve-month lease. The specifics will, of course, be spelled out in a formal contract."

"Restoration that's guaranteed to meet the deadline in the condemnation order?"

"The restorations will be completed by the first week in February."

"Impossible! Not in the middle of winter."

"Mr. Wellington, there are construction firms that work year 'round in harsh climates. I've met with the directors of several of these in the northern US, Canada and Scandinavia. Not one sees a problem with my February deadline. Most are willing to take on what promises to be a very lucrative project."

"I didn't know outdoor work in winter was possible. We don't do anything in Louisiana if it's not at least sixty degrees. But you know more about the North than I do, so I'll take your word for it. Let me go over this again. The ladies will be restored by the beginning of February, and you will guarantee in writing that the condemnation order will be lifted."

"Precisely."

"Well, this is definitely something to think about."

Shiller drained his glass, put on his overcoat and walked to the door.

"Don't think too long, Mr. Wellington. Your decision, whatever it is, will determine how I run my campaign. I'll need an answer in three days, nine a.m. at the Historical Society. H. L. and my attorneys will be present, as well as representatives from the contractors I hope to work with. Final agreements will be signed. I'm sure I needn't point out that you should be accompanied by legal counsel."

Beau tried to think of a lawyer he could count on, but only one person struck him as up to the task of *really* representing his interests. That person was Aunt Lilly.

CHAPTER SIX

Even in high school William "Moose" Chapman dreamed of becoming filthy rich. When college did little to further his dream, he dropped out.

"It is, of course, your choice," his father said at the dinner table. "But William, you shouldn't put all your eggs in one basket. What if things don't turn out the way you want?"

Sitting on the patio of his oceanfront mansion in Solana Beach, California, just north of San Diego, Moose relived that evening three decades ago as if it had been last week. He shook his head, tried not to smile, took another sip of his dry martini. His father's problem was that he thought all the Chapmans were psychologically his mirror image. Well, maybe he was right about Freddy and Karl. He'd talked them both into careers in engineering, and both would be considered "successful" by the average Joe. They earned a couple hundred thousand a year, had pretty wives and sent their kids to the best private schools in Southern California. But Moose considered them abject failures, men who had chosen to live out their days in the dull gray world of American suburbia.

No winter down here, thank God, not even in December. A light breeze brought the smell of the Pacific to his nostrils, an invigorating smell. The sea stretched to the horizon, touched by the wispy red and orange clouds that often caught fire at sunset. Life was good.

When he heard Claire, his fourth wife, approaching, he slicked his hair back with his hands and sucked in his button-popping gut. He would divorce her soon, sure, but a little attention to his appearance now and then created a deceptive aura of normalcy.

She was going out for the night, some kind of woman thing, and wanted to know which bodyguards should accompany her. The question answered, he listened to the fading clack of heels across the vast tile patio. When it was quiet again, he inwardly mocked his father's egg and basket sermonette. If you wanted greatness, you had to go out and grab it. Having something to fall back on made it too easy to give up.

He obviously hadn't taken anyone's advice. He had known all along that a life similar to the one he now had could belong to him if he pursued it. Which he did, single-mindedly.

Moose attributed his massive empire to the insight behind its creation. He had been first to grasp a basic truth: the list of things the media believed most effective in causing man to part with his money was incomplete. Some of their favorites, such as sex and violence, worked. So did fear, betrayal, suspense, evil and, occasionally, love. While hate could be woven like filigree into these things, it had never been used in its pure enriched form as the main public draw. He changed that forever. Moose's take on human nature struck a chord with real people that baffled every sort of do-gooder. Its skillful application to the airwaves made him the country's most popular radio personality – and a billionaire many times over. Jews, Hispanics, Blacks, Gays, reporters, poor people, liberals, ambitious women and the government were only his most prominent targets.

Moose made himself another martini from the cart beside his deck chair, this one without vermouth. He thought, as he did each evening, about his swelling fortune. Fifty-two billion bucks, that's what his hard work and keen understanding of the market had earned him, *legitimately* earned him. What really pissed him off was that most people thought "billionaire" just meant "rich." They'd say the same thing about some nobody with ten million. Well, ten million was only one percent of a billion. What percent it was of fifty-two billion he'd let someone else figure out.

Time for an early dinner and bed. The morning show began at 5:00 a.m., and Moose needed to be up at four to prepare. He made himself a third martini and put in a call to the kitchen. He'd have his usual: a thick ribeye with the fat untrimmed, a couple white sausages and mounds of fried potatoes. Fuck all that fancy restaurant food. When you were Moose Chapman, you didn't give a damn what others thought. He ate to enjoy, lived to enjoy . . . and practiced his art of broadcasting hate to earn himself the good life.

The sun sank below the horizon, the evening turned chilly. Special heaters in the tile and awnings chased away the chill. Soft lights made up for the sun's dying glow. A more perfect existence, one that he had earned and had every right to, he could not imagine. Heaven, he thought, smiling to himself, would be like a National Geographic tour through the slums of

India. But no matter how great his life, there was one thing he never forgot. He might not be here to enjoy it if Destiny hadn't smiled on him the day of the assassination attempt.

It happened just outside his radio station in San Diego, and he forced himself to relive that moment at least several times a month. Why? Because you could not appreciate the best until you experienced – or nearly experienced – the worst.

It was almost ten years ago when several low riders boxed in his Rolls limo. The human garbage inside wasted no time opening fire with high-powered assault rifles. His driver and two guards were hit immediately, sending blood in random splatters. Moose's third guard pushed him to the floor, muttering that he should play dead, then took a shot in the eye that landed his corpse on top of the man who seemed to have Destiny on his side.

Moose decided then and there, flat on his stomach in the back seat of limo number 43, the hot blood of his guard pouring into his nose and mouth, that he had relied on Destiny long enough. He would fake injury and go off the air for however long it took him to regain his confidence. During this period, he would move the radio station into his mansion and fortify it in a way only a man of his means could do.

Back on the air he would ruthlessly assail his assailants. He had seen enough of them to know they were Mexicans. Like all members of inferior races, these guys thought life was cheap. Not surprisingly, they also happened to be morons. With their attack during evening rush hour, they obviously weren't going to get more than a city block before the cops carried out their death sentence. Material for dozens of hours of radio ridicule that would hit the so-called Hispanic community and its blathering organizers where it hurt the most. But reminding the inferior of their inferiority was just a start. He would have the nation up in arms, ending all government talk of "immigration reform" for decades.

He ate his steak in large bites that left his lips glistening like his slicked-back hair, then continued his reverie. A few hundred million was pocket change. It was also several times more than the budget of the Solano Beach police department. He donated those many millions in secret with the understanding that he would receive a level of protection unmatched in America. Then, to guard against the incompetence that came with mandated minority hiring, he had his castle converted into a fortress. It wasn't paranoia, he told himself, but rational good sense. The losers would never stop resenting success, never stop resenting the biggest winner of all. Why take a chance if you didn't have to?

With his radio station at home and his unannounced trips beyond the fortress walls enshrouded in a veil of secrecy, he could live as he always had . . . and never worry about a recurrence of the only episode that had ever caused him fear.

Actually, thought Moose, the attack had been a blessing in disguise. When he finally went back to work, his newly energized hate saturated the airwaves as never before. Money flowed into his banks from London to Liechtenstein . . . and Homeland Security interviewed him in search of ideas for keeping America safe. He wasn't just a radio personality any-more; he was a force, perhaps the major force, in his country's politics.

Moose stood, unsteady but happy, and wove a heavy course through a grid of gaudy statue-lined hallways. He was almost sleepwalking by the time he entered his favorite bedroom. His wife, he thought drowsily, would be at the other end of the mansion when she returned from her bull-shit reading group. She would be stopped from joining him by several of the night guards. When you had to speak to the nation from five until eight in the morning, you couldn't let late-night bitching interfere with your sleep.

***

It happened to him a lot. Sometime around two o'clock he became aware of his own dreams. These were often pleasant, but not always. The trick was to know which dreams to wake yourself from and which to leave alone.

This time it was a feather tickling his penis. No harm in that, so he'd let it be. As his dream went on, he heard muffled giggling beneath the sheets. The feather left his dick and headed down his leg toward his ankle. Strange but not unpleasant.

Then, suddenly, the dream turned ugly. He felt cold metal around both ankles. Time to wake up and shuck this crap.

It wasn't a dream. Moose sat bolt upright, his heart pounding and his gut straining at the buttons of his XXL pajamas. Something besides metal and feathers was under those goddamn sheets.

Before he could speculate any further, the room lights came on with a blinding flash. He saw two young boys emerge from the covers at the foot of the bed, still giggling.

"What the fuck d'you think you're – "

His words were swallowed by the earsplitting shriek of a chain saw. He looked toward a corner of the room. The little kids, maybe nine or ten,

47

had joined two Mexican teens. One teen couldn't get his chain saw started. The other left his saw idling on the floor and went over to help.

Moose saw that no one was watching him. He heaved himself out of bed and fell with a jarring crash to the floor. When he tried to stand, he saw that he had not gotten himself tangled in the sheets as he had believed. The little kids had not only tickled his dick with a feather; they had put him in the kind of leg irons prisoners wear. His ankles were bound to each other and to a stout post of the bed. He wasn't going anywhere.

The fear was back, that fear he had overcome ten years ago. He had to think fast if he was going to succeed this time. He struggled to his feet. "Listen, I'll put all of you through Harvard. I'll buy you any car you want. I'll . . .

It was then that he realized none of the four intruders understood a word of English. He screamed and shouted. The teens laughed, speaking excited Spanish, as the second saw roared to life. Suddenly they were coming, both of them, each brandishing a chain saw that could have cut down a sequoia. He flailed, shrieked some more. And then he felt the agony of ripping flesh, his own. He began to fall, but his arm beat him to the floor. He lost consciousness with a dull thud in his ears, unable to hear the saws snarling toward his neck.

CHAPTER SEVEN

"Doing okay, Aunt Lilly?" Beau asked from the back seat of General Shiller's sliding and bouncing Land Rover.

"Yes darling – if you take into account we're on another planet with a madman at the wheel."

Nellie, who was seated beside Beau, laughed. Who else in the world would talk that way to a man headed for the presidency? Equally surprising, she thought, was Shiller's reaction: like everyone else, he seemed charmed by her.

"I know how you feel, Mrs. Prideaux," the General said. "I'm from the hill country of Texas, a small town near the Mexican border. Growing up, snow was something people read about in books."

"General," Lilly said, paying him no mind, "you'd better stop talking and concentrate on where you are going."

Beau expected Shiller to take unkindly to the remark. Again, he was surprised by what he heard. "You're right, Mrs. Prideaux. I'll slow down and keep my eyes straight ahead."

"An excellent idea, young man."

This time Beau and Nellie both laughed. A young man? Shiller might be in great shape but "young" was definitely a stretch.

Lilly craned her neck toward the back seat. "Children, aren't you both glad the old lady decided not to come?"

Beau couldn't restrain himself. "Aunt Lilly! That 'old lady' is a year younger than you."

"Well, she certainly doesn't look it. Did you see how she came to the meeting? No jewelry, men's pants, a ratty turtleneck and *gray hair*. She obviously had no upbringing. We should restore **her** before we start on the houses."

Nellie said, "Mrs. Prideaux, I – "

"Nellie, darling, please call me Lilly. You too, General. Now go ahead, dear."

"H. L. cares about other things, not her appearance. You saw at the meeting today how the men in charge of all of this stuff, the guys from the city and county, didn't say a word. H. L. has done such a good job preserving Aspen that everyone has ceded powers to the Historical Society it isn't supposed to have."

"And what about the name H. L.? Why would any self-respecting female allow herself to be called that? It sounds like she's a janitor. I saw her full name in the contract. Harriet Leigh something or other. So she has a name, Hattie Leigh, an acceptable name. Using it would be a good place for her to start."

"Please, Aunt Lilly. You're talking about a person we both admire."

"Well, honey, it's still unpleasant to spend the day with someone who looks and talks like she's on death row. When I'm gone, maybe Nellie could help her find a clothes store with a staff that understands fashion . . . and, of course, a beauty parlor that has a recipe for changing women into ladies. They'll have to work harder than John Henry in Hattie Leigh's case but maybe, just maybe, something will come of it."

Beau and Nellie ignored the ridiculous part of Aunt Lilly's tirade; but buried in those very Southern words was a scary allusion they both picked up on. "When you're gone?" Beau exclaimed. "You're going to live to be a hundred – at least."

Now it was Lilly who laughed. "Child, I didn't mean it that way – unless the General sends me to an early grave. I mean, gone from here, gone from Aspen. I'd love to stay but I have bridge group Monday, Junior Auxiliary Wednesday and a shower for Dottie Yerger's niece on Thursday. I also have to have my hair done so I don't return from up North looking like your Hattie Leigh. My plane leaves sometime around noon. General, I hope you'll arrange for me to get to the airport – preferably with a driver other than yourself."

"Certainly. One of my men who hails from Mississippi will take you."

"But Aunt Lilly, you just got in yesterday."

"Yes, Beau, but now our deal is done and I don't have a charming young thing to keep me here."

"You've got the wrong idea. Nellie and I just met. We're friends, that's all."

"Perhaps for now. Lord, look at that castle up ahead! It's almost as big as the antebellum homes in Natchez."

"It's a ranch house," General Shiller said. "Very different inside, no doubt, from Scarlett O'Hara's abode – but I think you'll like it."

50

"And if I don't."

"Then you don't. I will be disappointed, of course, but the important thing is that we made it here safely."

"I had my moments of doubt."

"Well, they're behind you now. Let's have dinner and work out those last details regarding the post-lease décor. I have no problem doing what you want and paying for it – if we can get it past Nellie Vaughn and Ms. Harriet Leigh."

***

"We hadn't expected anything soon," FBI Director Forsythe said. "More precisely, we hadn't expected anything at all. It appears we may have been wrong."

"Wouldn't be the first time," Connor grumbled. "Christ, Jason, it's still night in Colorado."

"Randall, you're FBI. The time of day – or night – is irrelevant. Will you please shut up and listen."

The Director's voice was either too soft to hear or too loud to listen to. Today it was several decibels too loud. Connor held the phone away from his ear and waited for the next barrage of incoming fire. He didn't have to wait long. "The SAC in L. A. doesn't know yet. I wanted to speak with you first."

"Hang on a sec while I get my bearings."

Hatch and Connor had only been in Aspen for three hours after a long late flight from New York, and Connor's exploration of their quarters had ended with bedroom number one. Totally unfamiliar with the layout of the place, he groped in darkness for the kitchen. After a few collisions with walls and tables, each accompanied by a ringing outburst of the vernacular, he stumbled into the right room and switched on the lights. To his surprise, the Pitkin County Sheriff had remembered his telephone request. The coffee maker was ready, and a can of Maxwell House sat like a gift from Heaven on the counter beside it. He punched random buttons until a green light came on. Naked, he made dog circles looking for a place to sit. He ruled out his bare ass on a chair: that wouldn't feel right, not even to him. He grabbed a section of yesterday's *Times*, slapped it onto a stool and let himself down. Without coffee pulsing through his veins his aim was poor and he almost landed on the floor.

"Shit!"

"What are you yelling about? I haven't even told you what's going on."

"I'm a clumsy son-of-a-bitch, that's all. Tell me everything."

"Okay, Randall, here's the skinny. It's twenty after six Mountain Time, morning in case you're not accustomed to rising before dawn. This means it's twenty after five on the West Coast. Moose Chapman's morning talk show hasn't come on the air. Know why? According to his wife, he's dead. Cut into pieces. We're going to treat it like we treated Keenan, at least for now. Foul play was involved so we need to make sure it's kept quiet. This guy talks to half the country. If word gets out that no one could protect him – or Keenan, or Kelly, for that matter . . . well, you get the idea. I've had the few Feds I could round up secure his place to keep local law enforcement out. You know the best people in L.A., and the best at keeping their mouths shut. I want them in Solana within the hour. And I want you to give the orders."

"Me? Why me? Isn't that Richard's job? Or yours?"

"I believe you know why I'm asking. Your SAC out there isn't universally respected and I've heard rumors the same might apply to me. Remember, it's five in the morning in California. For some incomprehensible reason, you're well-liked by your colleagues. Having you call will get us the fastest response."

"Maybe."

Connor heard the coffee maker emit a death rattle. About time. With a mug of Maxwell House in his hands he could summon the alertness to do what the Director wanted. And he *would* do it, though his stock answer to such requests was no. He would depart from convention because, for once, he agreed with Forsythe: this could be the celebrity assassination predicted in the letter from Libya.

***

Shiller's ranch house was unlike anything Beau had ever stepped inside, even though most of the place could not be seen. Many rooms and passages were hidden behind heavy wooden doors. But it didn't matter. What you could see was more than enough. The sitting room had ceilings at least 30 feet high, enormous windows, two gigantic stone hearths and, supporting the roof, huge round beams of some exotic wood. A study, its walls lined with books, occupied a recessed part of the parlor. And there was art everywhere you looked, all kinds of art. Beau wondered idly if the paintings and sculptures were originals. Perhaps Nellie knew. Asking her would be a good conversation starter if he could ever get a moment alone with her.

Nellie. Even with all the exciting stuff going on, he couldn't get his mind off her. To him, she was a lot more interesting than old houses and politics. Whether she was approachable or not . . . well, that was a question yet to be answered.

In the dining room, a table for four was set. It reminded Beau of the Commander's Palace in New Orleans – by far the best restaurant he had ever come near. That, he recalled, had been his 30th Birthday – and Aunt Lilly insisted he accept as his gift a proper meal. Now he was starting to wonder what she thought of the General's place. She had a way of finding fault with every home she entered, but he couldn't imagine what she would criticize in this spectacular almost dreamlike setting. She'd find something, no doubt, but he hoped she didn't say anything to Shiller. She had been awfully direct all day, as if she had hired Shiller to pick up pecans in her yard.

"It's late," the General said. "After drinks, Lilly, you are going to experience a meal I hope you'll like. I've had two chefs from Langlois flown up here in anticipation of our deal. You're familiar with the restaurant, yes?"

"Of course, General. It's a rare soul in Louisiana who isn't. It's very kind of you to have gone to the trouble and expense."

"No trouble at all. Not for me, at least. The men in the kitchen are doing the work."

"As it should be. I think, General, that we're going to make good business partners."

"But Aunt Lilly," Beau objected, "you deeded the places to *me*. *I'm* the business partner."

"Yes, dear, formally that's true. But you'll need my advice."

"Don't forget me," Nellie insisted. "The deal we reached puts me in charge of approving all changes and upgrades. Normally it would be H. L. but she can't get around like she used to."

"Of course," Shiller said. "You misunderstood Lilly's remark, both of you. It's clearly spelled out in the contract that the partnership includes The Historical Society and its representatives, which would be you and H. L., and that Mr. Wellington is the owner of the homes. I suggest we put all imaginary dogs to rest and celebrate our success.

"Nellie, I know you prefer white Lillet. Beau, Scotch neat. But Lilly, your preferences are unknown to me."

"Well, General, since you have two chefs from New Orleans here, I'll order as I would at home: a Sazerac."

***

53

"Hatch, I need you in here," shouted Connor.

"Has something happened?"

"To put it mildly. I just got off the phone with the Director."

"Coffee's over there," Connor grumbled, frustrated. Of all people, Hatch had knocked over a lamp and waste paper basket making his to the tech room.

"And?" Hatch said, inhaling the vapors from his mug while he waited for the black brew to cool. The men sat down across from one another in straight-back computer chairs.

"You remember that letter Forsythe talked about when we were in New York?"

"Letter? The note from Libya predicting the murder of another celebrity?"

"Yeah."

Hatch blew into his mug. Even unshowered and half-dressed, he looked like he was ready to give testimony before a Senate committee. He touched his silver wire-rimmed glasses, blew into his mug again and took a sip. "Go on."

"It seems to have happened last night."

"No kidding? Who was the victim?"

"Moose Chapman."

"Moose Chapman, huh. Well, off the record, you can't say he hasn't been asking for it. My first reaction is that this particular murder has nothing to do with the letter."

"That was my first reaction as well."

"And where did it happen?"

"In his home. He moved his broadcast studio there awhile back. Seems to me it was right after an attempt on his life."

"It was," Hatch said. "But the place is a fortress from what I've been told. Guards 24/7, alarms of every kind, 'round the clock protection by the local police department."

"A fortress, but evidently not impregnable." Connor stood and paced, his movements infused with a sort of animal ferocity. "You didn't hear what Forsythe just told me."

Hatch signaled with the coffee pot when Connor thundered past for the third time. Connor uttered a rare word of thanks as he stopped for a refill. Hatch glanced at his wristwatch – silver, trim, as unobtrusive as the man himself. He was about to say something when Connor distracted him, dropping into an armchair with an upholstery-splitting crash.

"Jesus, partner," Connor said, "someone's got our number."

"Did they make another video?"

"Yep. Copies went to Forsythe in D.C. and Trafford at the NSA. It's pretty clear whoever did Keenan masterminded this."

"No doubt. What's on the video?"

"I haven't seen it. Forsythe says they cut off the guy's arms and head with a chain saw."

"Jesus."

"Amen. More incredible because it was done by kids. Mexicans, Forsythe swears, as if he'd know a Mexican from a Malaysian."

"Listen, Randall, the thing must be a fake. How could kids breech his security?"

"I don't know but they did. One of our people has seen their work – not a pretty sight."

"He wants us out there, I take it."

"Not yet. He's putting an elite West Coast crew on the initial phase. Too bad we don't have one. As far as the press and local law enforcement know, the man had a massive heart attack. Same protocol as with Keenan. I feel like you, Hatch. I'd like us to be in on this from the start. But the man says no, repeats himself with more volume and hangs up."

"In other words, we're still on Kelly?"

"Right. He thinks there's something that ties all three cases together. I don't."

"Nor I. His murder doesn't seem to fit the pattern."

"Well, I guess we'd better dispense with the assumptions. He might know something he's keeping to himself. Anyway, we're flying to Crested Butte at noon."

"Why?"

"Hell if I know. We're being briefed by the CBI upon arrival."

"Maybe they've found something that explains Forsythe's decision to keep us here."

"Don't count on it. Listen, the Pitkin County Sheriff gave me directions to a café where the local cops hang out. Duff's it's called. Bacon, hash browns, eggs, sausage – the civilized man's breakfast. Wanna join me?"

Hatch glanced at his watch. "Sure. Just give me a sec to pick up something non-lethal."

"Health nut. Aspen's your kind of place. You fit right in."

55

CHAPTER EIGHT

General Shiller had announced his candidacy for President in a rural Colorado village the previous summer. Six people were present for the one-sentence presentation, among them the managing editor of the *Haxtun-Fleming Herald,* circulation 1,191. The national press, if they reported it at all, were unanimous in their opinion that the announcement was not serious.

Shiller, pleased with their response, quietly filed the required forms that made his candidacy official. He then moved to meet the registration requirements for ballot access in state caucuses and primaries. Later, when a groundswell of support for the General emerged, his announcement remained unknown even to his most fervent supporters.

The day the restoration of the painted ladies was completed, Shiller announced a press conference to clarify his position. He knew the media would be awaiting his formal announcement to enter the race. Better to keep the vultures guessing.

He scheduled the event for 10:00 a.m. January 29, adding a detailed if irrelevant description of its venue: the Molly Brown Conference Center in Aspen. Knowing commercial flights were booked months in advance during the ski season, he expected only the representatives of major news outlets who could travel by corporate jet to be present. Sure, a few hotheads would manage to show up. But apart from this inevitability, his first meeting with the national press would take place among known reporters in a setting whose tenor he could control.

***

Connor and Hatch had received a special invitation and seats up close. The agents were surprised. They didn't know their presence in Aspen, although it was not meant to be secret, held any interest for the man who would be president. But they'd met him on several occasions in the J-Bar and gotten on well. He had some interesting thoughts on where the attacks

56

might have originated, and he listened carefully to their own hypotheses. Shiller knew they were FBI here to investigate Kelly's murder. He must have wanted them to hear – and perhaps later critique – his plans for the country. Whatever the reason, they were glad to have been invited.

The room filled as the ten o'clock hour approached. When General Shiller strode to the lectern, he already looked presidential. His tailored suit was slim in the waist, broad in the shoulders. His walk was dynamic and his demeanor serious. Yet none of these things explained the air of authority that made him stand out from the field.

Shiller began without the usual throat clearing and water sipping. "I apologize for the wait at the front entrance. I'm sure you understand the need for security these days, and setting up arrangements to my satisfaction took longer than expected. I also want to apologize to those of you expecting some kind of announcement. There will be none. I declared my candidacy for President of the United States in July without fanfare, and subsequently made all required presidential and primary filings. You might want to think of this as an unconventional exploratory venture. At the time it did not seem my entry into the race held out any chance of success. But, as you know, History is a composite of unexpected turns. In the event the electoral landscape changed, I wanted to be ready."

The *New York Times* senior Washington correspondent jumped to her feet. "Respectfully, Sir, could you be more specific regarding your July announcement? I've seen no record of it and don't know anyone who has."

"Ms. Alvarez, I would like to outline my domestic agenda without interruption. I will then entertain your questions. He surveyed the crowd, which numbered around a hundred. "I would appreciate it if those of you standing would sit down until we open the meeting up for questions."

Which they did, to their own surprise.

"Thank you," the General said. "Our country is under attack. Last year we lost to terrorism and other forms of violence directed at random civilians more Americans than we lost on 9/11. According to government spokespersons, this heightened state of violence appears uncoordinated. It isn't. Too much has happened in too brief a time to be explained away by coincidence. If someone is to make our schools, shopping centers, highways, concerts and sports stadiums safe again, that someone must devote his or her life to the task.

"When we have healed our country at its core, terrorism – domestic and foreign – will no longer haunt our daily lives. We will understand its causes and eradicate it. This cannot be done by businessmen or real-estate developers no matter how often they manage to utter a word of truth. And it can't be done by politicians. Why? Because their understanding of such complexities – assuming they have the intelligence to understand – is incompatible with their constant need to raise money.

"So let me be direct. When you hear the words 'fund raising' you will know that the person associated with those words will have neither the time nor the focus to save . . . *yes, to save* . . . America. There are ways to fund elections that do not turn those who govern into the puppets of those who bankroll them.

"When you hear a candidate has made a traditional campaign stop, you will know you are looking at someone whose political existence is rooted in the past – a past that has brought us to our present state of dysfunction. Let's be blunt: in this new world of cutting-edge technology, we are no longer able to defend ourselves

"When you hear of candidates who have agreed to participate in the debates arranged by their party, you will know that time put into debate preparation is time that can't be wasted if we as a country are going to survive. There are other, more effective means of expressing personality and policy.

"If you hear of a Congressman or Senator whose sons, daughters and grandchildren are *not* serving, or have not served, in a branch of the Armed Forces, you will know that you are not dealing with someone who cares about our country. These are the people deciding who goes to war. Should they not make that decision for their own as well as for those they do not know? And should not the sons and daughters of those who have benefitted most from the American system contribute the most to its survival? You will no doubt find any such proposal unconstitutional. But affirmative action has been with us for a while, so let's not jump to conclusions.

"I will conduct as much of my campaign as possible from Aspen. Advances in communications technology have made it unnecessary, counterproductive in fact, to spend months in transit making disingenuous speeches to help one's electoral chances in this state or that. Such behavior, like that of fund raising, severely diminishes the time for study and thought needed to grasp what is happening to us. It is a guarantee of failure, not for politicians, but for the country they purport to represent.

"My campaign will be conducted by the national, state and local party leaders who care to meet with me here. A groundswell of American popular opinion will help them in their decision to join me; and will strengthen their efforts to make me your next President. I will accept no money because I am here to serve you, not special interests.

"There will be national service for all Americans between the ages of eighteen and twenty. This is a necessity if we are going to rebuild our country, its schools, its infrastructure, its military. Great nations die when they are unable to defend themselves; they also rot from the inside. Both of these things are happening. With me at the helm, neither will continue.

"To this end, we will work together as Americans. To collaborate successfully will require putting all social and moral disagreements on the back burner for a period of four years. This means no talk in the political arena of abortion, gay rights, gun rights, states' rights – all of those things that divide rather than unite us. Is such a limitation of free speech unconstitutional? Of course, unless it is undertaken voluntarily."

The press questioning that followed was harsh, as Shiller expected. He treated each questioner, no matter how rude or insulting, with respect. However, it didn't always come across that way: his answers were cool pointed daggers of intelligence. Men and women, accustomed to humiliating those in power, suddenly found themselves outgunned.

CHAPTER NINE

The past several weeks had been an emotional roller coaster for Beau. Aunt Lilly, not long after her visit to Aspen, had died suddenly, and without warning. Her 'when I'm gone' remark on the drive to Shiller's ranch did not mean 'when she got back to Louisiana,' as she had claimed. She must have known something was wrong. If true, it explained why she suddenly deeded over the Victorians . . . and why she made sure, by virtue of the renovations, that they would remain in the family.

Beau, along with everyone else, first learned at the funeral that she had succumbed to an aneurysm too advanced to treat when the doctors found it. At first he felt betrayed that she had not told him during her visit. But now he saw it differently. He saw that she had wanted to live the days she had remaining as she had always lived: on center stage. Her impending death, if others knew about it, would make her the object of pity. For her, that would have been another type of death as real as her physical demise. And so she kept her secret until the end. When she collapsed at Mattie Palmer's bridge party, she was in the middle of telling one of her inimitable tales. Four tables of women she had known all her life had to swallow their laughter. As usual, Aunt Lilly had gotten her way.

Beau rolled over beneath the heavy down comforter and pulled Nellie close. She didn't wake up, but her warm body in his arms helped fill the void his Aunt's death had left. Nellie had been with him since his return from Louisiana, the upside of his emotional roller coaster. While he was away she worked with Shiller's crews, devoting every spare minute of her time to the restoration of the carriage house. Beau knew nothing of this.

She phoned him in Lake Providence only once, and that was to let him know she or a friend would pick him up at the airport. When he arrived, Nellie was waiting. She drove him to his new residence, renovated, refurnished, decorated and well-stocked with food and drink. A gift, she said as he looked around in disbelief. She'd talked Shiller into letting his men work on the carriage house while he was gone. Yep, a gift because she cared for him. Beau suspected ulterior motives. His first thought when she asked if she could stay the night was that she felt sorry for him.

But she was in his bed the next night and the next, her legs wrapped tightly around him and her passion inexhaustible. It wasn't long until they became a couple, something Beau had secretly wanted from his very first night in Aspen. Nellie's friends seemed happy for her. Not so H. L., who made no effort to hide her disgust.

Their oversight of the restoration of Beau's houses did not suffer from the distractions of love. By the last week in January, the painted ladies were again the beauties they had been long ago. The condemnation order became a thing of the past, and the General declared them ready for the important people he hoped to bring to Aspen. And none too soon, if you listened to Shiller. The political system of the world's oldest democracy was not only deadlocked; it was dead.

***

Nellie pushed down the plunger on the French press more forcefully than usual and filled their travel mugs. It was 4:50 on the morning of February 4, just three days after the Iowa Caucuses. Already Shiller wanted to meet with them.

"I see why he's in a hurry," Beau said. "If he's going to stay in after that horrible Iowa showing, he needs to get some help ASAP. I'll bet he's already got people lined up to stay in the houses. What I don't get is why he insisted on such an ungodly hour."

Nellie kissed him on the cheek. "Why don't you ask him?"

"I might piss him off. I always have the feeling I might. He's nice to me, super nice, but the feeling just won't go away. Strange, isn't it?"

"He's a General, Beau. Those people live in a different world."

"You're telling me."

"We'd better hurry. He wants us outside at five sharp. You *will* piss him off if you're late."

"Me? What about you?"

"I'm not going to be late."

She grabbed his parka, opened the front door and walked out. He yanked on his boots, and caught up to her on the sidewalk in front of the Emma Claire. She held his travel mug for him while he fought his way into his coat.

"Okay. I'm on time. Impressed?"

"More like surprised."

61

Beau looked at the sky. The stars seemed close. They glittered like tiny ice prisms, so bright the crescent moon couldn't dim them. A night like this in Louisiana, he thought, would have been as black as coal. Here it glowed, so much so you didn't even need a flashlight.

He glanced at his watch. Almost five. He hoped the General would be late for his own meeting. No such luck. Seconds later the purr of a car engine reached his ears, and he saw the cool bluish headlights of Shiller's Land Rover rounding the corner.

Beau considered himself a casual sort of guy, not given to punctuality measured in seconds. But the General had messed with his mind more than he wished to admit. As Shiller pulled up to curbside, he felt a great sense of relief that he was on time and not dallying around in the carriage house. He held the front door open for Nellie, then climbed in back with a briskness absent from his DNA.

After a ride through the sleeping town they turned onto a narrow road made invisible by the snow. It must have been plowed before the last storm, Beau thought, or they'd already be high centered. Skillfully using the gears and throttle, the General inched ahead in a sort of controlled uphill slide. When the road closed in on them so tightly that the snow-laden pine branches to either side began dumping their loads on the jeep, Shiller finally spoke. "You're wondering about the hour?" he said, not taking his eyes off what had become little more than a trail.

"Not the hour but where you're gonna turn around."

"I come this way several times a week for a predawn hike. There's a turnaround a couple hundred yards ahead. We'll park there and continue on foot. Have you ever tried snowshoes, Mr. Wellington?"

"Are they anything like water skis?"

Shiller laughed. "You're in for a treat. And one hell of a workout. I wanted to reassure both of you when I asked about the hour that nothing is wrong. I merely wanted to discuss whether you two might work for me, and under what terms. Nellie, if you don't mind, help your friend into his gear. We'll discuss my proposal when we're at the top."

***

That eerie light of the moon and stars, brightened by a world of snow, was enough to illuminate the path. That didn't make snowshoeing easy, Beau thought. Sure, you could see exactly where you stepped. But sometimes, without warning, your shoes failed you and let your legs drop to your crotch in the deep powder. Then you faced the problem of how to fight your way back up to the surface. You couldn't lift both snowshoes up to crotch height. If you tried, even with one leg, you'd topple sideways into the three-foot deep powder, making the crater your fall had created twice its original size. Now you were on your knees or ass in a deep hole. You could reach the edges, but they gave way to the slightest touch.

What the hell could he do when the last visible part of him became the tip of his stocking cap? The first, last and only course of action he could formulate was to cry out for Nellie, who marched along with the General a hundred yards ahead. Each time he caused Shiller to wait, each time she hauled him to the surface, each time she lectured him on reading the terrain and feeling ahead for holes hidden by the snow, his humiliation grew.

"Okay, okay. I'll learn to swim. But slow the madman down. Please, Nellie, or I'll miss the entire meeting I came up here for."

"You'll get the hang of it," she said. She struck out up the path and disappeared around a curve.

He started ahead, carefully, tentatively, doing all the things she had told him to do. He thought he spotted an indentation in the softly glowing snow and triumphantly moved to the left. Something didn't feel right. Where pale light had shown earlier was now blackness. His eyes adjusted in a few seconds, and Beau realized with a pounding heart that he had moved to the side of the trail delineated by a near-vertical rock cliff.

He'd better get as far away from that chasm as he could. He was either getting the hang of it or just plain lucky, but he managed to traverse to the other side. A pine forest rose steeply, a wall that would save him. His forward progress? Well, it wasn't impressive, a foot at most. But what the hell. He was safe, and the cotton candy beneath his feet felt like reinforced concrete.

Beau willed himself forward, covering a mile on the forest side of the trail without a fall. Better not get cocky; better stop to rest. He was catching on, no doubt about it. The last thing he needed just now was a setback.

When his breathing slowed, he heard it. A twig in the undergrowth snapped, a mini-landslide came off a tree. He was cold and sweating at the same time. A chill went down his spine but it felt hot. Better an alligator than this. At least you knew what to expect, what to do. He tried to pretend the sounds were in his mind until he caught a glimpse of an animal with tawny fur slinking through the pines. It could be a deer, couldn't it? Deer didn't slink back home, but this was Aspen and everything was different here.

Silence. Was the thing waiting for him or had it gone away? He couldn't just stand here and freeze to death, so he'd better put his bet on number two.

***

The thing hadn't come back, and the former starting tailback for Ole Miss continued to transfer his skill from turf to powder. Rounding the corner minutes later, exhausted but unscathed, he saw Shiller sitting on a flat boulder unpacking breakfast. Nellie sat beside him, facing the other way, her legs dangling off the cliff. He could only imagine what those two were saying about him.

When Beau finally joined them, Nellie stood on tiptoes and gave him a much-needed kiss.

Shiller spoke without looking at him. "The 'sink or swim' order was from me, not your friend. Was I right, Nellie?"

She smiled broadly at both men.

The General said, "Mr. Wellington, regardless of what you may think, I'm glad you pulled yourself together. You've shown me a lot about yourself I wouldn't otherwise have known. Now, however, I must ask you to quit rasping."

"I can't help it, Sir. I'm out of breath."

"Then we'll wait. Not a word."

The breakfast Beau had watched Shiller take out of his pack was big enough for three. But being closer now, he could see that it wasn't breakfast at all. It was a large piece of raw meat. When the General deemed the environment silent enough, he leaned down and picked up a long pointed stick he had stashed behind a rock. Its tip looked like the flint of an overused arrow.

"Both of you, watch," Shiller ordered in a low steady voice. Be quiet, don't move, but watch." He skewered the meat and walked to the center of the path. The noises and little landslides off the trees Beau had attributed to a deer started up again. They didn't subside until a sleek mountain lion with a tail that stretched forever ventured out of the forest. The lion looked first at Beau and Nellie, let out a blood-curdling hiss, then turned his attention to Shiller – or rather to the meat. The General backed up, and the lion followed in the stealthy crouch of a hunting feline. As soon as Shiller extended the stick, the cat lunged at the meat, ripped it away with a swipe of its paw and disappeared into the forest. Shiller turned to face his hiking companions.

"That was Rommel. Impressive by any standard, isn't he?"

"Yes," Nellie said, "especially in his natural habit."

Beau kept silent: he didn't want to start speaking in tongues.

64

"Our first meeting was less cordial," the General explained with visible pride. "I'm not naïve. I kept a hand on my service revolver. But I took a step forward, speaking in the calm voice you heard me use today. Neither one of us moved for at least ten minutes. Then, finally, he took off. The next time I came armed with meat. Even so, establishing dominance took months. Now he trusts me. Against all odds, I might add. You find this an isolated incident. Or perhaps a random case of good luck. But neither is correct. My encounter with the lion is foreshadowing of the fight I've chosen to pick with the political establishment, a fight I'm going to win with unflinching will. I'm going to stare down Washington, and they're going to blink. My poor showing in Iowa is not the beginning of the end but, rather, the end of the beginning."

To the east, the first hint of dawn stretched along the horizon, still too young to extinguish the night sky. Beau felt uneasy, having just experienced the strangest few hours of his life. The eerie glow that had cast a soft light on their trail now seemed to acquire a substance of its own, like mist – or gas. Sunrise, he thought, could not come too soon.

***

Shiller, still on his feet, stared into the distance. "I would now like to make the proposal I mentioned earlier."

"An offer we can't refuse?" joked Nellie. She seemed at ease with Shiller: polite, respectful and at ease. She'd grown up in a military family; he had been raised by Aunt Lilly. That, he supposed, was the difference. When there was rational talk, she saw Reason behind it. He, on the other hand, saw the Reason behind rational talk as another layer of deception. He saw it as a veil hiding some hideous threat slithering toward him in eerie silence, hidden from sight by sunken tree stumps and tall marsh grasses.

He realized at that moment the source of his dread. He had been listening to Shiller's well-reasoned words rather than watching the veil . . .

"Of course not," the General said. "This is an offer you *can* refuse. It's an offer I want you to refuse if you don't believe in my cause, or if you don't find the substance of the job to your liking.

"As you know, the New Hampshire primary is next week. Within a day, all of the painted ladies will be occupied. You will recognize the names of the state's two senators and perhaps those of the agency heads arriving from Washington. The state pols, perhaps most important to my campaign, you have probably never heard of. Not to worry. You won't be using names, even names you know. If you're asked by a politician or member of the press about any aspect of my politics, *you don't know*. You're merely helping with the logistics of my campaign. You will refer them to a spokesperson I hired yesterday."

Shiller fell silent, paced a few steps and again peered into the distance. Behind him, the rising sun set ablaze streaks of high wispy cloud. The stars had vanished, and the moon hung over the high peaks like a faded X-ray of its former self.

The General clasped his hands behind his back. "I need someone who knows the town well to make arrangements for my private talks. Some will be larger gatherings than others. Some will be longer. Some will involve high-level intelligence people from D.C. Others will be with US Senators and Representatives. You can imagine the paparazzi-like reaction of the press. Nellie, your excellent working relationship with the management of the Jerome will be invaluable for all of these meetings. Once in a great while I will also need you to help with the catering of larger events at my ranch. Not one person on my regular kitchen staff speaks English, and I'm not going to have time in the middle of a heated election campaign to fly cooks in from New Orleans.

"As for you, Mr. Wellington, I need someone to help ferry people to and from the airport – important people in many cases. And, of course, Nellie will often require a helping hand.

"I also need eyes and ears around town – and perhaps, on occasion, in other localities. The jobs I am offering you will put you in a perfect position to be those eyes and ears."

"You mean we're going to be spies?" Nellie asked, excited by the prospect.

"Reporters would be more accurate. Undercover reporters, if you like. As my candidacy picks up momentum, there is going to be a tidal wave of scrutiny. Why? Because what I am doing is not supposed to succeed. A lot of this scrutiny will come from the press. Some of it will come from the other campaigns. And some of it may come from the nation's law enforcement and intelligence organizations. In short, those who have based their careers on conventional thinking will wish me to fail and will go to extremes to make sure that I do. This is a small community. You'll learn things I should know about, things that won't be true but can be dealt with more effectively if I have advance notice. A lot of attention is likely to settle on the security service I plan to assemble. These are dangerous times, and I'm not going to put my safety in the hands of drunken philanderers. You will have heard of the recent incidents involving the Secret

66

Service, the official Secret Service. So, that's my proposal. Mr. Wellington, I know that you are a millionaire. I also know that your inheritance is tied up in probate and that your deal with me regarding your homes will not produce income until the lease has run its course. If you join me, we will discuss your compensation.

"I realize that you will need time and privacy to reach a decision. I'll go ahead and wait at the jeep. But please. Have an answer when you arrive."

CHAPTER TEN

"Hatch, I need you over here."

"I'll be there in a moment. We've gotten the results on Kelly back from Washington."

"Kelly will have to wait. Forsythe just called. A video feed is going to start any minute, and Herr Direktor has ordered both of us to watch it."

"Video of what?"

"I don't know, but the Man says it's important . . . just shot by a news helicopter above New York."

"New York? Isn't the coast still socked in?"

"Nope. Frigid but clear."

Hatch, as always, moved quickly and quietly. In seconds he stood with a hand on either side of the door frame, straining to focus in the weak fluorescent light of what Connor called his Aspen geek room. "Jesus, Randall, throw whatever you're looking at onto the wall screen. I can't see the monitor with you in front of it."

"That's exactly what I'm doing. Have a seat. I'll join you before the show starts."

The picture on the enormous wall screen, when it appeared, would be enhanced. The system, which was meant to show in minute detail things that otherwise might be missed, had been designed to CIA specs and distributed in small numbers to the Bureau and its state counterparts. Presently, however, the screen was blank.

Connor sat with a thud, launching droplets of coffee in all directions. "Quiet!" he barked preemptively. "It starts with just audio."

"Randall, you're losing it," Hatch objected. "I didn't say anything,"

"You just did."

The audio from the chopper began, off-air audio, not meant for broadcast. "Jennifer, did you notice anything unusual out your side?"

"Just a normal Friday evening rush hour. The Cross-Bronx and Trans-

Manhattan are creeping along until the stream pools at the GW bridge."

"How about you, Chad?" asked the male half of the news team. "See anything?"

"Negative, Ted," the pilot shot back over the clatter of blades

"Both of you, take another look. A small plane is crossing into Manhattan right now. It's almost in the water."

"I see it now," the woman reporter said. "Can he make it to the Hudson?"

"If he does, I hope he's another Sully. Chad, can you drop down a few hundred feet?"

"Sorry. LaGuardia air traffic control. Look at that! He's not having mechanical problems. He's following the Trans-Manhattan, staying low, dodging buildings when he has to."

"I'll radio the station."

"Good idea."

Word came back a few seconds later. "Okay, Ted, start transmitting. Use the telescopic lens."

Connor and Hatch looked on, mesmerized. The new system proved its worth. What TV reporters and viewers alike took for a private plane was clearly a gray drone. It began to take on altitude as it neared the snarl of cars and trucks waiting to cross the George Washington Bridge. The agents heard the helicopter engine straining to pick up enough speed to follow.

Then something happened that caused the male newscaster to gasp before a live audience of millions. The drone climbed, exposing its familiar shape to the regular camera. After clearing the toll plaza, it descended between the great cables of the suspension bridge and levelled off only a few dozen feet above the stalled traffic.

"Holy Madonna," Hatch said. "That's one of ours. An MQ-9. The drone we use to target terrorists in the Middle East."

"Listen to the reporters," Connor said. "We can play this thing again. Remember. It's a recording."

"Okay, but one quick remark. Those mounts for the Hellfires seem to be fitted with anti-aircraft missiles. Some kind of upgraded Stingers."

"I noticed. Not good."

The male newscaster, trying to regain his composure, reported that a gray wisp had come out of the bottom of the drone.

"Not a wisp," the pilot said while they were still on the air. "That was the separation puff of a bomb. Delayed action warhead so the drone out-lives its work. JESUS CHRIST! It hit a tanker truck. Hang on, we're in for some turbulence when it blows."

A retired military pilot, thought Connor. Most of these guys were.

The woman spoke to the producer on a frequency the public could not hear. "Ethan, should we shut off the camera?"

"Are you kidding? We may be able to scoop the *Post*. Biggest story since 9/11."

"Oh, my God."

The tanker truck erupted. The massive fireball and several secondary explosions mangled a tar and steel bridge span supporting tons of stalled traffic. Without warning, the upper level of the span collapsed onto the lower bridge, taking with it dozens of blazing cars and trucks. The female reporter tried without success to give a professional-sounding description of the nightmare below.

"Turn off the sound," Connor grumbled. "That hysterical bitch is driv-ing me crazy."

"Ignore her, Randall. The audio might contain something we need to hear."

The agents watched the drone disappear into the arch of the bridge's last pylon. At nearly the same time, a fierce blaze erupted beside a truck waiting to move east. The drone reappeared, climbed through the parallel suspension cables and started a leisurely descent toward New Jersey and Interstate 95. Then the fireworks began in earnest. They were so violent it looked for an instant as if the pylon would give way and the entire bridge would plunge into the river. "That was ordinance, partner. What the hell is an ammo transport doing on the bridge?"

"Eyes ahead, Hatch. Follow the drone. What's there was there."

"And our drone boy seems to have known it."

"Possible. Where the hell is the Air Force?"

"Randall, this whole episode has taken less than three minutes – too little time to for a fighter wing to scramble."

"True. But something must have already been in the air."

"I think you're right."

The roar of two F-16s grew to a crescendo as the fighters passed over the bridge and banked into a sharp descending curve. Connor almost lost it when he saw the drone's air-to-air missiles blast out of their mounts and lock on the jets. The pilots, caught by surprise, had no time for evasive action. Both were hit. Fiery pieces of wreckage and randomly exploding weapons tumbled toward Fort Lee, New Jersey.

"Not even time to punch out," Hatch groaned. "If only someone could have warned our guys about the retrofit."

"The news chopper pilot should have noticed. He was a military guy. Besides, you see these drones on TV every night armed with Hellfires, not Stingers. Incompetence, Hatch. It's gonna take us all down."

The screen went momentarily blank, the audio switched to Forsythe. "The footage you'll see next was shot at the Port Authority's Teterboro Airport on the Jersey side. Relevant scraps from several sources were pieced together by our techs."

The camera on the control tower of the small commuter airport followed the tiny gray drone, which was flying a few yards above the adjacent freeway, I-95. Suddenly, the drone made a sharp turn toward the airport, picked up a little altitude and landed. On the ground it looked as frail as a praying mantis.

Airport police cars rushed out to surround the gift that had come their way. Both agents assumed that someone had done the calculations and that the death machine had exhausted its supply of bombs and missiles. For once, they were right.

A second camera scanned the drone's exterior. Something caught Hatch's attention. "Randall, look at the underside of the wings." He picked up a pointer to illustrate a scarcely visible line of light green letters, Arabic letters.

"I suppose you can read that shit."

"Not really, but I had a course in it once. Two years of hell. I think the word 'traffic' is in there." "What about 'problems'?"

"No idea. Why?"

"Time for some traffic problems. I'd bet what's left of my manhood that's the translation."

"Could be. If you're right, it's another episode of taunting."

A third camera, this one accompanied by good lighting, moved through the drone's ordinance bays. A note in English was etched into one of the exposed metal panels: "Americans should learn what they are inflicting on others. Our teachings will continue until they do."

Before either agent could comment, Forsythe's voice intruded: "I hate to tell you this, men, but the bad news doesn't stop there. The videos of the Sean Keenan and Moose Chapman murders just appeared on YouTube. They'll go viral in minutes, making this another day of infamy.

Unless we figure this mess out, it won't be long till we're living in a country of 300 million people afraid to go out of their houses. As for us, the legendary crime solvers, we'll be lucky if we even have houses to go out of. Yes, that's right. I'm talking about immediate dismissal with no pay, no pension, no nothing. Sure it's illegal, but who gives a shit at this point? So, gentlemen, one more plea, this one from the President. Do your job or lose it. The same goes for me, if it's any comfort. Have a pleasant evening."

Surrounded by silence, Connor stared around the room without seeing – or wanting to see. But one thing he could not escape. It was the light in this goddamn geek room. There was a bluish tint he hadn't noticed before. It seemed to shimmer a moment, detached from a source. Then it got inside his mind and rendered it useless.

Hatch noticed. "Snap out of it, Randall. Our work hasn't been a total failure. In a little more than a month, we've uncovered and prevented an attack on the St. Louis airport; we've found the culprit in the bridge demolition on I-80; we've supplied the information that led to the Denver sniper's arrest. And, as of yesterday, we've gotten to the bottom of the Tulsa school shooting. We must be doing something right."

"No. Those were routine cases. Without the taunting, you'll notice. None of them are connected."

"And Kelly?"

"A random murder we haven't cracked."

"Randall, remember what I told you when you pulled me into the geek room?"

"What? I'm shutting down."

"I said the results from reading that thing the CBI found near Kelly's murderer's snowmobile had come back from Washington."

"That thing? I still think it was the black box from an old plane crash."

"You're half right. It *was* a black box, but it had nothing to do with a plane. It had been gutted. No disc inside, nothing but a note. Paint in the scrape marks show that it had been on the snowmobile."

"And?"

Hatch held out the paper, which Connor unfolded like a letter from his ex-wife.

"Aren't you going to read it?"

"Why don't you read it aloud. My eyes are killing me."

"Give it here."

Connor snapped out of his daze midway through the first sentence:

72

We endorse America's commitment to equality, even if Americans don't. Our teachings will honor that commitment. We will not discriminate against political orientation or geographical setting, North, South, East or West. More importantly we will offer our help in bringing equality to your economic life. A good place to start is with the elimination of the obscenely rich. You have exactly one week to achieve this yourselves. If you don't, you might want to warn CEOs, thieves on Wall Street, lobbyists, wealthy political donors and holders of inherited fortunes that they are no longer safe. We want you Americans to know how it feels to practice at home what you preach abroad.

"How's that for taunting?" Hatch said. "With this material, I think we can safely say we've linked the three murders to one another. I don't know what it means for our investigation, but at least it's a start."

"I suppose," Connor said, falling back into his stupor.

"You need a drink," Hatch pronounced, correctly reading the situation. "Let's go across the street. If it's any consolation, I'm buying."

CHAPTER ELEVEN

Their second day on the job Beau awoke to a smell he loved, the smell of bacon. It was the smell of his boyhood, his youth, his college days. It was the smell of mornings in Louisiana. No one seemed to eat this magnificent delicacy in Aspen, the global center of dietary hypocrisy. No one but an occasional vegan hiding in the corner of the greasy spoon where all the cops went. The bouquet drew him to the kitchen, where Nellie stood over a hot iron skillet, dodging the grease showers after each pop. She wore the same long T-shirt she had helped him struggle out of the night before – and nothing else.

Had Saint Peter asked him at the Pearly Gates what he wanted in heaven, he would have answered, "This, just this, nothing more." He couldn't believe he wanted her again already after their marathon session the night before. But he did. He was naked, ready; she might as well have been naked. He came up behind her, slipped his hands over her breasts and whispered into her ear.

"Beau! Stop it! I'll burn the bacon."

She would burn the bacon . . . she actually had a point. She would still be here in 20 minutes; why not have the two things on earth he loved unconditionally on the same morning? The kitchen table would do quite nicely for both.

"Only one thing could make me wait. You know what that is, right?"

"I do. You can't believe the trouble I went to finding something that wasn't made out of turkey, shiitake mushrooms or God knows what else. Today's your Birthday. Had you forgotten?"

"You made me forget everything last night. Thanks for remembering."

"*I* made you forget. It's not my fault you're thirty-one and senile." She brushed a quick kiss across his lips. "To work. Hand me four eggs from the fridge, please. I'm trying to have the bacon and biscuits ready at the same time."

He noticed while he was reaching for the refrigerator handle that she had already set the table. The butter was out, not some kind of yak milk health spread but the real thing. The flowers in the center of the table were lilies. She'd done that on purpose, he thought, knowing how much his Aunt had meant to him. And the white linen tablecloth he was already imagining as a bottom sheet.

He handed her the eggs, which she cracked with one hand and slid into the hot grease. One perfect woman in the world, he thought, and he'd managed to find her in a place as foreign as Aspen.

Beau counted his lucky blessings again when she walked toward the table with two steaming plates. Her hair was a mess, the way he liked it – piled on top of her head with long blonde strands escaping and tumbling where they would. Her legs were sensational, her breasts full. She was a goddess, at least to him. Nothing else had ever threatened to interrupt his sacred relationship with bacon, but she was coming damn close.

He'd been with plenty of girls down South, some of whom he hadn't even told Aunt Lilly about. He remembered the smudged eye shadow and misshapen mascara on the faces of the strangers he awoke to find in his bed; remembered the pinkish face paint on the pillow beside him; remembered the occasional fake eyelash or painted fingernail lurking like a fishing lure beneath the sheets. He supposed that was why he never made love in the morning to a girl he brought home at night.

But Nellie . . . she was incredible. She was Nellie when she went to bed, and a slightly tousled but equally beautiful Nellie in the morning. And just like now, she unleashed in him an early morning torrent of desire. That's why the phone call after the best breakfast he had eaten in Aspen came at such an unwanted moment. She was on her back on the table now, his T-shirt above her breasts and her legs slightly parted when that shrill ring barred his path to paradise.

She rolled off the table. "Answer it, Beau. Don't forget the promise we made the General."

"Okay, goddammit. Okay." He picked up the receiver as though he wanted to strangle it. "What?"

"Mr. Wellington," H. L. said, "are you aware of what is happening outside your houses?"

Beau cracked the curtains, then hit the floor. "Get down, Nellie! Reporters!"

She started for the bedroom, then glimpsed a tiny gap in the curtains and disappeared into the john.

Beau crawled to the phone, that had skittered across the room when he

75

went down. "Sorry, H. L., I dropped the phone. I see a couple of reporters on the sidewalk. What's the problem?"

"You have a liberal definition of 'a couple.' I want you and Nellie at the Historical Society in ten minutes, even if it necessitates a communal shower."

"If there's a communal shower, you can expect us around noon."

"Don't get smart with me, Wellington. This is serious." She slammed down the receiver.

Bad luck, he thought. Something strange had transformed this woman he had worked so hard to get along with back into the terror she'd been when they first met.

"Nellie," he called. "Where are you? We are being ordered by your boss to take a communal shower. We're supposed to be at the Historical Society in ten minutes."

"I've just showered, Beau. Find your community with soap and water. Your jeans aren't dry yet but wear them anyway."

***

"It doesn't sound *that* bad," Beau said. "Lawns are private property, even if they're covered with snow – right? Call the Sheriff and have him dispatch a few cops."

"You're not getting it, Mr. Wellington, so let me repeat myself. The General called here just before I called you. He's putting up two dozen important people in those houses of yours, and a couple hundred reporters are harassing them. He wants the reporters to back off and give his guests some breathing room. Since the attack in New York yesterday, the media is desperate for his reaction."

"Attack in New York? Do you know anything about an attack, Nellie?"

"Of course she does," H. L. said bitterly. "She's been out of the South long enough to – "

"Actually, H. L., I don't. We didn't get back from snowshoeing until late. Then we cooked supper and turned in. The *Times* hadn't come this morning when – "

"Spare me the details. We can't have cops out there bludgeoning anyone who mouths off. We can't have some fool lighting up a reporter from the *Washington Post*. The General is a *candidate for President*. He needs the press and wants them treated with kid gloves. But they have to be moved outside the perimeter fences and onto the sidewalks."

"Yeah, okay," Beau said. "Explain that to the Sheriff. He'll know which cops are right for the job."

H. L. looked down at her hands. "I can't. We've been having a nasty row – and he's a vindictive son-of-a-bitch."

"Row about what?" Nellie asked.

"That can wait. Right now we have to solve the reporter problem. ASAP in the General's words. Remember: he's someone who can help the Historical Society with its mission, especially if he becomes President. The Sheriff isn't going to cooperate with me. Which is where you come in, Nellie. I'd like you to go over to his office with your Southern gentlemen, the owner of the houses, and explain the trespassing situation. He's obligated to take care of it. You, if anyone, can convince of the need for delicacy. A little later, I'd like you to drive by the places and confirm that good things are happening."

"So what about this attack?" Beau said. "We should know something about it before we walk into a den of cops."

H. L. shoved the *New York Times* down the table. "Get going. One of you can read while the other drives."

***

"You gotta be kidding. One of our drones almost took out the George Washington Bridge?"

"Incredible, huh," Nellie said. "Then there are two YouTube videos posted at around the same time. They show Sean Keenan and Moose Chapman being murdered."

"I thought those guys both had heart attacks."

"So did the rest of the world. This is getting bad, Beau. A lot of people are going to feel better if we have a military man as President."

"You're saying you think he has a chance."

"That's what I'm saying. We'll know more on Tuesday."

"Why Tuesday?"

She looked at him, horrified. "Beau! That's the day of the New Hampshire primary."

"Sorry. I was thinking of something else. So where's the Sheriff's office?"

"Near the Jerome. But he won't be there. He hangs out at Duff's Diner until ten. Find a place to park. It's just around the corner."

Don Cousins, the Pitkin County Sheriff, was one of those walking contradictions a lot of Sheriffs seemed to be – at least in Beau's experience. He sat at a big round table with two other men in full view of anyone who happened to come into Duff's. That could be someone who had the power to fire at him or someone who had the power to get him fired. In Louisiana you expected the local cops to be in a greasy spoon most of the workday, but this was Aspen – a long way from the Mason-Dixon Line.

In front of Sheriff Cousins was a plate heaped with eggs, potatoes, bacon, sausages, biscuits and a ribeye steak that was more marbling than meat. When you saw a plate like that, you expected to see a person of considerable heft behind it, like the other guy at the table with a 5,000 calorie cholesterol heap on his plate. But the Sheriff was one of those skinny guys with veins in his forehead from being in good shape and a belt that went right over the center of his midsection without making a flesh gully. The third guy at the table . . . well, you couldn't really describe him. He just looked like a regular guy – not fat and not thin; not tall, not short; not handsome, not ugly. The only memorable thing about him, the only thing that stood out in this temple of grease, was the bran muffin on his plate. The bag where he had bought it – the health food bakery around the corner – lay neatly folded beside him.

But these two guys who weren't the Sheriff, they had something in common. It wasn't at all clear what that something was. Beau looked on for a while trying to figure it out while Nellie went over and charmed Don Cousins. He slid an empty chair close to his and invited her to sit. Trying to look at him rather than his plate, Nellie explained the situation.

Within a minute or two, deputies from inside and outside the diner were surrounding the Sheriff. He was still eating but mumbled something in Nellie's direction. The message was clear: he wanted her to explain to his men what she had just explained to him. No problem there. Everyone who knew the Sheriff knew you didn't interrupt his breakfast.

Beau had taken a seat next to the big guy. "Terrible what's happening in New York," he said. "In the whole country, for that matter. Are you all from here?"

Connor laughed. "We're from everywhere, my partner and me. He grew up in some Podunk place in Arizona. I was lucky enough to call Memphis my home until school and work dragged me away. Used to look at that big ole looping river every day on the way to school when I was a kid. Say, I hope you don't mind me saying this, but you've got quite an accent. You look vaguely familiar too. Were you ever at Ole Miss?"

"Yeah, a long time ago. How about you? Did you go to school there?"

"No. UT in Knoxville. Which reminds me why I recognize you. SBW Three! That was you, right?

"Right."

"Connor stopped in mid-sausage. "Well, I'll be damned. You're the guy who cost me my first ten grand."

"Sorry about that. I sure as hell wasn't on the receiving end."

"What are you two talking about," Hatch asked. "SBW III? Ten grand lost?"

"Come on, partner. This is that guy I told you about, the guy who took down the Big Orange. We were undefeated, three TDs up with twelve minutes to go. So they hand the ball to a younger version of the man you're looking at. No fancy stuff, no passing or trick plays, just handoffs. And he scores four running TDs in less time than it takes you to get off the john."

"No fruit sucks like the Big Orange," Beau said, smiling. He turned politely to Hatch. "That was the chant from the stands, started by our very proper cheerleaders. But it wasn't me who made it happen. It was their line. Tennessee left holes I could've driven a cement truck through."

Connor stood and hauled Beau to his feet. "Hatch, don't listen to his modest nonsense. I want you to meet Sir Beau Wellington the Third, the best college back I've ever seen. So, Sir Beau. What happened? How come we never heard of you in the pros?"

"Injuries. My Aunt suggested graduate school at Vanderbilt instead. Probably just as well."

"And what brings you to Aspen, of all places?"

"My family owns four Victorian houses here, and our local presidential candidate needed places to put up people during his campaign. To make a long story short, I leased them to him. Everything was fine until the attack in New York, but now we have a problem I have to solve ASAP."

"And that would be?"

"The reporters swarming all over the General's guests. My girlfriend's trying to get the Sheriff to move them back to the sidewalk without pissing them off. So, how about you guys? What brings you to Aspen?"

"We're FBI," Hatch said. "It's no secret. We're here to help with the crackdown on narcotics."

"Well, I guess you'll be heading back to New York soon."

"Could be. Say, isn't your girl one of the bartenders at the Jerome?"

"Nellie? Yeah. She loves being around people – all types"

"Then maybe she won't mind us," Connor said, "Listen, Sir Beau, while we're waiting on the next set of orders from Washington, we'd gladly drive around and check on your houses. You know, make sure the trespassing problem gets solved. FBI credentials speak more loudly than armed local cops – especially to those pushy bastards from the East."

"That would be great, really great. But why would you bother?"

Hatch said, "We have our own history with the press. We're not football stars. In other words, we don't like the way we're treated."

"Amen," Connor added. "So any time we can make their job a little harder is a good time. Besides, we're interested in your man, Shiller. We'll see how he does in New Hampshire, but I have a feeling he'll surprise the people we're going to help you deposit on the sidewalk. I don't need to tell you this, but we're getting hit from all sides. Maybe the General is what we need. Anything we can do to help him, like getting the press out of his guests' faces, we'd like to do."

CHAPTER TWELVE

Jake Hollis wasn't accustomed to wearing a suit, much less a tailored suit. Normally he hated to dress up, but he had to admit he liked the feel of this magnificent creation of merino wool and Italian design. Shiller had sent a tailor from a place called Ermenegildo Zegna last fall to have him measured, saying only that he wanted his man to look his best.

When Shiller made his final plans known, he informed Hollis what his bit part in the larger operation would be. He also asked him to wear his new Ermenegildo Zegna suit in New Hampshire the night the primary results came in.

Years ago, when Hollis served under the General on active duty, he knew exactly what was expected of him, both in dress and behavior. But as spokesman for a presidential candidate . . . well, that was something new. He had the credentials, sure. But his political science doctorate from Harvard had become, after two decades, a meaningless piece of paper, and his resurgent passion for politics was no guarantee that he was equipped for the job. He had never answered questions from reporters, never even appeared on TV. All he had to buoy his confidence was Shiller's assurance that he would surprise himself once he dove into the mêlée. He had doubted the General's judgment on many occasions when he had been assigned to missions he considered impossible. But he had always succeeded and made it home alive.

Shiller seemed clairvoyant when it came to reading the strengths and weaknesses of others, strengths and weaknesses men often didn't know they had. That meant a lot to Jake Hollis: if Shiller thought he would perform brilliantly in the post for which he had been chosen, then he *would* perform brilliantly.

By the time Hollis jogged down the stairs of Shiller's private jet at the Manchester-Boston regional airport, he had put self-doubt behind him. He had been offered the chance to be a known representative of his country's historic transformation, an honor few could dream of. But it was more than an honor; it was also a path to power. He had tasted power in the field and liked it. Now, suddenly, he was ready for more – a lot more.

***

Followed by a small but pushy gaggle of reporters, most of them local, he checked out the facilities at the Castleton Banquet and Conference Center. True, the establishment was frequently used for celebrity weddings. Looking at photographs, he had feared the place might have an indelible air of levity that would stop him from doing what the General wanted. But now he could see that Shiller had chosen well. With a few minor changes, the Center would become a lush but somber venue. A post-primary speech would stand out because of its non-traditional delivery, not because of the environment in which that delivery took place. This was of critical importance to Shiller: if he was going to survive as a candidate, he had to demonstrate from the start that a campaign could be carried out with technology rather than time-wasting travel. If he failed in New Hampshire, there would be no second chance.

It was Sunday evening. The enormous screens and the AV systems that would allow questions to be answered by Shiller had been prepared for delivery and testing the next day. But Hollis still had his hands full. He was to make arrangements for transporting the General's local supporters here without hassle. He was to ensure that the bar, kitchen and hors d'oeuvres tables were set up as the boss wanted them; and most importantly, he was to decide, in concert with the state party chairman, who would speak, in what order, and for how long. It was a lot to get done in such a short time, but he had done more in less pleasant surroundings. Jake Hollis answered a few questions from the reporters, then retired to his hotel to sketch out how he wanted to proceed.

***

"Would you look at that," Beau said, throwing open the shutters. "It's Armageddon in white."

Nellie glanced up from the ham and cheese panini she was making. "Actually it's a snowstorm, not exactly abnormal in the Rockies. I told you yesterday it was predicted. That's why the reporters are gone. They got out of town while they could. Up for a little skiing this afternoon? When we get powder like this, the whole place goes into party mode. *Mardi Gras* in white."

"I've never seen anything like it, not even here. I think God decided to bury us in talc. I can't even tell where the gate is. I hope this doesn't mess up Shiller's transmission tomorrow."

82

"It won't. The man's a contingency artist. So, how about the skiing?"

"Look, Nellie, I'm just learning. You'll be hauling me out of drifts the whole time. Why don't we stay here after lunch, have a little nap, build a fire and make love until morning? You're off tonight, aren't you?"

"And tomorrow night. Here's a compromise. We warm up on ham and cheese panini and hit the slopes for a couple hours. Then I'm yours."

Beau stepped close to the window and squinted into the whiteout. "What the hell is that?"

Nellie joined him at the window. Shadowy figures were visible just inside the gate, moving slightly but going nowhere. A snow blower choked a few times, then buzzed to life. Pushed by one of the shadows, it came toward them, plowing the sidewalk to the carriage house before continuing toward the rear entrance of the Emma Claire. The two men who weren't pushing the thing followed, wrapped up like mummies.

"Beau, we'd better get out there and see what's going on. This is the perfect time for a robbery."

"Hang on. That's Shiller, the one in the Russian hat and sheepskin coat. Looks like he's paying us a visit."

Nellie opened the door. "General, what are you doing out in this weather?"

He didn't move from the tile entryway, didn't take off anything but his hat. "Sorry to barge in like this. Any news?"

"Only the FBI guys," Beau said. "The two that helped the Sheriff's men push back the reporters. They said they'd met you already."

"Nothing else? Nellie?"

"Well, what I've been hearing at the bar is that you're a dreamer who'll be out of the race any day now. But there's less talk like that since the attack in New York. Actually, quite a bit less. I've overheard a few regulars saying you might be what the country needs."

"It will soon be more than a few regulars. You must be wondering about the hubbub outside. I'm putting up three of my men here, the men you just saw. I asked them to watch the primary tomorrow on TV, and I'd like you to join them. We'll discuss the reasons later."

Without another word, he put on his fur hat and left.

***

At five o'clock the following evening TV coverage of the New Hampshire primary began. As the General had asked – or ordered – Nellie and Beau sat with three strangers in the parlour of the Emma Claire. The men were all roughly the same age, around fifty, and looked to be in awesome physical condition. As for their social graces, they had none. Nellie asked them if they had been in the military. They all responded with a curt 'yes miss' before sinking back into an awkward silence.

A fire crackled in the old stone hearth. Heavy pieces of Gothic and Rococo style furniture crowded a space already filled with intricately patterned rugs, marble-top tables, and an upright piano that could have come from a Wild West cathouse. The walls had wainscoting at the bottom and a cornice at the top. They were covered with dark oil paintings in carved frames. And there was a large flat-screen TV, apparently delivered for the occasion. The room was so full it felt suffocating, and the presence of Shiller's men added to that feeling.

"You fellas eaten?" Nellie asked during a commercial. "I can have something yummy delivered by one of the hotel restaurants. It won't be a hassle. I work with these people."

"No thanks, miss. We brought our own provisions."

The man who had declined dinner turned to his buddies. "Imagine the disaster if it hadn't stopped snowing. No satellite link, no television coming in and no streaming from the ranch."

"He's always lucky. I've never seen him blindsided by anything."

"Quiet," the third man said. "The results are starting to come in."

Everyone stared at the TV. With 7% of the precincts reporting, the General was in second place. Something had changed since Iowa.

The night wore on, the men drank some kind of health smoothie one of them made in the blender. Mercifully no one offered Nellie or Beau anything, so Nellie used the phone to call the Jerome. By the time their pasta and wine arrived, Shiller was in first place.

The crew covering his campaign began broadcasting from the Castleton Center, which was filled to overflowing with the General's backers.

The refrain among national reporters maintained a steady rhythm. Who were they? Where had they come from? Shiller had no ground game in New Hampshire, so what explained their presence?

The beltway media speculated with increasing frequency that the General had hired people to attend. But no one interviewed on camera made the impression of acting, and no one in the local press mentioned the absence of a ground game. To anyone watching the enthusiasm in the hall, it was clear that a candidate who had come out of obscurity was in the race to stay.

With 87% of the precincts reporting, Shiller's lead had become insurmountable. He had garnered a fourth of the vote in a field of 14 men and women. The size of his victory was underlined by the fact that only two other candidates had escaped the purgatory of single digits; and that Shiller's 25% nearly equaled their combined total.

Shiller's spokesman, Jake Hollis, stepped to the podium a half hour after the race had been called. His masterful presentation was greeted with wild applause that reached a crescendo when Shiller appeared on large screens placed strategically around the hall. He was standing beside a massive stone fireplace in his Aspen ranch when he began his victory speech. It became evident in the first minutes that he could hear the crowd as well as they heard him. He behaved exactly as a live speaker would, waiting during periods of applause and responding with sincere words of gratitude to the most intense outbursts. In fact, as one of the TV newsmen reported, it was easy to forget he was hundreds of miles away.

According to a woman interviewed after the event, watching him gave the impression that he was speaking exclusively to you. It was easy to understand why. Wherever you sat or stood, a screen was near. No one jumped, stood on tiptoes or climbed on tables to see him. Waiting for him to turn his gaze in your direction was like waiting for him to find you in the crowd and single you out as the recipient of his words.

The General bestowed the normal round of thanks on those state and local politicians who had come to Aspen and helped him formulate a viable alternative to the traditional ground game. That was the end of the prepared remarks. He now asked for questions from the press and his supporters. Several of Shiller's men circulated with microphones so that all who spoke could be clearly heard.

Hands went up everywhere. At that moment, the television picture being broadcast across the nation went into split-screen format, allowing viewers to watch the General and crowd simultaneously.

"Jeremy," Shiller said, nodding at Jeremy Pollack of the *San Francisco Chronicle*. Before Pollack could utter a word, a member of Shiller's staff moved close to him and held out a microphone.

The reporter, a tall gaunt man with thinning gray hair, was not startled by the sudden appearance of the mike. "General Shiller, I'm sure we'll get into questions of policy soon. Before we do, however, I want to ask why you – on such a momentous occasion – why you are not here in New Hampshire."

"Given the results, I think it more interesting to know why the other thirteen candidates *are* here."

Laughter, both in the hall and in millions of American living rooms.

85

"You know what I mean. Do you really think you can continue to run your campaign from afar?"

"I have no choice. If I am going to figure out the root cause of our vulnerability to attack, I can't waste the time it would take to run a traditional campaign. Let the others travel around the country shaking hands with voters they'll never see again. Let them eat hot dogs at county fairs, speak at fundraising events and prepare for debates to gain media exposure. While such foolish antics are going on, I'll be working on ways to save our country."

Now the questions came fast and furious:

"General, in light of the horrific things that have happened in the last days, have you changed anything in your agenda?"

"No. Do you have another question?"

"Yes, thank you. I think it's everyone's question. How would you, as president, protect us from attack?"

"One can't protect an open society when people are willing to die to harm it. We're not North Korea and never will be. What we can do is remove from the face of the earth those willing to die."

"And how would you do this? You're up against a billion people."

"Excuse me? You are making the assumption that the world's one billion Muslims are all terrorists. Nothing could be further from the truth. God's Wrath and its affiliates don't have enough fighters to fill a football stadium. We hear how youth in the West are being mobilized by social media to join this dead-end cause. Let me give you an example of one of the many ways to stop this. For every God's Wrath video that appears on YouTube or in any other format, we will make a thousand videos that will bury it. We also have the means to redirect websites of the enemy to our own, which we will do. The end of the terrorist organization's ability to communicate will mark the end of its success in foreign recruitment."

"And the content of your videos?"

"Let's start with cowardice. I've been a military man all my life. Bravery is almost always found in honorable men and women. Those who go around beheading people and shooting civilians are behaving like frightened dogs. So let's show them to the world and its social media for what they are, not what they pretend to be. Example. We put a hundred of these cowards in a cage and hang them by their ankles, as they did to our aid workers last month. Five Marines approach the cage with flame throwers *while we film*. You'll see the faces and hear the screams of cowardice writ large, and so will those God's Wrath wants to recruit."

86

"So you plan to take a few prisoners from, say, Afghanistan in order to carry out your video stunt? That strikes me as an inadequate way to win the war."

"It would of course be inadequate, but I have not mentioned a stunt. We won't be dealing with Afghan prisoners. We'll be dealing with the heart of the Wrath's fighting machine, a tiny organization we can defeat in months. How? I called for a program of national service for a reason. If we're going to save our country, we're going to have to fight. We didn't start this fight, but we can easily finish it. Let's say we build rapid deployment forces of 10,000, 50,000, 100,000. Let's say we push forward programs now underway that will allow us to deploy and remove each force within 72 hours. We're not going to get bogged down anywhere; we're going to work quickly, annihilate and leave. With cameramen, of course. Once these would-be warriors have their Toyota trucks shot out from under them, they'll be running around like frightened chickens, running until they're caught and filmed at their own beheading. Among those Americans doing their national service, there will be thousands of website designers. They'll have content and they'll have work."

"But, Sir, we in the West don't go around incinerating and beheading people."

"We will – for a short time," Shiller said. "Remember that the eradication of God's Wrath, though necessary, isn't our main problem. Rather, it's putting on hold our domestic disputes so that we can rebuild a country that has seen 30 years of decline. When we are again what we once were, we can return to squabbling and deadlock . . . if we still want to. One last question."

"General, how does it feel, after your showing in Iowa, to win the New Hampshire primary?"

"Ms. Baker, I did not win the primary. Seventy-five percent of the people voted against me. True, I received the most votes . . . but far from enough to predict the mass movement that lies ahead. One more thing before I close. I have been approached by the Secret Service with an offer of protection. I'm not naïve. Our enemies, however insignificant, know that my election to the office of president would be synonymous with their demise. However, in light of recent episodes of whoring, drinking and security lapses that could have led to our president's assassination, I prefer to assemble my own team."

"General, some of the things you said tonight are reminiscent of Hammurabi, an eye-for-an-eye and so on. Are you suggesting a return to the earliest days of civilization?"

"We will go where we find those who have harmed us, and we will use the techniques against them they have used against us. Only against them. This small contingent of tech-savvy barbarians is an obstacle to the continued flowering of our civilization. A tiny cancer, when excised with methods that seem invasive, can be the salvation of the sufferer. We're not going to operate on those aren't part of the cancer. We bear no grudge against anyone of any religion who seeks a more civilized world. But the United States must again clear the road for the advancement of Good. Thank you, good night, and God bless the United States of America that is waiting to emerge."

PART II

CHAPTER THIRTEEN

They were sitting on the patio of a restaurant in the hot dusty Mexican border town of Rio Bravo, having just met for lunch with the country's Minister of National Security, Arturo Diaz. Brightly colored hanging baskets and pink stucco walls shielded the patio's diners from curious passersby. Umbrellas blazed with the green, white and red of the Mexican flag, a fine display of national pride for the Minister and his guests. Beside this pleasant cocoon was a concrete square, cracked and overgrown, which the government helicopter had used to land and take off.

The secret encounter was supposed to be the kickoff of a serious collaboration between the US and Mexico in hunting down El Lobo. But before the first bowl of *pico de gallo* hit the table, Connor saw it for what it was: a chance for the Minister to get himself photographed with American law enforcement officials. And before the tortilla chips landed, all three agents sensed that El Lobo and the Minister were in cahoots. Nothing frustrated Connor more than corrupt politicians and their publicity stunts. He came close to expressing his feelings, but managed to suppress them at the last moment. Today he had more important things on his agenda.

***

"I think," Connor told the FBI Director, "that people in Aspen are getting the wrong idea,".

"People?" Forsythe said. "*People?* It's not like you to be so vague."

"He means Shiller," Hatch chimed in. "We like him. We both hope he's the Republican nominee. I'm not saying we'd vote for him in the general election, but he should know the way we feel."

"You're losing me. What difference does it make?"

"Jason, if he becomes president and sees us as enemies, we'll be out on the street."

"You'll be there sooner than that if you don't hurry up with Kelly.

Christ, guys, it's *April* already and you're still where you were in December."

"Not exactly," Connor objected. "We just got some interesting results from the forensics lab."

"Why didn't I hear about this?"

"Because we wanted to give you some context first. We're almost there, and it's thanks to Shiller. But I shouldn't have put the question to him the way I did. Now I get the impression he thinks we're in Aspen to spy on him."

"Come on, Randall. You're imagining things. The man has a lot on his mind. He's preoccupied. That's what you're picking up on."

"I don't believe that's it," Hatch said.

"Randall?"

"I told you. He probably believes we're in Aspen to spy on him – or at least on his campaign."

"Have you thought about talking to him?"

"Yep. I've also thought about how he would feel if I did."

"And how's that?"

"Like I'm trying to patch up a cover I'd blown."

"What do you want me to do? Transfer you to the Denver Field Office?"

"Now there's an idea."

"Well, it isn't going to happen and I'll tell you why. You've just been assigned to the hunt for El Lobo. That *requires* you to stay where you are. So get over your paranoia. Think about the major crimes you've helped with all over the West. You've been on the road as much as in his backyard. Sadly, you're still on the Kelly case. The public, congress and the president are demanding answers. Kelly alone would justify your long-term presence near the scene. Shiller's not stupid. If he ever believed you were there to spy on him – *which I very much doubt* – he won't believe it for long. Unlike you guys, he doesn't fight facts. Trust me."

"Trust *you*?" Connor grumbled. "We trust facts. But I've got to admit, Jason, that you make a strong case – except for one thing. Why would our El Lobo assignment require us to be in Aspen instead of, say, Tucson?"

"Give me a large break. Since his tunnel escape, Señor Kingpin remains a huge news story. Everyone in the country knows who he is. More to the point, the media never fails to mention his ties to a specific US distribution center – ASPEN. That suggests a Hollywood connection, meaning the possible involvement of big-name movie stars. You've located where these people hang out. If I were you, I'd stop worrying about how you come off to Shiller and start worrying about El Lobo's boys hacking you into bite-sized pieces."

"That might happen if we don't get out of here soon," Connor said. "In case you didn't notice, your Mexican Secretary of Public Security belongs heart, soul and wallet to Lobo."

"No doubt, Randall, which is why our trip home will be the safest you've ever made."

"Excuse me?"

"I'm serious. El Lobo's got our backs for now. If something ugly happened to us right after our meeting with Minister Diaz, it would look like Diaz passed information to the Cartel, especially after all the trouble he went to meeting us out here in the sticks."

Connor did a rare thing: he agreed with Forsythe. "You're right, Jason. I'm not thinking straight. I shouldn't have had that third chimichanga."

"You shouldn't have had the *second* one," Hatch quipped.

Connor looked irritated enough to suck Hatch into one of their legendary verbal wars. Forsythe was quick to intervene. "Look, guys, this is a good place to talk. I want to tell you about recent developments in the other investigations, review your findings in the Kelly case and try to come up with a common thread. I can't believe there isn't one."

***

Forsythe said, "Hatch, you go first."

"Well, we know the same group is responsible for Kennan, Moose, Kelly and the GW bridge. We know this from the taunting videos and messages, almost identical in tone, that the perps left behind in all four instances. No concrete assumptions here, but we would seem to be dealing with an Islamic terrorist group. Some of its members are very familiar with the States. They know more about our own country than we do, and their English is superb."

"Maybe not superb, but better than my partner's," Connor added between sips of carbonated water.

"Stop fucking around, Randall. Hatch, continue."

"Thanks, Jason, I will. The point is this: their English in notes and videos was indistinguishable from the English of a native speaker, Arabic specialists assure me their Arabic is just as good, maybe like the language of a professor or some other professional. I know, I know. That doesn't tell us much. We know we're dealing with smart people. So what hypotheses are we left with? First, we're being hit by an Islamic terrorist group that has recruited one or more Americans. Second, the perps are American-educated Arabs. Third, there's a remote chance it's an American group familiar with the Middle East that hates the US. Such a group would have to be made up of military personnel, civilian converts to Islam or both."

"Thanks," Forsythe said. "What about the new stuff, Randall?"

"It might be something, it might not, but forensics found a speck of DNA on the 'black box,' that thing with the note in it. I'm not totally convinced the DNA is from the guy driving the snowmobile, but our lab says it is."

Forsythe sat up straight. "How could the lab be sure?"

"If you ask me, they couldn't. If you ask them, they'll tell you the snowmobile explosion caused the thing to graze the driver's hand. I didn't understand the scientific shit that proved it was *his* hand and that his glove got blown off it before the box hit it. Seems to me a lot of people must have messed with that box before the snowmobile exploded. But we didn't let our doubts stop us from looking for a match. We didn't know anything about this match when the El Lobo affair came up, but the DNA, wherever it came from, belonged to a retired Army Ranger named Bret Smith."

"Regiment and specialty? I'm guessing you looked into that."

"Hatch did. The 75th in Afghanistan . . . officially."

"And unofficially?"

"Pakistan, the tribal regions. He specialized in the use of snowmobiles to locate Taliban hideouts. Got himself wounded nine years ago and went civilian with an unblemished military record."

"I imagine you're thinking what I am," Forsythe said. "His background is why someone had him sneak up on Kelly in a snowmobile."

"Probable. There's no evidence he joined the other side while he was over there, but it seems like he did. That would make the Kelly murder consistent with the Islamic terrorist hypothesis."

"And you've interviewed some of the soldiers who served with him and his commanding officer?"

"Jesus Christ, Jason. We've had the DNA findings for three days. Those were the three days you wanted us to get familiar with the Lobo case. We're trying to approach both investigations systematically – and not go crazy in the process.

93

"Understood. Nevertheless, as I said before, don't *ever again* wait to inform me of a potential breakthrough. I might know things you don't that will 'put it in context.' Let's take five before we finish up here. By the time we leave, you'll understand why El Lobo might have a role in the assault on our country. If I didn't believe that, I would have left him to ICE and Immigration."

***

"First New York," Forsythe said. "This may or may not be relevant to the Keenan murder, but it has to be ruled out before we dismiss it. The agents working the case kept digging further back into the past. It turns out an upstairs neighbor hired a new housekeeper in June of last year."

"And?"

"The housekeeper was someone we wanted to interview. Did she notice any changes in the people coming and going, were there any long-term guests of other occupants, stuff like that. We couldn't find her, and no one had seen her since the day before they found the body. Employment records kept by the building manager identified her as Maria something or other, Mexican but legally here. He had a photocopy of her green card in the files. It turned out to be fake. All we have are photos of her from security cameras. We know she was in Keenan's apartment when he was away, and not just once. So we've got nothing to go on but face recognition based on fuzzy pictures. That's not going to cut it. However, we can't exclude the possibility that she was one of El Lobo's people. She had the codes to a dozen infallible security systems. She would never have become a person of interest if she hadn't run. That means our perps managed to hack into data banks thought to be as secure as any on earth. Any idea what that augurs for the future?

"Anyway," Forsythe continued, "that's the latest on Keenan. Let's turn to the drone attack on the GW Bridge. *This* is the incident that puts your snowmobile findings in context – and provides an example of why I want all new results of your investigation passed to me without delay.

"The CIA lost a drone being shipped overland to one of its facilities near Kandahar. You probably remember the attack on our supply convoy in Pakistan last year. It happened near the Khyber Pass, and it was worse than publicly known. An MQ-9 Reaper and its control module, disassembled and packed up for shipping, fit into a normal container. This particular drone was being shipped. When the fires were finally put out, our soldiers noticed that the container carrying the drone was empty. It turned out to be the same drone that pulled off the bridge attack. We know this from its serial number, verified by General Atomics. So we can put Kelly's killer and the lost drone in the same area of Pakistan – though not at the same time."

A gust of hot wind rustled the hanging baskets and sent a puff of dust onto the patio. Evening was near; time was short. Connor, who had been silent for Connor without his Casa de Maxwell, seemed to come alive. "Excellent, Jason. We've got two maybes for Hatch's first hypothesis, and one for a Lobo connection. Is there more?"

"You bet. I don't want any questions from here on out. I'm going to tell you what we know about Moose, then we're done for today."

"A productive day," Hatch said.

"I thought it would never come," Connor added.

Forsythe said, "We've got a scenario similar to the one we have for Señorita Maria. Someone had to know the codes held by the Solana Beach PD, as well as those of several top-notch security firms, to get anywhere near the compound. The guards and dogs were gassed. We can't say yet exactly what the substance was, but that's not critical. Gas is easier to get hold of than 32-digit rolling security codes. From the video of the murder, we know four of those present were from south of the border, probably Mexican.

"Here's where it gets even stranger. Thanks to a few late drivers, we know the Border Patrol ran down, cuffed and loaded into their van four Hispanics fitting the description of the subjects on the video. The van was clearly marked, easily recognizable, sirens up top. And, in fact, a missing van was reported from the Patrol's San Diego Region maintenance facility the next morning. The van was found empty about a hundred miles up the border from where we now sit. Then, barely a week ago, a tunnel under the border fence was discovered nearby. Lights, rails, you name it. All the marks of an El Lobo project for bringing drugs into the US. But does it serve another purpose, one in our domain? Lobo is known for his tunnels but not for his hacking. That honor goes to Middle Eastern groups.

"So now we have what appears to be a definitive link between the Mexican drug lord and whoever is hitting us from Pakistan. Moose's filmed murder further supports our conclusion. The Moose film was made by the same professionals who shot Keenan with his dick in his hand – verifiable by our own analyses and by the forensic work of the best in the private sector. And in each case, Mexican nationals were involved. So, gentlemen, that's where we stand at the moment. We're lucky there hasn't

95

been a major attack for a few months. It's time to turn on the afterburners and get to the bottom of this mess before we're hit again."

Forsythe put a stack of dollars on the table – the FBI was short on pesos – and put Connor's glass on top of it. "Let's go home," he said.

CHAPTER FOURTEEN

"**I** have an idea," Beau said. "We've spent the last hundred nights or so in the carriage house. How about we take a break?"

"Well . . . sure. What exactly do you have in mind?"

"A suite at the Little Nell. Everyone's cancelled because of the warm weather. The place has the right name and so much more. I spent my first night in Aspen there – and that was the night we met."

"Beau, listen. I like the plan, but let's find another place. You know, something *really* different. A hotel would make me feel like I was going to work. I hope you're not offended."

They were walking along a path that had been covered with snow in the middle of March. Now it was early April of an early Spring. The snow had melted, the mud had mostly dried up, and the late afternoon sun had not yet sunk behind the peaks. Budding leaves added a splash of color to the white bark of the aspen trees. Tiny wildflowers covered meadows that were, until recently, fields of snow. Even the Roaring Fork River, having shed its blanket of ice, danced with the sound of spring.

"Not offended in the least. But, Nellie, I'm not camping out. Not now, not ever."

"Not even in my old office at the Historical Society? We haven't christened it yet. We definitely should, especially since it's your office now."

"Now that's an idea! But we'd have to get word to Shiller."

"And it would have to be late. I work tonight."

"Maybe you could call in sick."

"I can't. I'm the eyes and ears of the General, remember? Now would be a lousy time to go deaf and blind."

"But you've done it before. I'm not seeing the difference."

"It's the Wisconsin primary. He won it with minority support."

"You're killing my idea. Politics and sex don't go together."

"Really? Tell that to congress."

"Okay. Politics creates sex junkies. But why is tonight so important?"

"You know there are five big eastern primaries coming up in a couple of weeks. I'm supposed to eavesdrop on the state and county operatives who are already here to meet with him – especially African-Americans. He needs their vote to win in the northeast, so he wants to know what they're saying. Think about it, Beau. Those states are 'winner take all.' Five victories would put him within a stone's throw of the nomination."

"It would. And you, my love, are a shameless spy – a damned sexy one."

"Well, it's something I never pictured myself doing, and maybe it's a little unethical. But if I can help him, I don't care. How about you? Burnt out on writing for him yet?"

"You keep asking me, like you're waiting for it to happen. No way. I'm working my ass off and liking it better all the time. So let's get back to the christening, okay?"

Nellie laughed. "Okay, but I'm afraid it's back to the drawing table. I wasn't thinking. We won't be able to get into the Historical Society without triggering the alarms."

"I know how to shut them off. H. L. showed me in case I ever had to work late. I might even do some actual work while I'm waiting for you, assuming I can concentrate. I've already got this picture in my mind. You coming up the creaky old stairs with nothing on but boots."

"Pervert. You can undress me in the office. What about the security cameras? I don't particularly want H. L. seeing us."

"Nellie, she never looks at the tapes. Cameras are only there in case someone breaks in. But we could pretend she's watching and put on a real fireworks display."

"This sounds . . . fun. You get the champagne. I'll bring some bed stuff over from the Jerome."

***

After a burger at Zane's Tavern, Beau walked to the Carlyle House, the Historical Society's permanent residence. He'd never properly appreciated how beautiful the three-story brick Queen Anne was. Probably, he thought, because he'd grown up among antebellum plantations homes. Whatever, the place was perfect for sex away from home. Her arrival was hours away, but he could already feel her naked body in his arms. He unlocked the ornate front door, entered the code to kill the alarm and, leaving the door open for Nellie, climbed the stairs to his third-story office.

***

Beau had been working for Shiller since New Hampshire, researching the backgrounds and preferences of the state officials Shiller planned to invite to Aspen. He didn't have to select these individuals; Shiller and his growing staff did that. Instead, he put together a personal document for each operative, a document Shiller depended on to make his "personal" video presentation its recipient could show to his potential supporters at home. In this fashion, Shiller was able to escape the anonymity of a campaign run almost exclusively from Aspen.

The movers and shakers at all levels of state politics, usually unknown on the national scene, felt flattered being addressed personally by a presidential hopeful. Their expense-paid trips to Aspen inflated their self-images and won over to the cause legions of skeptics.

It didn't take Beau long to realize that he and his "worthless" degree in journalism were important to the campaign. Shiller's converts, seduced as they were, invariably accepted Shiller's choice to run his 'ground game' in the states where it did not spontaneously emerge. This gave the General an army of foot soldiers to knock on doors, distribute publicity and arrange rallies that would attract major press coverage.

Even the beltway media, habitually late to identify new trends, came to understand the wisdom of Shiller's choice to eschew a traditional campaign. The General, as they now liked to report, wasted no time travelling, fund-raising, eating corn dogs at county fairs and shaking hands with thousands of strangers for an evening news photo op.

Local newspapers, especially important in presidential primaries, were also recipients of Beau's writing and Shiller's videos. Editors, reporters, office managers and spokesman found themselves being addressed from afar *in person* rather than being schmoozed up close by candidates who had learned their names that morning.

By the time of the Wisconsin primary at the beginning of April, Shiller seemed to be everywhere. Just as important, he was always armed with a keen understanding of those whose support he would need to win a given state. Criticism of his physical absence from the campaign trail morphed into praise for his ability, using modern communications, to be even more present than the flesh-pressers.

Beau took off his shirt and began working on the reports due the next morning. He always had a hard time getting started, especially tonight, but once rolling he was hard to stop. When he heard Nellie come in hours later, he'd almost forgotten his real reason for being where he was.

***

99

She showed up just after two a.m., not naked but for her boots as he had imagined but dressed in tight jeans and a low-cut blouse. She had dragged sheets from the Jerome up the stairs in a laundry bag. What happened next needs no telling, but it went on for an eternity, punctuated by cries of love and sighs of exhaustion.

"Look at the stars," Beau said before Nellie dozed off. "They look brighter than usual."

Nellie walked to the window, wrapped in a sheet. "You know why?"

"Cause it's so late."

"It's never late in Aspen. It's because the city's black." She flicked on the room switch. Nothing. "A power outage. Strange. I've never seen it happen in good weather."

***

Connor had scheduled a breakfast meeting with two CBI agents who were in Aspen to discuss their recent findings in the Kelly investigation. His alarm clock hadn't gone off yet, but he felt rested enough to begin the day. He heaved his naked bulk out of bed, groaned, stretched, and started down the well-traveled path to the kitchen.

The light on the coffee machine was red. Of course it was red: he'd gotten up earlier than usual. But the machine ignored his attempts to start it manually and did not respond to his slapping. The thing, he thought, was either broken or the power was out. He flipped a light switch: nothing. Jesus! A power outage when he needed it least.

He got more bad news when he opened the blinds. The sun burned brightly in a cloudless sky. He'd not only overslept; he'd missed the meeting he had insisted on. With the mid-morning light pouring in, he saw Hatch's note:

Randall, trying to get you up was like wrestling a rhino. I thought I'd better get over to Duff's and hear the latest on Kelly. Not to worry. I'll say you had a call from Washington you had to take.

When the going got tough, Hatch got going. Connor vowed, as he had often done, to ease up on the teasing of his best friend. He didn't dwell on his vow: the important thing now was coffee.

His salvation was the gas stove. Connor brought a pan of water to a boil, pivoted the drip basket out of the machine and had his morning fix. His thoughts quickened. The alarm hadn't gone off. Must be a cheap

100

piece of government crap without a backup battery.

In the bedroom he glanced at the clock. Its hands were stuck at 4:11 a.m. A piece of junk with no backup battery alright, but at least it told the exact time the outage hit. He stepped into the shower. The water was hot. For the second time that morning, he thanked the gods for natural gas.

Still, gas didn't mean these electrical blackouts weren't a monumental pain in the ass; they were. His irritation was on the rise again. These events were the fault of a deadlocked congress. Without a cent from Washington, electrical companies couldn't fix the nation's obsolete power grid. Maybe Shiller was right: a government that couldn't keep the lights on needed a major overhaul.

He knew he'd missed the breakfast meeting, but he didn't know by how much until he had dressed and looked at his watch. Jesus, it was almost lunchtime! Duff better have gas stoves. He needed to make up for the lost breakfast with a big-league lunch. Through thick and thin, he never forgot the words of his grandfather: each man has a finite number of meals; to waste even one is a sin.

The phone, a land line, rang moments before Hatch came into the room. Connor answered, listened for a few seconds, then held a hand over the receiver. "It's Forsythe. Looks like we've got more than just a local outage. Get on the line."

"Randall, Hatch, are you both listening? Good. Here's the lowdown, and you're not going to like it. When we lost power in the East, it was during rush hour. You can't imagine the chaos, worse than 2003."

"Excuse me, Jason," Connor interrupted, "but we're in the dark too."

"I know, I know. The blackout is nation-wide. All three grids are down: Eastern, Western, Texas. But the Mountain and Pacific Time Zones at least avoided the rush hour catastrophe. We were hit in other ways too – hard. We'll need time to assess the damage, no small job under the circumstances. Anyway, you will have guessed that all airports are closed to commercial traffic. Homeland Security can use them, but only during daylight hours. An FBI plane is on its way to pick you up. I need you in Washington."

"Do we have an ETA?" Hatch asked.

"I wish. Too much going on here to keep track. Both of you, get your asses out to the airport and wait."

Forsythe hung up.

"I brought you treats from the health food store," Hatch said. "I knew you'd be hungry when you woke up. Duff's was closed. Only the healthy survived the outage."

"The diner's closed? The man doesn't have gas?"

"Hell if I know. The deep fryer and griddle could be electric. You'd better eat this stuff. It might be the last food you see for a while."

Connor opened the paper bag and peered inside. He thanked his partner before he sent it sailing toward the waste basket.

***

Captain Jennifer James, J. J. to her colleagues, felt as she always did boarding the enormous C-17 Globemaster: tiny. But when she pushed the throttle levers into takeoff position, that feeling evaporated. She and her craft became one, a charging behemoth of 500,000 pounds, 500,097 if you included J. J.

It was 2:34 a.m. Pacific Time when she taxied into takeoff position at McChord Air Force Base. She was to deliver this particular Globemaster III to the Australians, who had acquired it for their own Air Force. They had gotten it for nothing, the half-baked base commander told everyone in the bar last week. Now that these giant transporters had fallen out of favor with the Defense Department and production of the C-17 had ceased altogether, foreign militaries were encouraged to buy Globemasters from late production runs.

This was nonsense, according to the commander. Just because the last few wars had been fought in regions that couldn't always accommodate such large aircraft, did that mean the same would apply to future wars? Hell no! The Globemaster III had cost Boeing almost 200 million bucks each to build; now they were handing them out like raffle tickets at a church supper. Stupid. It was just plain stupid . . .

Well, J. J. didn't entirely disagree, but her job as she saw it was not to criticize Air Force policy. That wasn't the way for a woman, even a woman as gifted as she, to rise to the coveted position she now held.

Rain lashed the windshield. She didn't mind the weather; in fact, she was accustomed to much worse. There was nothing unusual about a takeoff in rain as long as the mist didn't reduce visibility close to zero. Tonight the rain actually helped, opening large gaps in the fog. The lights marking the runway, which had momentarily disappeared in a bank of gray soup, again shone clearly. Even the glow from the nearest city, Tacoma, flitted in and out of view. No problem with the ceiling either: it was well above the required minimum for takeoff.

The only thing that bothered J. J. tonight was the co-pilot assigned to her for the trip. He was one of those big ripped gym rats who strutted around like his only concern in life was his body.

She'd seen enough he-man braggarts like 1st Lieutenant Paul Smith during her twelve years in the Air Force. She'd also seen too many of them crack when under fire. Thank God they were just delivering a plane, not heading into a battle zone.

"Lieutenant," J. J. ordered, "run the takeoff checklist."

"In this weather?"

"We've been cleared by the tower. Hurry up."

When he had finished, she shoved the power controls forward. The huge plane shuttered while she held it back with the brakes, waiting for the engines to reach full thrust. No rolling takeoff tonight. The Globe-master carried 35,000 gallons of aviation fuel and a full load of 2,000 pound laser-guided bombs the Australians had bought along with the plane. Their maximum allowable take-off weight was 560,000 pounds. Judging from the way the craft handled on the ground, she wouldn't have been surprised to learn that it was heavier.

When she let the beast loose, the lights marking the runway's end seemed miles away. But when the Globemaster finally lifted off it had eaten up all but a few hundred feet of tarmac. Clearly overweight, but the aircraft could handle it.

J. J. climbed as steeply as possible without stalling and flattened their ascent when they were far enough from Tacoma to cut the engines to 80% thrust. From here on out, she knew the flight would be routine, boring in the vernacular. A fueling by aerial tanker every 2,500 miles was the only excitement she had to look forward to; Paul's sexist joking was the only thing she had to dread.

"Twelve degrees left, flaps at five."

"Captain."

"What?"

"My controls aren't responding."

"Nonsense. You've somehow managed to lock them up."

"I haven't even touched them. They're dead."

"Okay. I'll fly for a minute while you get your problem figured out."

J. J.'s first indication that something really was wrong came when she saw the artificial horizon: it showed them banking at eleven degrees. She moved the stick to correct their course, but her input had no effect.

Craning her neck, she could only see the tip of the wing. She was about to send Paul back into the cargo area where he might have a better view. But why? She could tell from the odd behavior of the aircraft he

103

would see nothing she didn't already know. The ailerons, flaps and every other component of wing reconfiguration could not be manipulated from the cockpit.

One more idea before she got on the HF radio: she would let down the landing gear.

Again, nothing.

Her co-pilot had no comment when he saw that even the most basic functions could not be executed from the flight deck. J. J. glanced at him while she busied herself connecting with the tower and instantly knew why. In the bluish light of the instruments, his face seemed to belong to a terrified stranger. One thing was clear: whatever was wrong with the aircraft, she would have to handle it herself.

At last, contact. She didn't realize until she spoke that she had lost some of her legendary cool.

"Calm down, Captain James. An autopilot malfunction would be my guess. I'll splice in the tech rep for BAE Systems. We'll get Boeing's assessment, too. You're absolutely certain the autopilot wasn't turned on by mistake?"

"Absolutely certain."

Could anything else go wrong? she wondered. The answer came immediately as the pitch of the engines changed. All four engines simultaneously, as if she had pulled back for the initial approach to an airfield. Nothing wrong, nothing unusual – if you overlooked the complete absence of pilot input.

"While you're splicing in people, Sir, get me someone from Pratt & Whitney. The engines might also be implicated."

"Roger, Captain. If you can keep her airborne for a few minutes, I'm sure we'll be able to diagnose and repair the malfunction from this end."

"The aircraft isn't under my control. Seems like a drone flown from a control module located God knows where. I have no idea what will happen. Get those reps on the line. Fast."

"Captain, Greg Williams from BAE."

The guy sounded clueless. "Captain, my guess would be a locked autopilot or defective FMR."

"Already checked the first. I can't do much about a defective Flight Management System. Other possibilities?"

"We've had no similar incidents."

"Where's the Boeing tech?"

"This is Mike Brady, Captain. No hypotheses from our end either. As

Greg said, you seem to be experiencing some sort of abnormal locking of the autopilot – or a defective Flight Management System."

Greg Williams suddenly became more animated. "Listen, Captain, we can reinstall your instrument software from here. It's possible you have a corrupted file."

"Roger that. Good idea."

"Captain, this is Jerry Rundell with P & W. The 100 series engine has been in service for years without malfunction. Catastrophic engine failure is of course a possibility, but unlikely. However, if that's what you are experiencing, shut down the implicated engine, its generator and anything else that might cause a wing fire. We're following you on radar. You should be able to land at SeaTac in a few minutes."

J. J. was getting frustrated, even mad. Weren't these people listening to her? "Look, there's been no catastrophic engine failure. They're all in sync. The problem is that they are totally unresponsive to pilot input. I can't land at SeaTac because I have no control over the aircraft."

"Captain, this is Commander Abbot at McChord. We have ships in the area. If you and your copilot can figure out how to keep the craft from coming down in a populated area, you have my permission to parachute."

"Commander, not being in control of the aircraft, I can't know where it will come down. It might fly anywhere and there's fuel for another 2,200 miles. I will, however, order my co-pilot to parachute."

"Hang in there," Abbot said. "You're going to be okay. BAE found the corrupted file. They're preparing to overwrite it as we speak. God bless, Captain James. When you again have control, return to McChord."

"Not when, Sir, but if." A moment of silence on the flight deck. "Paul," J. J. ordered, "go to the back of the plane and parachute. In case we don't regain control, we need someone who can testify as to what went wrong." Her co-pilot wasted no time moving to the rear of the aircraft.

Several minutes after the conference, J. J. heard familiar sounds. Flaps shuddering as they moved toward landing position, another cut back in engine power, the unmistakable feeling of a final approach. She came out of the overcast and gasped. This was not possible. Ahead were the lights of the coastline. From Seattle, they ran south past Tacoma and north to Everett. She could see water below, the Puget sound. On her present course she had three minutes at best until the aircraft, with its cargo of bombs and aviation fuel, took out the heart of the great city in which she had been born.

She had an idea. Reaching for the HF radio, she caught a fleeting glimpse of the clock: 3:12 a.m.

"Sir"

"Lieutenant Grayson here. The software is presently uploading."

Without warning, the Globemaster banked into a sharp turn to the north. It was then that she knew what the plane had been programed to hit: Boeing's largest production facility in Everett. Triple Sevens, Dreamliners – those wonders of commercial flight . . .

"Shoot me down," she screamed. "The plane's on target to wipe out Boeing."

Her words went unanswered; she had lost contact with the tower.

In that moment, the millions of lights along the coast flickered and went out. A chill ran down her spine. Something she didn't understand was going on.

Chin up, goddammit. She had been in no-way-out situations before and always managed to pull through. This would be no exception; it couldn't be.

J. J. flew past the eerie silhouettes of buildings and over fishing boats whose tiny orange lanterns offered her the illusion of warmth. They became her God, those lanterns, but she had no time to pray.

She crossed the coastline near Mukilteo, still on a heading with disaster. She jumped in her seat when a blinding flash of light split the darkness. The diesel generators at the Boeing plant had finally kicked into gear. She tried the controls a final time: nothing.

She saw her husband on the day they married, her kids at play in the backyard, herself on the sofa with a photo album of her youth. And she saw the great rectangle of light that would soon be her grave.

CHAPTER FIFTEEN

After two days, the situation was becoming dire: grid operators, electrical engineers and computer experts could not figure out how to turn on the country's lights. Everywhere the diesel generators that supplied backup current to hospitals, military bases and other facilities indispensable to the nation's health were running out of fuel. The pumps that delivered gasoline and diesel were electric; getting the liquid out of underground tanks could sometimes be achieved through improvisation, but the quantities were scarcely worth mentioning. The only dependable power came from generators powered by Conner's latest love: natural gas.

As a result, federal intelligence, the military and some state law enforcement agencies were able to sustain a near normal flow of electricity. But that was it. Cars had only the gasoline in their tanks, and many had already used up that meager supply. Cell phone towers, even those with backup capacity, were so overloaded that they crashed. Televisions, refrigerators and electric ranges stood useless in the dark of most American homes, stranding their inhabitants in a prison of anger, boredom and hunger. In several cities, looting began after sundown. Without power, the police were unable to hold back the tide.

In Washington, after two days of mind-numbing speculation by public utilities experts, digital-age geniuses and cyber-security officials, Conner and Hatch were sent to different parts of the country. As the Director explained, he wanted to put his best men in charge of the investigations being conducted by FBI Field Offices in every major city. Hatch got Phoenix. Connor was sent to New York to cooperate with Deputy Director Barnes.

Both Field Offices had power from gas-fired generators, a precautionary change ordered and paid for by government before it was paralyzed by a short-sighted group of tax cutters. You get what you pay for, Connor told Hatch whenever his partner shopped at discount stores. It hadn't occurred to him that the same applied to countries.

Forsythe, who loathed Washington and liked Connor, accompanied him to Barnes's facility at 26 Federal Plaza. Interstate traffic had almost entirely ceased, and they arrived in record time. When Barnes finished their briefing, an aide opened the curtains of the large conference room. Six hours had flown by. Already it was dark. The city rose around them like the shadow of a giant cemetery. Below, a flashlight probed the sidewalk. A few cars bounced down Lafayette Street. Several lights shown in windows. Otherwise nothing, as if the world had sunk into the fog of time. But the stars were as bright as Connor had ever seen them in New York, and a tiny sliver of moon hung above the skyline. That, at least, was something.

"Shut those blinds," Barnes ordered. "How do you think it makes them feel out there when you remind them that we've got lights?"

"Sorry, Sir. I wanted to give our guests a peek at what they will never see again."

"Never see again? I'm not sure such remarks are justified."

"Sorry again, Sir."

"Okay, enough. Sit down and be quiet. Jason, you and Randall are in luck. We booked a couple of suites at The James for our joint intelligence discussions with British Security. The meeting is off, but we've kept the rooms. It's at the corner of Thompson and Grand, a leisurely stroll."

"The James," Conner exclaimed. "Please, not The James. Isn't there anywhere else?"

"The sidewalk," Barnes said. "The hotel is the only accommodation within walking distance that has reliable backup power."

"Gas generators?"

"That would be my guess. Jason, Randall, you'll need to get online. The new software from Internet Security Systems should protect you from cyber peeking."

"Let's hope," Forsythe said. "We'll be ready to give you a summary of our Washington testimony in the morning."

"No *Casa de Maxwell*," Connor mumbled under his breath.

"Relax," Forsythe said. "Your buddy came up with a stockpile from the old days. Don't ask me where he got it. Maybe from a junk room in the Hoover Building. Maybe from looting. I don't know and I don't care, but he apparently thought you would need it."

"Hatch did that?"

"Yes. Hatch did that for *you*, Randall. Treat the man with a little more respect. He deserves it."

Connor on this black evening did what he had never done before: he used his FBI credentials illegally – but for a noble purpose. They got him into the kitchen of The James. He cornered the executive chef, demanded that his fish be headless and fried, and that only Maxwell House be sent to his room when he ordered coffee. When the chef replied in an unsteady voice that the hotel had no Maxwell House and no place to get it during the blackout, Connor hoisted his swollen briefcase onto a butcher block counter and took out two of the cans Hatch had found for him. Abuse of power was a crime, but in this case it sure as hell didn't feel like one.

The corner suite on the 12th floor again! Jesus, it was bad enough he couldn't escape the hotel he despised; he couldn't even manage a different room. But enough whining about his fate. Fuel was on the way, via room service, to lift his thinking to a higher level.

A gentle knock at the door. The same Hispanic-looking girl who had delivered his first meal five months ago wheeled in a cart laden with a silver chafing dish and large pot of coffee. He apologized for his previous outburst just in case she remembered. To no avail. She didn't understand enough English to grasp what he was saying. It finally dawned on him that he was speaking to a different girl. Betty, his insufferable bitch of a first wife, must have been right when she accused him, one of the top investigators in the nation, of an offensive inability to tell one pretty young Latin woman from another. He tipped the girl thirty bucks, ten to make up for his earlier behavior, ten to apologize for his ethnic blindness, and ten for tonight's service.

He ate quickly and downed a pot of Maxwell House, irritated that he was thinking of Betty when the love of his life, Kristýna Sondheim, hid her pretty face from his memory.

It was hot. A note on the door explained that the backup generators didn't produce enough current to operate the central air. Just getting to work tonight was proving to be a challenge. He shut the drapes to hide from Betty's transatlantic stare of disgust and circled like a dog in distress to find a cooler spot in the sprawling suite. A vent that breathed warm air at least created a breeze. He dragged a desk and chair beneath it, fired up his laptop, opened his briefcase and went to work.

By the time he hit the first key, he had a plan for organizing his thoughts. The blackout he could forget: it was clearly a cyberattack. No substations had been physically damaged, meaning that there was no other

109

possibility. Everyone in the Bureau, the CIA and the NSA agreed. No reason to involve himself in an investigation for which the experts were better equipped.

There was, however, the big picture. He believed his intuition and investigative skill could help bring that picture into focus. He reviewed the list of known attacks that had taken place around the time of the blackout. First, there was the destruction of the Boeing plant in Everett. Military aircraft weren't built there, but commercial airliners critical to America's economy were. Second, there was the devastating attack on a tanker train of liquid sodium cyanide from Nevada. Its destination was in Canada somewhere, but it had stopped at a railyard outside of Chicago. The train, his research revealed, had done nothing out of the ordinary. An American crew brought the train into the yard every night; a Canadian crew hauled it off with a different engine every morning. No one could determine the number of deaths until the lights came back on, but it was evident the explosion and poison gas had taken an horrific toll.

A similar explosion had occurred in a sodium cyanide manufacturing plant north of Memphis. Connor had grown up in Memphis. He still had family and friends there, or hoped he still had them. He took the attack personally, and it made his blood boil.

Apart from Boeing and the cyanide targeting, the remaining hits had been on refineries. The list included five of the country's largest facilities, all of them around New Orleans and Houston. He called room service for another pot of coffee while he tried to find dots connecting the attacks. Only one thing stood out: they had all been caused by aircraft that had somehow been hijacked from the ground and flown like drones, hitting their targets with absolute precision. There might be a clue, yet unexplored, if he could link the types of aircraft to one another instead of the types of attack – or so argued his intuition.

It *was* known that all of the aircraft except one, according to the reports from military installations around the country, belonged to the Air Force. It was also clear that the same transnational terrorist group that had targeted America since the previous summer was the culprit. But there were still questions that had not been answered. For example, thought Connor, did the flights that did the damage target recurrent trips, predictable trips like those of the cyanide trains from Nevada? What about the makes and models of aircraft? Were they identical or similar in some way? If he could come up with a "yes" to either of these questions, he might have found information that would help the cyber experts probe in the right places.

He spent the next two hours waking up base commanders whose planes had been in the air at the time of the blackout but had never reached their destinations: A C-17 Globemaster from McChord Air Force Base south of Tacoma; an A-10 Warthog from Moody Air Force Base near Valdosta, Georgia; an F-15E from Seymour Johnson Air Force Base near Goldsboro, North Carolina; a C-5M from Kelly Air Force Base near San Antonio; a C-130J Super Hercules from Wright-Patterson near Dayton, Ohio; two F-16s from Luke Air Force Base near Glendale, Arizona; and, strangest of all, an MQ-9 Reaper belonging to Customs and Border Control from the Naval Air Station near Corpus Christi. The drone, according to the Station Commander, had taken off on its own just after the lights went out. It was the same type of drone that had struck the George Washington Bridge, but that told him nothing he didn't already know.

Connor realized why no one had traveled further down this particular investigative path: the planes had nothing in common and had taken off from bases thousands of miles apart. Where could he go from here? He was stumped. The image of a plume of sodium cyanide gas over his native city gave him a momentary surge of physical energy. Unfortunately, that energy bypassed his brain.

It was approaching 2:00 am and room service was closed. In desperation, he unlocked the refrigerator door and took out three tiny and obscenely expensive bottles of Southern Comfort. The Bureau wouldn't like seeing these on his expense account, but what the hell did he care? He poured the three mini-bottles into a glass and downed them in one swallow. While he waited for them to kick in, he speculated idly, and for no real reason, on which planes had hit what.

The three giant transporters, he guessed, had been sent to those targets chosen to sustain maximum damage. They would be Boeing, which he already knew, the big Exxon Mobile refinery in Baton Rouge and the sodium cyanide plant in Memphis. The C-5M, which could take off with a 380,000 payload and carry over 50,000 gallons of aviation fuel, would have been the perfect bomb to destroy the Exxon Mobile facility. The slightly smaller C-130 Hercules would have been more than enough to blow up the sodium cyanide plant in Memphis. The remaining targets could have been torched by the smaller aircraft. And there was this to think about: the terror group was limited to the planes that happened to be airborne that night. God knows what they could have done with an entire fleet of C-5Ms.

The Southern Comfort came on with a rush. His body went limp. Miraculously, though, his mind became Maxwell-House sharp. Kelly, he thought. We know these guys murdered Tim Kelly. Thanks to DNA evidence, we also know the actual killer reached the murder site in a snowmobile. When he served in Afghanistan, he belonged to a small unit of Special Forces that pioneered the use of snowmobiles to sneak up on seemingly inaccessible caves in the mountains around the Khyber Pass. So . . . we can put him in Afghanistan six or seven years before Kelly was hit.

What about the aircraft used in the present attack? Were they also over there?

Bagram Air Base had been mostly dismantled when the US withdrew from Afghanistan. Connor had no idea who would be on the other end of the line if he tried a secure telephone call. Instead, he opted for an Internet search of the aircraft stationed at the base at some point during the Afghan War. Perhaps it wasn't important, he thought, since about every Air Force asset had used the sprawling facility at one time or another. Still, he felt better after he determined that all of the planes – not specific planes but identical makes and models – had been stationed there. Hatch's least likely hypothesis, namely that some of our soldiers had hooked up with God's Wrath, was beginning to seem credible. That could well be what had happened. The terror group, with American help, had years to develop software that would allow the aircraft to be flown from the ground.

Suddenly he was exhausted. Connor made his way to the bed, still naked, and fell asleep. When the room service girl arrived with his breakfast, he was too groggy to remember that he wore nothing but his underwear.

After she screamed and ran off down the hall, he examined the breakfast cart. There was one pot of coffee, hardly unreasonable. But a pot held only half the amount his brain needed to emerge from the morning fog. He was debating whether he dared call room service after his bodily display when Forsythe walked in through the door no one had bothered to close.

"Randall, you look like hell. We're already late to the office. Let's go."

"Like this?"

"Get your ass in the shower and get dressed. I'm leaving with or without you in ten minutes."

CHAPTER SIXTEEN

"I hope you don't mind being kidnapped," Shiller said, glancing at the couple in the rearview mirror of his Land Rover. It was early morning the second day of the blackout. The sun had not yet crested the horizon, but a luminescent pink dawn silhouetted the peaks to the east.

"The kidnapping, no," Nellie said. "But we'll have to check on H. L. She's alone without power and isn't exactly young."

"I assume she has a land line."

"She does. She wouldn't be caught dead with a cell phone."

"You can call her from the ranch. I'll have my driver take her whatever she needs. If she'd like to stay here for a while – or at least join us for lunch – I would be honored."

"Sounds good. I just want her to know we didn't bail on her when we started working for you."

"Of course."

"Sir," Beau said, "did you see those lights behind us? Are we being followed?"

Shiller, when he spoke, seemed amused. "You might say that, Mr. Wellington. The Jeep trailing us belongs to three of my permanent body-guards. Now that my candidacy is being taken seriously, I sometimes have them accompany me."

"You're worried about an assassination way up there at this hour?"

"Worried? I don't think that's the right word. But things happen, and I don't take chances."

"Ah, those morning walks," Nellie sighed. "I hike a lot, but the only mountain lion I've ever seen was on your snowshoe excursion last winter. Does the one you were feeding still show up?"

"He does," Shiller said, "if I take that same trail and leave my men at home. These cats are as shy as they are they are beautiful. Which doesn't mean they're harmless, especially in the hours just before sunrise."

"I hope you don't have any more predawn walks planned for us." Beau said. "You scared the hell out of me last time."

"But you survived," the General said. "I take care of my people."

Nellie shook her head. "I was fascinated, unlike Bayou Boy here." She jabbed Beau in the ribs. "Don't listen to him, Sir. I would love to accompany you again. Is that a possibility?"

"I'm sorry, not during the campaign. I plan each day while the world sleeps and I am alone with Nature, 'alone' being the operative word."

"A good strategy," Beau joked. "I'd rather have an incurable disease than be eaten by one of those things."

"Where's your backbone, son? I hear you were a college football star."

"My aunt had it surgically removed. Seriously, General, what's behind this kidnapping?"

"Work as usual. I have electric power as well as access to the Internet. You'll need both of these to continue what you've been doing. We have six important primaries on April 26th, assuming power is restored soon. I say 'six' because the New York primary has been postponed a week."

"Because of the blackout?" Beau asked.

"Yes. That gives us almost three weeks to prepare for a day of critical importance. We need to make good use of the time."

"How will we do that?" Nellie wanted to know.

"By moving forward with what your friend has already started – at an accelerated pace. While the others are groping around in the dark, I want to gather all relevant information on state and local political players, from precinct captains to party bosses. Now that Skidmore's win in Wisconsin has put us a few delegates behind, we might need some negative material on his donors and advisors. If we can manage to win all six of the upcoming states, we have a clear path to the nomination.

"It's effectively some form of winner-take-all from here on out. Four candidates are still running. Do the math. In such a fragmented field, 35% percent of the votes should suffice to take all or almost all of a state's delegates. And let's not forget about our other advantage: California hasn't voted yet. I have good people on the ground already; Skidmore doesn't."

"What about this terrorist attack?" Beau asked. "Seems to me people are going to want a military man instead of a blowhard real-estate developer or a professional politician."

"I was going to bring that up. We could also have Caskey to deal with. He was an effective general before his retirement from the Air Force. You

114

might not remember this, but he was considered the likely choice for Commander of the Joint Chiefs. He has done well in both the House and Senate since he entered politics. If anyone will benefit from the unspeakable act, I think he's the one. He has both military *and* political experience.

"But let's take it one step at a time and concentrate on the 26th. With your help, we'll uncover the best and the worst of all state people involved. And I mean *all* – from the lowest operatives to the kingmakers; from my supporters to my detractors. Now, let's have a good breakfast and get started."

"But General," Nellie said, "what you're talking about hasn't been part of my job before. You act like it has, but I won't have a clue where to start."

"That's not correct. You're fast on the computer. Mr. Wellington, the Historical Society and the Jerome have all confirmed this."

"Fast, right, but this has been Beau's job. I'm not even sure what he does."

"It's a straightforward task of providing me with verifiable profiles of the individuals I've singled out. Your friend has the list. I'm sure he won't mind getting you started. Now, come inside and have a seat at the kitchen table. Jesús and Manuela will take care of you."

***

Shiller did not join them for breakfast, but the bodyguards did. They were the same three taciturn oddballs the General had stuck in the Emma Claire during the blizzard. Big guys, clearly in top physical condition, who seemed content to chat among themselves.

Beau felt irritated that he and Nellie were being ignored again. He decided to start a conversation – or at least try. "Hey guys, we work for the General too. It would be a lot less awkward if we knew each other's names."

One guy glanced up from the dice game they were always playing. "We know your names."

"Fine, but shouldn't we know yours?"

They looked at each other in silent consultation. "We're not as asocial as we appear," one of them said. "The General asked us to disclose nothing. I suppose first names among employees isn't a violation of his order, but no more questions."

"No more questions. Just names we can call you, even if they're fake."

"We don't use fake names. I'm Kent, the man to my left is Doug, and

115

to his left is Kyle."

"Okay." Beau mumbled, wondering why he had bothered.

Nellie paid them no mind. "Manuela," she said in Spanish, "could you make a big plate of *huevos rancheros* for the two of us? And coffee, lots of coffee."

"Si, *Señorita*."

"And those men, what do they eat?"

"Always the same thing. *Huevos*, but not *huevos rancheros*. Five raw eggs each man, whipped up in the blender with some kind of powder the boss gave us. I can't watch them drink that stuff."

"I won't be able to either," Nellie said. The women laughed. They had gotten to know each other during Nellie's food runs from the Jerome to the ranch and her occasional help preparing meals. Since neither Manuela or Jesús spoke or understood a word of English, they only conversed in Spanish.

"You guys," Beau said when he had tasted his breakfast, "you should try these. Talk about good!"

"And you should eat something healthy," Kent said. "Have your girl ask the Mexicans to fix you one of these drinks. They slide right down your throat. Twenty minutes later you feel like you could take on the world. The General insisted we have at least one before a Special Ops mission."

"Special Ops mission?"

"As in killing Bin Laden."

"Different formulas for different jobs," Beau quipped. "Oysters slide too. So you guys were in on killing that bastard?"

"I didn't say that. It was an example. Besides, we had an agreement: names but no questions."

The General appeared at the entrance. "Men, it's time for your morning routine."

They stood, saluted, belted out a simultaneous *Sir!* and hurried off without a word.

"Morning routine?" Nellie said.

"They search the perimeter of the ranch – twice during daylight hours, twice after dark. We call it a paparazzi hunt. It keeps them entertained – and in shape. Fortunately their tasks aren't affected by the blackout. There are other things they do that I'd rather not discuss."

"I don't care what they do," Beau said. "But aren't they a little strange?"

116

"You don't know them, and I have asked them to keep it that way. However, I will say this: at the ranch they provide a level of security hard to come by these days. When I served in Afghanistan, they saved my life more than once."

"The three of them together," Nellie asked, "or different ones at different times?"

"Does it really matter? Enough chit-chat for now. I'll show you to your work room."

***

"So here's what you do," Beau explained after Nellie had gotten off the phone with H. L. "You take a name on Shiller's list, look for everything you can find on the Web and pick out the important stuff. Like he says, we'll be looking at Skidmore's people too. I haven't done this before, but for them it's easier. You write down negatives and positives for everyone who's with the General or against him, note your source and move on. What helps a lot is Shiller's unlimited access to the kind of public records you usually have to pay for. Maybe it's some kind of military Internet."

"So why are Skidmore's operatives easier?"

"Because you're done when you finish what I just described. With Shiller's people you have to write 200 words on each one, and what you write has to be good. You know, like he really knows them. With the big names in a state's politics – he has them stared – you write 500 words. He looks over what you've done, makes the changes he wants, then has you print out however many copies he thinks he'll need. It might be thirty or forty for precinct captains, enough for them to pass out. If they need more they can make copies. For bigshots he'll want thousands. The printers are in the other room, so they won't bother you. He'll tell you after he reads each blurb how many copies he needs. Then there's the tricky part. Where he's got two stars by a name on the list, you have to write a second blurb, only no one but Shiller will see it. You're supposed to make it real informal so it sounds like someone speaking. You know, sort of like a screenplay."

"Why in God's name does he need that?"

"You'll see when we come out for lunch. He has professionals here to make DVDs about himself. They're tailored specifically to the recipients. According to him, they're really effective winning over the politicos who bring in the voters, especially because the films aren't all the same. He works his ass off to get these scripts like he wants them, I mean *exactly*

117

like he wants them. Sounds crazy, right? But he says these DVDs have done more than anything to help him make converts and put together his ground game."

"So where do we start?" Nellie wanted to know.

"Why don't you take Connecticut, Maryland and Rhode Island? I'll take Pennsylvania, New York and Delaware. We'll be at this right up to the 26th."

Nellie was a quick learner and natural writer. When he read some of her stuff, Beau could almost hear the General's praise.

Shiller came in when the film people arrived, picked up what they had done and looked it over. "Good, especially these. Keep up the pace. Lunch in three hours."

***

Shiller liked good food; he also liked his servings small. Jesús and Manuela knew his preferences well: they had worked for him an entire year and the General, who spoke perfect Spanish, spent the first month in the kitchen with them.

Today the lunch menu was light and simple: sea scallops on forbidden rice, Swiss chard braised in a skillet with olive oil and a touch of garlic, sorbet and espresso. The film people, two men and a woman, could, thought Beau, have been in a TV commercial for Aspen. They were well-dressed, tanned from the ski season, and comfortable making small talk with Shiller and his guests.

Waiting for lunch in the main dining room, they sipped *amontillado* sherry from small copitas. At each place was a bottle of spring water, a sign that no additional alcohol would be served at lunch. Shiller promised drinks when the day's work was done, though he added that it could be as late as midnight.

"It will be quite a shock to go back into the power outage," the woman said. "Everything seems so normal here."

"General," one of the men asked, "do you have any idea how long this is going to go on?"

"I don't think anyone does," Shiller said.

"Any thoughts as to the cause? I mean, I know it was terrorism. But what could they have done to pull this off?"

Shiller seemed to be reflecting on possibilities when the doorbell rang.

"Our guest of honor," the General said. "Excuse me while I escort her in."

When an old woman using a cane entered the dining room the men from the film company looked stunned and disappointed. Idiots, thought Nellie. "Special" meant for them "glamour," as in Beyoncé or Adriana Lima. Aspen was filled with beautiful people, so much so that their numbers made them anything but special. Even Beau now agreed that the one special person in town, apart from Nellie, was H. L. Gibbons.

"Friends," the General said, "we have the honor of being joined by Ms. Gibbons of the Aspen Historical Society. She is single-handedly responsible for the preservation of much of the downtown in its original form."

"Nonsense," H. L. said coolly as Shiller helped her into her chair. "What are these pathetic little glasses your sycophants are sipping from? Don't tell me, just spare me having to drink from one. I'd like a Johnnie Walker – neat."

"A double?"

"A triple, if you don't mind."

Jesús brought H. L.'s drink with exemplary speed, and she intercepted it before he could place it on the table. While she drank, the General introduced the members of the film crew. H. L. didn't like the spotlight or the camera, which, as Nellie knew, explained her utter lack of response. The prospect of a pleasant meal was quickly disappearing.

"After lunch," Shiller said, looking a bit uncomfortable, "I'll ask Manuela to take you on a tour of the house."

"General, you know modern dwellings don't interest me. Instead, I'd enjoy seeing your political command and control center. I would also like to hear how you, as president, would handle the ongoing crisis – not just the power outage but the other attacks that have killed thousands of Americans."

"Certainly. Now, is there anything else you would like before lunch?"

"Another of these," she said, draining her glass. "A more liberal amount. You know, General, I *am* a liberal."

119

CHAPTER SEVENTEEN

Three days into the blackout they were still discussing how to proceed with Connor's hypothesis. Forsythe, suddenly feeling claustrophobic, got up to open the office blinds. "Natural light," he mumbled. "I read somewhere it can stimulate neurons in the brain. We've got about an hour to test the theory."

"Testing the theory," Connor said, "presupposes the existence of a brain. I don't know about you, but mine's fried."

"Randall," said Deputy Director Barnes, "your brain's been fried for decades and it hasn't stopped you from solving crimes."

"Or bringing home and bedding glamourous fugitives," Forsythe added.

"That too," Barnes said, "but his brain wasn't involved. By the way, Randall, are you still living with that woman?"

"He prefers it if you call her Kristýna Sondheim," joked Forsythe as he returned to the conference table. He flashed a mischievous smile in Connor's direction.

"Goddammit, would you both shut up. There was no relationship. Even if there was, so what? We're not in grade school."

"Sensitive, are we?"

Connor ignored his punch-drunk superiors. He looked out at the great city. The blaring chaos of late afternoon traffic had been replaced by an eerie calm. Pedestrians and cyclists sifted peacefully down streets meant for motorized stampedes. There was, he thought, an aspect of tranquility to it all. But this was an illusion. Shops that had managed to open for a few hours were already preparing for another night of looting. Metal security doors began coming down in rapid succession; iron latticework storefronts slid over display windows of luxury boutiques; a deep sense of foreboding seeped like gas through the veneer of calm. When, Connor wondered, would this all end? When and how?

"Okay," Forsythe said. "Let's get back to work. Sorry, Randall, everyone's feeling the pressure."

"No excuse, but okay."

A coded knock. Barnes studied the image from the security camera, then turned on the intercom. "What is it?"

"Sir, we have two important pieces of new information that came in minutes ago. Could I speak with you out here."

"No." Barnes pushed the remote to open the steel door. "Come in and sit down. Brief us all so I don't have to fill in the blanks later."

"Yes, Sir." Special Agent Nelson, immaculately groomed and dressed, walked to the conference table with his attaché case and took a seat. "First, El Lobo is dead. Shot by a sniper from over two thousand yards."

"Two thousand yards?" Forsythe was incredulous. "Randall, is that even possible?"

"With the right combination of rifle and ammo, it sure as shit is. Don't you remember that British sniper who took out two Afghani insurgents from almost *three* thousand yards? Two insurgents with two separate shots, like he was trying to prove the first kill wasn't just a lucky hit."

"I remember reading about it a few years back," Barnes said. "Agent Nelson, give us a summary of your other piece of information before we get into the details of Lobo."

"Yes, Sir. There has been an unprecedented hit on the banks. The large ones have enough backup power to handle critical internal tasks, but they are evidently still vulnerable. There appears to have been a cyberattack like those on the aircraft, only this one was on money. Large portfolios, some worth billions, are now empty. Well, almost empty. They either have $17.76 or $20.16 left in them."

"How can anyone calculate the value of a portfolio?" Barnes asked. "It might contain thousands of different bank accounts, plus stock holdings, derivatives, credit default swaps and whatever Wall Street has come up with since the crash."

"Sir, it didn't seem possible to me either when I first got briefed. But these figures were provided by the largest financial institutions in the United States, Canada and the Cayman Islands. They took into consideration all of the things you mentioned. I was told it can't be coincidence that all of these different institutions using different accounting methods came up with exactly the same numbers. It's sort of like the Brit's double kill in Afghanistan. It can't be coincidence that he hit the second guy."

121

Connor, who had been uncharacteristically silent for a time, stood so abruptly he knocked over his water. "Jesus! You guys are asleep!" He ripped a sheet of blotter paper he had been doodling on from his desk pad and held it up. "Get it? GET IT?"

"Calm down, Randall."

"Not a chance." His sketch showed a gravestone with the lifespan 1776 – 2016 on its face. "Nice, eh?"

"Son of a bitch!" Forsythe barked. "They'll be playing our requiem mass if we don't shut them down soon."

"They're probably playing it already," Connor snarled. "Prematurely. No one fucks with us this way and lives to tell about it."

"I hope you're right, Randall," Forsythe said. "These bastards, I hate to admit, are cyber geniuses. Why aren't any people like that working for us?"

"Budget cuts," Connor repeated. "Remember? You get what you pay for."

"Okay. We'll get back to this when we can get someone up here who understands computer language. Barnes, make some calls. While we're waiting, let's hear the details on El Lobo. Agent Nelson?"

"It went down like this, Director, and it's not pretty. He was sitting at an outdoor café wearing a senior Mexican police officer's uniform. Just sitting there, drinking coffee. Trouble is, he was chatting with a couple of our DEA people. These men had been reporting to Washington that they had recruited an informer from the leadership of the Mexican police."

"You can't be serious," Connor said. "You're telling me these clowns didn't recognize him? No one's that stupid."

"The evidence, Sir, would suggest otherwise. They didn't recognize him until he hit the ground and his hat came off. Or maybe it was his wife, who came from across the street screaming his name."

"Back to the shooting itself," Forsythe ordered. "Let's not waste time getting ourselves worked up over what's already happened. Agent Nelson, please continue."

"Yes, Sir. Like I said, it took place at an outdoor café. They were in the town square of a village near Sinaloa. After he was shot and identified, the DEA agents seem to have followed protocol. They found the slug in a telephone pole and dug it out. Looking from the pole to the place where El Lobo's head had been, they could tell which direction the shot came from. In that direction, about 2,000 yards away, are some hills with trees and gullies."

"Which tells us nothing," Barnes grumbled, "absolutely nothing about the shooter's distance from Lobo."

"That's not the DEA's position, Sir. They used our ballistics lab and our experts in Washington to get this data, so it's probably reliable. Anyway, they were able to take perfect close-ups of the slug and email them home. In the meantime, they're on their way to Dulles with the real thing."

"Fewer words, please," Forsythe said. "Why does Drug Enforcement believe the shot came from those hills."

"Like I said, the bullet was in good shape. They identified it as a .338 Lapua Magnum military issue. When a sniper shoots from that far away, the slug isn't going very fast at the end of its trip. We have computers that can tell us exactly *how* fast from the shape of the slug – if the composition of whatever it hits is known. The DEA agents found a company in Mexico City that came out and gave them the stats on the telephone pole. Once you know how fast the bullet is going when it hits, computers can figure out how far away the shot came from."

"You're leaving a lot out," Connor said. "You have to know the muzzle velocity, speed and direction of the wind, relative humidity, temperature, specifics on the earth's rotation, and about a thousand other things."

"These were all taken into account." Agent Nelson dug through a stack of documents. "Here we have some hard data. The bullet came from an L115A3 AWM. They know this from the rifling and several other identifiers."

"Son of a bitch," Forsythe snapped. "That finishes off my theory of El Lobo's involvement."

Connor was quick to respond. "Listen, Jason, that's not right. We have two high-profile murders at the start of this mess, both filmed, both featuring Mexicans or almost-Mexicans from down there. The rifle Nelson identified as the weapon used to knock off El Lobo was also used by the Brits in Afghanistan. I know for a fact a crate of these things disappeared along with military issue Lapua Magnums. So let's stick with the proposition that El Lobo helped with Keenan and Moose. Those were big jobs worth big money. God's Wrath has cash, lots of it. Now, it would be reasonable to assume someone would capture El Lobo at some point . . . and that he might sing. We don't know how much he knew about this terrorist group that's hitting us now, but it might have been a lot. He'd done his job for those assholes. The smart move for them was to deep-six him. So, Jason, I'd say his murder is totally consistent with your theory."

"Randall," Barnes said, "it's getting on twilight. You're closest. Please close the blinds before we continue."

Connor almost bumped into Nelson, who was on his way out. Something distracted him before he could apologize.

"Jesus Christ!" he shouted. "Get over here, both of you. Tell me I'm not seeing things."

"Don't stroke out, Randall. What is it?"

"The lights! They're on!"

CHAPTER EIGHTEEN

The translation of an article published by the Italian Communist maga-
zine, *Il Manifesto*, and endorsed by God's Wrath as representative of
Western journalism, appeared the first week of July in *The New York
Times*. The White House and others argued that the article was not "news
fit to print" and should be shelved. But the editorial board, citing both
First Amendment rights and journalistic obligations, disagreed. A seg-
ment of that article is reproduced below:

Although the darkness had lifted, the nation was still paralyzed by fear. The home of the brave, if it ever existed, was
nowhere in sight. Citizens stayed away from shopping malls,
airports and concerts. The economy remained in a tailspin,
and foreign competitors positioned themselves to take advantage of new opportunities certain to emerge. Military aircraft were still grounded for fear they would be taken over by
cyber-intellects and crashed into critical components of the infrastructure. Financial institutions closed, shutting down their
heavily networked computer systems to avoid a repeat of the
portfolio adjustments that had been realized during the blackout. Billionaires who supported political campaigns tried in
vain to recoup inherited or fraudulently earned fortunes. Their
heavily leveraged investments and giant real-estate holdings
collapsed, creating a ripple effect that impoverished the entire
donor class and most other wealthy citizens. The United
States of America became the type of egalitarian society to
which it had always paid lip service. Money was now out of
politics; wealth distribution saw its shameful extremes re-
duced. These changes, claimed those responsible, had been
made in the name of global justice. This contention greatly

disturbed the citizens of a land allergic to its own professed values. The United States, on the verge of total dysfunction and probable collapse, became for the first time in its history a beacon of despair rather than hope. And not without reason: the country that had until recently thought of itself as the greatest nation on earth struggled without success to survive the only real crisis it had ever faced.

**

On July 17, 2016, General Gordon Schiller arrived in Cleveland for the Republican Party's 41st National Convention. His victory in the Indiana primary of May 3rd had lifted his delegate count above the number needed to become his party's presidential nominee. Although there had been a handful of terrorist attacks since the cataclysm of April, these originated domestically and were relatively ineffective. The perpetrators – whether they were Americans radicalized by God's Wrath, white supremacists or mass shooters of questionable sanity – had all been tracked down, captured and jailed. Most admitted to being inspired by the April attacks and were thought to be copycats.

**

Americans of all political stripes quickly became accustomed to a military man as the presidential candidate of a major party, most even welcoming it. What caught everyone by surprise, however, was Shiller's choice of William G. Caskey for his running mate. Not only did the two men hold antithetical positions on many important issues; Caskey, during the primaries, had made no secret of his distaste for the centerpiece of Shiller's platform – national service for all young Americans. He also opposed the creation of rapid intervention forces, some consisting of several divisions, to be deployed for *blitzkrieg*-like strikes in the Middle East. Caskey wanted to destroy God's Wrath, as did Shiller, but he argued that this could be accomplished without putting American boots on the ground. How the relationship between the two men would play out at the convention and during the general election campaign remained a question of intense speculation.

**

Connor and Hatch, reunited and transferred to the Los Angeles Field Office, continued to uncover evidence of close collaboration between American soldiers and Islamic fundamentalists. In Afghanistan, a number of highly decorated Special Forces men from all branches of the military had gone missing. This was not unusual, as Special Forces often ventured into hotspots no one else dared go near, sometimes in small groups and sometimes alone. Disappearance in places where bodies could not be retrieved and identified did not result in an official 'Killed in Action' designation, but this was unofficially assumed to be the case.

However, one puzzling fact could not be overlooked: during two months in the Fall of 2009 there was an unusual spike in disappearances. This was enough to convince Connor that members of the American military elite had joined God's Wrath.

To prove he was onto something, Connor bet Hatch a case of 50-year-old Scotch that a soldier from this select group would be on the list of those who had disappeared in 2009. Hatch dropped off the Scotch the next day, his legendary frugality no match for his delight over their apparent breakthrough.

***

The months after the blackout had been a frenetic time for Beau and Nellie. Though they always managed at least an hour a day in the sack, other activities they loved had to go. After Shiller became the unofficial nominee of his party, the campaign shifted from recruiting state and local political operatives to winning over the American public and important people in the federal government.

The painted ladies could not sleep all of the Senators, Representatives, agency heads and military brass the General brought to Aspen. As a result, he began using his ranch to accommodate the overflow. Nellie, as event organizer, had her hands full. Her duties included arranging catered meals from the town's best restaurants, setting up Shiller's private meetings at the Jerome with groups of his guests, helping Jesús and Manuela keep the freezer, walk-in cool room and bar properly stocked, making arrangements for the General's first in-person visits to battleground states and, finally, editing Beau's articles and scripts promoting Shiller's agenda.

During television coverage of the Republican National Convention, there was a brief suspension of political visits. Only the men and women Shiller called the "heart and soul" of his personal security detail were invited to stay at the ranch.

The General told Nellie he wanted his guests treated with special care, his way of thanking them for their exemplary service. He asked her to coordinate the work of the chefs he had brought in from New Orleans, and stressed the need that she maintain a functional "chain of command" in the kitchen. As for her hours, she was to arrive at the house at noon and leave by midnight.

Beau, while continuing his written work for the campaign, wanted to help Nellie with her four-day marathon. Shiller denied his request: the ranch, he explained, would already be too crowded. No offense, but Beau's presence would only make the situation worse.

***

The day before Shiller's elite bodyguards, who were stationed in different places around the country, were to arrive, the French chefs – the same two Shiller had flown in for Aunt Lilly's visit – were already at the ranch. They immediately began reorganizing the kitchen, barking orders at Jesús and Manuela when they weren't at one another's throats.

When Nellie arrived in Beau's truck, which was filled with fruits and vegetables from farmer's markets, meats from specialty shops and every alcoholic drink bartenders at Aspen's exclusive watering holes had recommended, she saw right off there was going to be a problem. Shiller had asked her to run the kitchen. The last thing she wanted was to let him down; but the last thing either of the French cooks wanted was an American girl in charge of what they considered their personal domain.

Arguments began immediately over who would unload the truck, what would go in the cool room instead of the freezer, who would work where; petty arguments she couldn't believe she was hearing. The struggle for dominance quickly spiraled out of control. Jesús and Manuela returned to their cabin, gentle souls unable to tolerate conflict. The chefs, when they weren't screaming at each other, united against Nellie. She yelled back, sometimes in French, managing to keep a tough façade but unable to establish what Shiller called a functional chain of command.

She left in frustration around ten p.m., glad only that the guests hadn't yet arrived. Driving the truck home, she could no longer fight back the tears. She was supposed to be in charge, but felt as though she couldn't get there. Maybe there was a way, but if there was she sure as hell hadn't found it.

***

When she got home, Beau was waiting with a chilled bottle of Bâtard-Montrachet, an exquisite bottle of white Burgundy Shiller had given him as a sort of consolation prize for not being allowed to help in the kitchen. He put it down unopened when he saw Nellie was crying. She went limp in his arms, sobbing like a kid.

"It's gonna be okay," he said. "Whatever it is, baby, it's gonna be

128

okay."

"It's not," she whispered. "Maybe you'd better open the wine."

"I was planning to. Shall we sit outside?"

"How about we snuggle up on the sofa?"

The Montrachet was cool and delicious. Beau's arm around her was warm and comforting. Still, it took her fifteen minutes to utter a word. First it was literally just a word, then a few, then a torrent. He expected her to start crying again when she finished her kitchen story. Instead, she got mad.

"Those bastards," Beau said. "I'll set them straight. We'll go in there together in the morning."

"No, please. You can't do that. Shiller nixed the idea of you at the ranch. He's got mega-security all over the place. And now one of those weirdos at the gate is driving around photographing any journalists who try to talk to someone at our place or the Historical Society. He'll find out and . . . well, you know how he is. Remember how you used to be scared of him? You said it was something you felt but couldn't explain."

"Oh, that. That went away a long time ago."

"For you, maybe, but now I've got it."

"Don't be ridiculous. The three of us are friends. I think he'd want me to put those pricks in their place . . . especially if I was doing it for you."

Beau poured the rest of the wine. She sipped and thought, then shook her head. "It's a bad idea. You'll get photographed. He'll know you defied his order. He's a military man, Beau. I know how he'll react."

"It won't matter when I explain myself."

"It *will* matter. I grew up in a military family. It's a world I know and you don't."

"Yeah, but –"

"But nothing. You're not going to learn the hard way – if you live that long."

"Meaning?"

"The chefs. They walk around sharpening butcher knives. You could end up sliced to pieces."

"Right. Two Frenchmen flat on their backs won't be slicing up any-thing. I saw those little twerps when my aunt was here. At Ole Miss, I put linemen the size of bulls on their asses. These guys will stay on the floor until we've straightened out the chain of command. Let me open another bottle. It won't be a Bâtard but . . ."

"Beau, seriously. Something like that will definitely piss off Shiller Let's use our brains instead. Please. Help me come up with a plan that doesn't have you going in there. And also one where you don't beat up anyone. *Please*, Beau. I've never asked you for a favor, but I'm doing it now."

"You feel that strongly about it?"

"Yes, that strongly. I also have a lot of confidence in your ability to say things without really saying them. The stuff you write for Shiller does that. If you can say things without really saying them, I'll bet you can do things without really doing them. Let's get these guys the Southern way."

"Well, I guess it won't hurt to try. Grab a sweater. I can think more deviously on the porch."

She snuggled up to him again, this time in the old wooden swing. The stars and quarter moon bathed them in soft light. The high peaks behind Ajax Mountain sketched a dark line across the luminous night sky. A breeze had come up, warm and rich with the smell of pine. Beau said, "Back home they call it high-grass slithering. We all do it and we all know everyone else is doing it, but we never actually see something slithering, never know if something is really there."

"What in the world are you talking about?"

"I'll give you an example. Hear that rustling in the cottonwood trees?"

"Sure."

"Well, are those trees really all that's out there? Maybe someone is using the sound for cover and sneaking up on us. Maybe it's not a person but one of those mean-ass lions we saw in Shiller's winter wonderland. Maybe it's worse . . . and maybe it's nothing. It doesn't matter. Just thinking about it has the same effect. It makes you feel like you're on an island of quicksand and if you assert yourself you'll start to sink. It makes you uncertain and insecure. That's high-grass slithering, and that's how you're going to turn these Frenchmen into obedient little Frogs. It'll be like those pieces I write for Shiller: I didn't write it, the reader didn't read it, but he's got this funny feeling what I didn't write and he didn't read might be true. In other words, there *could be* something dangerous – I mean *really* dangerous – that the person you're dealing with doesn't see. Could be. Whether there is or not doesn't matter. Nothing's certain in the eye of the beholder. That's all that counts."

Nellie snuggled closer. "Know what, you should have written fairy tales from bayou land instead of wasting time on football. I really don't get what you're talking about, but at least you've got something to try.

130

That's more than I can say for myself. So let's go for it. Write me a script and I'll put on a high-grass slither that would make your aunt proud."

***

When Nellie arrived, the two chefs were sitting at a table on the patio off the kitchen sharpening knives and smoking Gaulloise cigarettes. "Don't get ashes on the flagstone," she said coolly as she went by. In the kitchen Jesús and Manuela were slicing and dicing at a furious pace. Nellie tried to lead them into the cool room, but they seemed frightened. "Señorita," Jesús said, "we have orders. That giant pile of vegetables has to be turned into little things with pedals that look like flowers."

"Get in here and let me talk. Who gave you those orders?"

"The chefs, Señorita."

"Listen, both of you, The General asked *me* to supervise the kitchen, and that's what I'm going to do. Those peons don't have any right to boss you around."

"But Señorita –"

"Shhh. Just listen. We're going to put those *pendejos* in their place. I'm not going to say it and neither are you, but I'm going to create the impression I could be Shiller's *amante*. Who knows? Maybe even the First Lady one day."

The Mexicans gasped in unison.

"I just want to create an impression. You know, raise the possibility. All this without speaking an untrue word. All I need from you are occasional knowing looks and smiles. Since I'll be speaking English, you won't know when to do this. I'll signal you by pushing an unruly strand of hair away from my eyes. You'll get the hang of it."

"But how –"

"Quiet. They're coming. Help me lift this crate."

No one was chopping at the butcher-block counter when the chefs strolled in. They immediately started yelling something about the price of disobedience. Nellie stepped between them, pushing a strand of blonde hair off her forehead. Her blouse was cut low, her jeans were tight, her sexy shapely self was front and center.

"Remy, Jean-Paul, be quiet or you'll find yourselves somewhere you won't like. The chaos in the kitchen is over. Help with the vegetables."

Jean-Paul, the larger of the two, stiffened. "Who tells a master chef what to do?"

"Who takes a cigarette break while others are slaving away? I don't know, but I'll tell you who doesn't. You."

131

"And you are the bullshitting person who is going to stop us."

"That's right. How could you have failed to realize that word of your behavior yesterday, yes *your behavior*, would reach the General? He has eyes and ears everywhere. How could you not have realized that you might disqualify yourselves from planning state dinners at the White House? And dumbest of all, how could you *not* have asked yourselves the reason I am here?"

"Like, you mean, like you could be his daughter."

"Like I mean I *could* be anyone."

Jesús and Manuela both giggled audibly.

"*Merde alors*," Remy said. "I am always wondering what relations that man has with women."

"Shit *alors*," Jean-Paul added.

"You haven't found out anything," Nellie said. "So don't go around spreading unfounded rumors. If the General hears talk like that, especially just before the election . . . well, you can imagine how he'll feel. Now, are you ready to follow the chain of command he has mapped out for the kitchen?"

"Yes *mademoiselle*. We were ready yesterday. You could have told us your position then, *non*?"

"I didn't tell you my position yesterday and I haven't told you today. Quit thinking about personal matters that don't concern you. You're here to cook for some of the General's most important supporters, period."

"But you were . . . I thought you were with a *mec* when we cook for his aunt in December."

"You thought, you THOUGHT? What did I just say? You're not here to speculate on people's private lives. You saw me come to dinner with a *mec* and his aunt. She was an important person General Shiller needed for his campaign. And that was in December, non? You're guessing about who was with whom seven months ago? *Dégeuelasse*. Now, both of you, get to work over there chopping vegetables. I need Jesús and Manuela for something else."

"I am not understanding any of this, *mademoiselle*."

"You only need to understand one thing. We've got five hours until dinner."

***

High-grass slithering, thought Nellie on her drive home. You learned something every day, which was kind of remarkable.

CHAPTER NINETEEN

Unlike the three taciturn gorillas at the gate, Shiller's elite bodyguards were easy with words and obviously intelligent. Still, Nellie didn't allow them to enter her workspace. After what she'd been through, she had no desire to upset the precise operations of a perfectly organized kitchen. From time to time, several of the male guests who were well-versed in the subtleties of exotic food stopped at the door and asked politely if she had a moment to come out and describe the preparations in progress. Usually, she did. She would, on these occasions, dry her hands on her apron and step into the hall to chat.

From the perspective of the two chefs, it looked as if those friendly foodies knew her "position," just another sign that they had reached the right conclusion. Nellie once saw them wink at each other and fixed them with a withering stare. They went back to chopping and mincing with renewed zeal.

Shiller was scheduled to give his formal acceptance speech on the last night of the convention. It would, as always, be the highpoint of the political gala. The last supper at the ranch was to be a similar highpoint. For this special occasion, the private dining room was unlocked. A note Shiller had entrusted to one of the guests detailed the way in which the kitchen staff was to serve each of the seven courses. The French chefs, both trained at the Cordon Bleu in Paris, had no trouble interpreting the note. Nellie was content to play overseer, watching them like a professor of gastronomy.

***

The ambience of the dining room, she thought, was strange. The weirdness began with the handle on the great wooden entry door: it had no place for a key or keypad. So how had the door been unlocked? She had watched a big muscular guy attempt to open it. No luck. But when he tried again five minutes later, it yielded easily.

133

And the dining room! It was a long narrow rectangle without windows, a striking anomaly in this elegant mansion of wood and glass. Even worse, the guests would be eating at some kind of refectory table. She had seen these depressing monsters in paintings of early Renaissance monasteries, but never dreamed she would come across one outside of a book. She could picture unhappy monks with reverse Mohawks sitting in parallel rows. Unhappy, perhaps, because they had to face each other; or perhaps because their only other option was to stare at the disgusting gruel in their bowls. Why a sophisticated contemporary general with impeccable taste would have one of these uncomfortable behemoths . . . well, that was something she would never understand. And why he would choose it for his special dinner was too baffling even to contemplate.

The guests, she mused, could have watched the acceptance speech in a magnificent living room with beautiful stone fireplaces, sleek Scandinavian furniture and 30-foot ceilings. When it was over, they could have retired to his comfortable modern dining room for the celebration meal. Instead, the General wanted them in a dreary Medieval cave that could have doubled as a torture chamber.

Nellie couldn't stop staring at the table. The top was hardwood, mahogany like her grandmother's chest of drawers, and it was two or three inches thick. You could see cracks and splits and a sprinkling of woodworm holes, but you couldn't bring them into focus. The rich patina of the surface made them look as if they were covered by a translucent haze. The stout table legs were ornately carved with crests and figurines she had never seen before. The chairs were carved the same way, but they didn't look as old. They had thick cushions of dark leather that showed no signs of creasing or cracking. Shiller must have had the original chairs reupholstered to make them comfortable for sitting – or he had acquired a fake. Which was the case? It felt important that she know, even if she had no idea why. Running her fingers along the wood of a chair back, she tried to find a clue. Nothing tactile. But when she held her hand to her nose, she breathed in the scent of time. This ghost from the past was real.

While she and Manuela laid out and ironed the tablecloth, Nellie counted the chairs: six on each side. One end of the table was not meant to be occupied. The opposite end had a chair that looked almost like the other twelve. But when she studied it more closely she saw that it was a little wider, with thicker and more ornately carved legs. Shiller's chair, she guessed. The thirteenth disciple.

"It is beautiful," Manuela said in Spanish. "I once saw such a table in an old church in San Luis Potosi."

"I've only seen them in books," Nellie said. "You've seen this particular table before, haven't you?"

"No, Señorita, I have never seen it. I didn't know it was here. I certainly didn't know the General was a religious man. This explains so much."

Nellie said, "Manuela, not to disappoint you, but he might just be an antique collector."

"No, Señorita, you do not understand. You know the meaning of my husband's name, but do you know the meaning of "Manuela?" It means 'God is with us.' I have often worried that God was not with the General, but now I know that He is."

"Even so, I wouldn't want one of these things in my house. They belong in very old monasteries. Don't you agree, Manuela?"

***

At least, thought Nellie, they were able to watch Shiller's speech in the living room. She made a point of enjoying the open, airy atmosphere while she brought out tray after silver tray of exquisitely prepared hors d'oeuvres. The pleasant surroundings, she knew, wouldn't last forever.

While Nellie served the guests, Jesús and Manuela wheeled around carts laden with every sort of drink imaginable. No one seemed to notice the endless flow of wonders from the kitchen, so intent were they on catching the General's every word. Their eyes remained glued to the television, even when standing ovations silenced the speaker.

Nellie wanted to take a break from serving and listen the speech but she couldn't. The dinner hour was fast approaching and her well-oiled kitchen machine was running low on fuel. Fortunately, both the kitchen and living room had televisions. This allowed her, as she hurried back and forth, to piece together at least some of the General's address.

Shiller thanked William Caskey, his choice for vice president, for coming around to his position. It wasn't exactly clear how the two men had managed to achieve such unity after a campaign that exposed their many differences. The press, which had been hoping for drama, knew they were out of luck when they learned of a Shiller-Caskey meeting the previous afternoon. The result of the meeting, as the deflated drama junkies of the beltway now concluded, was the normal coming together of a political party's disparate factions before a presidential election. Or was it? Nellie had her doubts – though, as usual, she couldn't say why.

Next time out with the hors d'oeuvres trays, she was able to hear

Shiller explain a few changes in the order of things he wanted to accomplish. National service for all young Americans would remain the top priority, as would a four-year suspension of the culture wars that had pitted countrymen against each other. But after the events of April, rebuilding the nation's infrastructure and educational systems would have to await the destruction of God's Wrath. To this end, the creation of rapid intervention forces would be accelerated and their numbers expanded. Changes in automated systems of military drones and aircraft were on track to be completed soon, meaning that engagement in the Middle East would not experience significant delays.

He deplored the way money had been removed from politics. It had been one of his primary goals – through traditional means, not terrorism. Nellie heard him promise to help restore the lost fortunes of those who had previously controlled the Republican Party, but only after new laws were passed that made lobbying and campaign financing from private sources illegal. Money had nothing to do with free speech, he said, and American democracy would no longer be for sale when he was president.

She wondered how this change would clear the legal hurdles it was sure to encounter, but she needn't have. He provided an explanation almost immediately . . .

The imminent vacancies on the Supreme Court due to illness would afford him three appointments to make within the first months of his administration. His appointees would be men and women who accepted his interpretation of the law: *anything that weakened America went against the intent of the Founding Fathers and was hence unconstitutional.* Myopic justices, brilliant though they might be, were unable to put the words of a different era into a modern context. Those living in the past would no longer hold a majority . . .

His victory in the presidential election was not in question. Just as important, House and Senate races were shaping up in a way that would give him a veto-proof majority in both bodies. As a result, the deadlock that brought America to its knees was destined to end. The implementation of his no-nonsense agenda would mark the beginning of a new Golden Age . . .

With that, Nellie was finished listening. The clamor coming from the kitchen announced the final preparations for dinner, preparations for which the future President of the United States would hold her responsible. Nothing, absolutely nothing, must be allowed to go wrong.

CHAPTER TWENTY

"*Alors, mademoiselle,*" Jean-Paul asked after the meal, "what did you think?"

Nellie could hardly contain herself. "It was spectacular, fabulous, better than the best I've had in Paris."

Remy winked at his fellow chef, then smiled at Nellie. "So, then, cooking at the White House for the First Lady, no guessing who – maybe young countess – we might still have the honor?"

Jean-Paul cringed, but the undisputed master of the kitchen was beyond anger. Instead of a withering stare, she treated the Frenchmen to a glimpse of her incomparable smile. "You jokesters know that others decide such things."

"But I hope others are not deciding who is First Lady."

"Listen, the First Lady is the wife of the president. General Shiller is not married. I haven't heard from anyone that this will change."

"So . . . no young countess?"

"No young countess. Like I said, who cooks at the White House is a decision others will make. The president of course will have the last word. But I intend to tell the General it was a pleasure working with both of you. In my book you are culinary geniuses."

"And you will be describing the dishes we made that are proving this, *non?*"

"He'll probably hear the details of the menu from his guests before he hears them from me. But, yes, when I see him again, I'll be sure to describe them."

The kitchen phone rang. Nellie answered. "I'll send them right out," she said.

"Our travel to the hotel?"

"Yes. Your car's waiting out front." She gave them each a kiss on both cheeks, French style, and thanked them once more. "You'd best hurry, now. I'm sure we'll see each other again. Maybe in New Orleans at your restaurant."

"*À bientôt*, then. No farewell."

"No farewells," Nellie said. "But now it's time for you to go."

***

She had pulled it off, the whole damned assignment, and this left her feeling a bit giddy. The final meal, her last hurdle, the hurdle she feared the most, had been a smashing success. Once they started the dinner service, she hadn't even been creeped out by the room and refectory table. She took a moment to think back on her little miracle . . .

The guests, all of them pleasant people, were in such high spirits, so appreciative of the food and wine, that they didn't seem to notice the bizarre room and table. But they did notice *her*. Each time she came with another course, they tried a little harder to include her in their circle of good cheer. By the time dessert was served, she felt as if she could have taken a seat in the empty twelfth chair and been welcomed into the group. Not in Shiller's chair, of course. He was the boss, the future president, a man who commanded the respect of everyone who knew him. His seat, even when vacant, was sacred – sort of like the Pope's. But that twelfth chair seemed to beckon to her. It would be the perfect place to take a short breather. She was about to ask why the spot was vacant when an explanation came her way.

"Hollis is going to be pissed when we tell him about the dinner," one of the women said.

"He shouldn't be," the guy beside her quipped. "He got the easy job. Shiller's spokesman! Never thought he'd be the chosen one."

Nellie realized then that these men and women had been here before. Twelve places; one empty. The good-looking guy in the expensive suits she'd seen on television, Shiller's press man, had gone to Cleveland for the Convention. Probably better she hadn't taken his seat.

This whole thing was a puzzle. It seemed incomprehensible to her that bodyguards would need a room as private as this one to meet in, especially when the room was inside an impenetrable house. But she was probably being naïve. The criminal underworld had now become proficient in all sorts of high-tech stuff, not to mention God's Wrath. Extra precautions couldn't hurt, and she knew Shiller was a cautious man. So why think about it at all?

"I saw you watching me from the door to the dining room," a man across the table said. He seemed friendly enough. "What you witnessed

138

was an exercise in primitive technology. Still, a fun trick for the uninitiated. Wouldn't you agree, Ms. Vaughn?"

"You mean how the door handle to this room wouldn't open . . . and then it would?"

"Yep, that's what I mean. There's a receiver in the handle you can't see. The General operates it with a cell phone. He dials a number from anywhere in the world to open the lock, which you can't see either. I guess he doesn't want us having unlimited access to his antiques. I don't know how we'd hurt them, but that's the way he is: smart as hell, unconventional as they come."

"I like him that way," Nellie said. "He's what the country needs. The polls are already saying he'll win at least forty states, maybe all fifty. It isn't going to matter who the Democrats nominate. What a privilege for all of us to be working for the next president!"

"You've got that right," a man who hadn't spoken yet said.

Everyone toasted her as she hurried back to the kitchen.

***

She looked at her watch, then at a wall clock – just to be sure. It was a habit she'd gotten into the last four days. Shiller was a precise man who gave precise directives. He had told her when to show up and when to leave. She didn't want to give him reason to be angry with her – not now, not ever.

Her watch and his clock were in perfect sync: both read 11:19 p.m. Forty-one minutes! She had almost an hour before she turned into a pumpkin. It was just enough time to do something special for the General's guests.

A nice gesture would be to lay out a few things for breakfast, prepare the coffee machine to start brewing at seven, leave behind a note with instructions on where to find the many other breakfast things, not easy for newcomers to Shiller's restaurant-size kitchen. But did she have enough left in the tank to do all of this? Probably, if she stopped thinking about her dinner triumph and stayed focused.

A little planning. For a start, she'd grab a few things from the cool room that would taste better if they warmed up overnight; Shiller's exotic fruits and melons, for example, and Manuela's *pico de gallo* – and, of course, the cheeses.

When she stepped inside the chilly vault, she felt revived. The door, which opened outward into the kitchen, closed behind her as it was supposed to do. It didn't slam, didn't reestablish its hermetic seal, but left a

139

slender almost invisible crack. The lights came on automatically.

Nellie surveyed the room. Crates of unused vegetables lined the wall to her left. Soufflés, quiches and frittatas were things the guests didn't eat unless they were loaded with bacon or sausage. Side dishes, such as those of kale, onions and mushrooms, didn't please anyone. The chefs said nothing: they simply stopped preparing vegetable dishes. That's why the vegetables were still there . . .

Nellie caught herself imagining that Shiller would ask her to take a couple of crates off his hands. Not good. Daydreaming was a distraction that stole your sense of time.

The back wall of the cool room was stacked with empty crates that a few days earlier had been full of meats, poultry, pâtés, and crustaceans. The wall to her right stretching back from the hinged side of the door held the items Nellie planned to bring out. She took two empty crates from the back wall – one for the fruits and melons, one for the cheeses. Incidentals, such as Manuela's *pico de gallo*, she could put in the small wicker basket that had held the truffles.

That basket! She had to laugh. She was imagining herself as Little Red Riding Hood swinging it by the loop handle. "To grandmother's house we go," she whispered to herself.

Stop fantasizing! Get to work!

***

She thought she heard something, even though the crack in the heavy door was so small that any sound outside the cool room was muffled. Nothing to worry about. The noise would be coming from the guests, who were either going to bed or heading for the living room to have a nightcap.

She admonished herself again to stay focused. Time was passing. Time was short.

While she was piling every kind of cheese into a crate, she heard something again. This time the sound of voices was unmistakable. A couple of Shiller's men were in the kitchen, not far from the crack in the cool room door which they must have noticed.

Apparently not: if someone had seen the crack they would either have looked inside or pushed the door shut. If they opened it later, so what? They'd find her doing just what she was doing – nothing Shiller would object to. And if they shut it without looking inside and didn't hear her yell, she wouldn't be trapped. She had seen the big lever-like handle on the inside of the door several dozen times a day; she could find it blind-folded. Still, it would be better to go out immediately, better not to risk

140

the appearance that she was eavesdropping.

She walked to the thick insulated door to shove it open, which brought her nearer to the crack. Not only could she hear voices: she could understand them.

Just a few more words, she decided, letting curiosity get the best of her. She would listen to a few more words before bursting into the kitchen.

The man who had been talking the most said, "Funny how you get hungry after a giant meal. Have you ever thought about why?"

"Never. But I know what you're talking about. I'm no stranger myself to post-gluttony scrounging missions."

"A universal human trait, I suppose. I've got a major craving for *coquilles st. jacques*."

"Mine's for crème brulée."

"Listen, Jim, before we conduct a raid on the fridge I want to ask you something I wouldn't bring up if I weren't this buzzed."

"Make it quick."

"I don't want you to take this the wrong way. I just need to know I'm not alone."

"Not alone? What are you talking about?

"You've doubted the ethics of Shiller's plan on certain rare occasions, haven't you? Like tonight, when we've had *way* too much to drink."

"Never. Drunk or not, never. I can't believe you have."

"Just in passing, and just once or twice. It's the 'means justify the end' element of the mission that bothers me. As a student of history, you're aware that the means has always colored the end."

"Look, Allen, we're not involved in a mission that replicates anything in the past. Shiller loves our country; we love our country. Before the emergence of transnational terror groups, we never hesitated to go to war to defend it. We've lost hundreds of thousands of American lives in the process. That's what we're doing now, but in a drastically changed world. History offers no parallel. Your worries about means tainting ends are not relevant. We're only doing what we're doing because Washington is paralyzed.

"General Shiller refuses to allow the greatest country on earth to be dismembered because we don't have the flexibility to change what shackles us. Sixty-five thousand Americans have died in a war to save their country. *We* killed them? Technically, yes. *But you can't start thinking like that*. It's just plain wrong. They sacrificed themselves to protect three

141

hundred million compatriots who would otherwise face a future of unimaginable horror, perhaps even extinction. There was no other way to proceed."

"Clearly, Jim, you're right. I'm no Doubting Thomas. I just had a few infrequent and insignificant moments of doubt. I guess I needed to hear what you've just outlined so well. Thank you."

"Sure, comrade. You've done great work. Don't come unraveled now. Shall we hit the fridge?"

***

Nellie, while listening to the unthinkable, went numb. She had to be dreaming. Such things did not happen in this country . . .

But happen they had. Her blood became ice water. Her numbness yielded to terror. A medicine ball from nowhere hit her in the gut. Reality cracked her in the head like a tire iron.

She could feel herself falling and grabbed a shelf. She had to do something to save herself but she couldn't. Fear strangled her like a Boa, fear made the earth spin, fear squeezed the air out of her lungs and paralyzed her.

Where was the kid she had been in grade school, the kid who had rebelled so fiercely against a military dad that he sent her to military school? She found that ferocious little girl buried under learned civility; found her at the core of her being; became her . . . and laughed.

Footsteps coming her way, footsteps of her resurrected dad. Kick him in the shins, bite his arm, stab him in the leg with a letter opener . . . or charm him. You've done it all before. You can do it again. MOVE!

She burst into the kitchen and feigned a startled look. "You guys . . . Jesus, you scared me. No one's supposed to be in here."

"Says who?"

"You know who."

"He didn't tell me."

"I guess it's no big deal. The cooking's over, the chefs are gone. Know what? You showing up like this, even if you almost gave me a heart attack, isn't all bad. You can help me get these crates out of the cool room. Or better yet, gentlemen, you can *really* help me and do it yourselves. I'm freezing to death."

"What's so important about the crates?"

"They're for your breakfast. The stuff in them needs to warm up, and I need to go home."

"So why are you shaking?"

"Oh, come on. That's a cool room, not a sauna. Would you please brave the cold and bring out the stuff. Or don't. I'll get it myself. I've got to hurry. The General asked me, ordered me, to leave the ranch by midnight."

"Okay, okay. We'll help. What was your name? It slipped my mind."

"Nellie. You guys do the heavy lifting while I get the coffee ready for morning."

"Okay, Jim, let's roll."

Nellie was careful not to make noise. She wanted them to hear "the sound of silence." They had to believe she didn't know or they would murder her. Her, Beau, H. L. and God only knew who else.

They were in the cool room longer than it took her to set up the coffee machine, no doubt to assess the acoustics.

She started trembling again, but the little girl she used to be yanked open the cool room door.

"Hey! I said *GOOD NIGHT*. Are you guys deaf?"

PART III

CHAPTER TWENTY-ONE

After the Convention, Shiller made a round of the largest victory parties. Wherever he showed up, he was met with subdued awe. This was a man cut from a different cloth, a man whose intelligence and strength radiated from his mere presence. Soaring rhetoric and brightly colored balloons were not necessary to announce his arrival on the world stage. So great was the authority he projected that many Americans turned to him rather than Faith for salvation. God had not shown up in their time of need; Shiller had.

At 3:20 a.m., while Jake Hollis mollified the press, the General boarded his private jet to return to Aspen. He wasn't going to waste time campaigning while the Democrats held their brokered Convention. They had no prospective candidate who could mount a challenge, no one the national polls gave a chance of winning more than one or two states.

The plane waited ten minutes for Shiller's press spokesman to break free of the reportorial feeding frenzy, then spooled up its engines and rolled into take-off position. The rain-slick runway pulsed with reflections of distant lightening.

It wasn't likely they would be able to get airborne before the thunderstorm grounded them. Shiller radioed his pilot to "misunderstand" air traffic control if take-off clearance was withheld. Five days spent with politicians in Cleveland had left him with a powerful need to get out of the place.

"Not necessary, Sir," the pilot radioed back. "Clearance granted." In seconds, the engines were at full thrust. They accelerated along the uneven tarmac, climbed steeply toward a ragged sky and cracked into an angry wall of turbulence.

"Good job, Ellis," Shiller radioed back to the pilot, unruffled by the creaking bones of the plane. He would not ask if it had been necessary to "misunderstand."

Hollis, so talkative during the Convention, fell asleep while they were

145

still bouncing around. The General, who was enjoying the exhilaration of escape, waited until they reached cruising altitude to shed his tie and call for a drink. The public be damned, he thought, downing the first swallow of Glenfiddich 30. He was human, not God. So human, in fact, that he allowed himself a mental journey into the past.

At first his reminiscences reached back only as far as the Convention. Everyone had been worried about security, and understandably so. But Shiller reassured the country in a press release that the threat was small. God's Wrath, after its crippling attack of April, would need additional months to prepare another strike. Just in case, though, tanks and troops would be added to security forces on the ground, and squadrons of aircraft newly outfitted to fend off cyber terrorism would be watching from above.

***

Well on the way to achieving his goal, Shiller remained somewhat surprised that his call for the suspension of culture wars had been accepted by majorities on both the left and right. Hell, he wasn't even president yet and already they were listening! Or maybe it was something else: when your country was on the verge of collapse, it mattered a lot less whether gay marriage was legal or there was a gun in every closet. What *didn't* surprise him was that most everyone agreed on the necessity to fundamentally restructure a political system designed for another era. When a government could no longer protect its people, the only possible conclusion was that something had to change . . .

The remainder of his agenda, at least the part of it known to the public, had gone over well. In droves, Republicans realized they were being duped by a handful of the superrich who couldn't care less about the average Joe. The Grand Old Party, long a bastion of anti-government sentiment, survived only because Shiller, friend of the little guy, had taken it over. That his agenda dovetailed at many points with the traditional objectives of Democrats either occurred to no one or bothered no one.

Perhaps, he mused, it was equally helpful to his cause that many liberals had softened their view of Republicans. He supposed they had gotten the message that the U. S., if it was to overcome the current crisis, needed a unified effort. This would require the support of former Washington haters, white and right, who lived in small towns, rural areas and large pockets of affluent suburbia.

Shiller did not doubt he would get a large percentage of left-leaning independent and liberal votes. No progressive had an answer for dealing with God's Wrath; and without an answer, high-minded policy agendas

146

were nothing more than pipe dreams.

So, yes, it had all worked out. It had worked because he dared to take the drastic steps needed to open the eyes of his compatriots. Much remained to be done, but Shiller knew he was now unstoppable.

Another Glenfiddich, and his mind travelled back through time. He had kept his thoughts focused squarely on the future for almost a decade, seeing no reason to look back on what had already happened. Now, however, he was far enough along with his enterprise that he felt like revisiting the past.

So he did, with pleasure, sifting through the seminal events of his life like a man leafing through old photographs of himself.

***

The order for him to board a waiting helicopter just inside the Pakistani border came as a complete surprise – and Shiller was rarely surprised. It was November of 2009. Nine months into his first term, the President of the United States had made a secret trip to Bagram Air Base. While there, he took several private meetings with General Shiller, head of SOCOM. The content of their discussions was never made public, and it remained unknown to both men's closest associates.

Shiller, after the third meeting, was abruptly relieved of his command. There was speculation that he had been fired for his unauthorized move from Kabul into a combat zone. SOCOM was the Command of all US Special Forces, and the importance of the man in charge could not be overstated. His firing made perfect sense: so critical a position could not be compromised by a loose cannon, a commander who insisted on placing himself in the middle of the fighting. Shiller was what he was: a brilliant tactician and fearless leader whose obstinacy made him impossible to control. No indication he would ever change.

He refused outright to live in safety when the missions he planned put his Special Forces troops in danger. His idealism might be admirable, but his lack of practicality would eventually lead to disaster. President Albrecht knew this and decided he must go. Or so went the most prevalent line of speculation.

But not everyone believed Shiller had been fired. He was far too valuable to the military. He and his troops had pulled off missions on the Khyber Pass and in the mountainous regions of Afghanistan that were considered impossible. Perhaps more important, his success protected big-name generals from accusations of incompetence. Because of Shiller's battlefield triumphs, they could avoid unpleasant and possibly career-ending appearances before congressional committees.

The official explanation for his removal from SOCOM – that he had been assigned to a classified mission he alone in the Armed Forces was intellectually and emotionally equipped to carry out – might actually be true. In fact, this interpretation became more and more credible over time.

Soon after the meeting, Shiller fell off everyone's radar. He was not seen or heard from again until Albrecht lost his bid for a second term. Schiller's position was terminated before the change of administrations; so too was any evidence that it had ever existed.

His resignation gave hope to the punditry that something newsworthy might emerge. But when the General settled into a quiet civilian life in Aspen, interest in "the missing years" faded. By the time of Albrecht's death, seven months after losing the election, that interest had all but disappeared. Yet, for Shiller, those years remained the most memorable of his life.

***

President Grant Albrecht was one of the few politicians Shiller respected. He was an ex-Marine who had become a Congressman and, eventually, Chairman of the House Armed Services Committee. In that capacity he had befriended Shiller, with whom he agreed on virtually every aspect of military policy. It wasn't long until their friendship became an unbreakable bond, cemented by trust and mutual admiration. In private they used first names, a practice they never abandoned.

When the door to the meeting room opened, Shiller saw only a crush of officers and Secret Service agents. But the President quickly dispatched the mob, and wasted no time closing and locking the door.

"Gordon, it's been far too long," the President said.

They shook hands, firmly.

"Indeed, Grant. The war has also been too long. I assume you came to be briefed?"

"No. It's something else. Let me pour drinks before we begin."

"Certainly."

The President opened a bottle of Wild Turkey the base commander had saved for his visit. "You'll join me?"

"I don't drink when I'm on duty, which is always."

"Water, then?"

"Yes, thank you."

The men sat in armchairs facing one another. Bourbon met Perrier as they clinked glasses.

Albrecht said, "You might want to reconsider your choice of drinks when you hear my proposal." Shiller smiled thinly. "Something of major significance?"

"Bigger. Something unprecedented. I'm not going to repeat the negligence preceding 9/11. Whatever the outcome in Afghanistan, the threat of transnational terror will continue to grow exponentially. If we don't make fundamental changes, the American Homeland – its military bases, vital infrastructure, its industry, institutions, everything we value – faces imminent destruction. Not tomorrow, but sometime during my eight years in office. The CIA managed to infiltrate a group no one outside of the intelligence community has ever heard of."

"God's Wrath?"

"You know. But are you aware Westerners are involved?"

"I am."

"Not just any Westerners. Americans and Europeans skilled in types of warfare we haven't even thought of."

"If you don't mind my saying, it seems a rather sensational claim."

"I know. But it was indisputably confirmed by our agents, two of the best, before they were ferreted out and beheaded."

"Give me the green light and SOCOM will take care of the these guys."

"Gordon, since our infiltration the group has divided itself into cells. These cells, we believe, have scattered to the ends of the earth. You might be able to destroy one or a hundred. I tell you, it'll make no difference. They'll continue to metastasize. Just as disturbing, we suspect they can communicate and coordinate in ways we don't have the capacity to monitor.

"These aren't black-clad kids who drive around in Toyota pickups scaring the hell out of unarmed civilians. They're unheralded members of the world's intellectual elite, determined to destroy the United States. Gordon, we are facing a cataclysm the likes of which is unknown to Western Civilization. And I *am* including Hitler. Unless . . . *you* can prevent it.

"Let me just say it. You are the one man I trust with the military savvy and intellectual prowess to direct another Manhattan Project. This undertaking will be more important than building an atom bomb to end a war that was already over, much more important. It will require and receive a commensurate level of secrecy. I realize I'm asking a lot. I'm also giving you the chance to rewrite History before it happens."

"Grant, I don't need convincing. Tell me in detail what you want me

149

to do."

"I'm coming to that, but the 'why' must precede the 'what.' Let me put things in context. We live in a world we don't understand. We face an invisible adversary we don't understand. In this new world, we don't have the means, will or imagination to defend ourselves. Hell, we don't even know what to defend against. My hands are tied as long as Congress is diddling around and the Court thinks we live in the same agrarian society we did when the Constitution was written.

"Gordon, I'm asking you to provide our public and private sectors with hard evidence of their own vulnerability. The secrecy of your operation will put it beyond reach of Congress and the Courts."

"I'm listening."

"I want you to prepare *and take to the very last stage* terrorist attacks against a number of targets without which America could not function. I'm not going to specify which ones because I want you to have the final word in their selection. Choose the power grid. Choose the heart of our industrial plant. Choose nuclear sites, airfields, the aircraft industry itself. Military bases are not off limits. The media, sports, concerts, all forms of entertainment – these are also legitimate areas to put in your sights. What things do our people depend on? What things do they enjoy? What would it take to end life as we know it in the United States? Your demonstration of exactly what is possible will lead to profound changes in Washington and beyond, changes any functional modern government would demand."

"This is a lot more complicated than the first Manhattan project."

"Yes it is. But you've worked with Special Forces people who are geniuses at cyber warfare. You have worked with men and women prepared to do what they must, whatever that might be, to protect America. I could go on, but you already know these things. I want you to recruit your most trusted, most competent warriors. I stress here 'trusted.' No one, *including* government intelligence people, can know of this undertaking's existence until we are ready to demonstrate that the push of a button, the pull of a lever, can – not could but can – destroy our country. We must behave in our preparations as we believe our enemies would behave, and this will require a significant overhaul of our political, military and technological worlds. It's the only way I see to spare our country an agonizing death. We'll begin our discussion of specifics tomorrow."

***

Before Albrecht's election loss in 2012, Shiller had planned to work with the president. Together, they would use the stunning achievements

150

of his recruits as shock therapy to awaken the nation to its vulnerabilities. But two things happened during the period between Albrecht's defeat and the inauguration of the next president, and these pointed Shiller in a radically new direction.

The first was the discovery in late December of Albrecht's incurable pancreatic cancer. The second was a series of events that showed the newly elected President of the United States to be a weak and ineffective leader, incapable of breaking the deadlock in Congress, let alone of stopping God's Wrath.

Shiller reassembled his people in February of 2013, confident that each soldier with whom he had worked for the past years shared his devotion to America. The twelve disciples, as they had come to be known among themselves, would no longer be relegated to a bit part in the larger scheme of things. Instead, they would shape History.

Shiller would "retire" to a spot where he could receive frequent guests without attracting attention. In subsequent meetings, he and his disciples would devise and implement a strategy to restore America's greatness.

* * *

The General felt the beginning of their initial descent into Aspen. He would have time for a short night's sleep before the next stage of his enterprise began.

CHAPTER TWENTY-TWO

"Beau, wake up!"

He groaned, rolled onto his side and coughed. She'd pounded on him, slapped him, yelled at him – all with no effect.

"I said, we're about to be KILLED! Wake up!"

Miserable Southern slouch, she fumed, whacking on his arm. Southerners! They slept when they were awake, and when they really were asleep you couldn't wake them up with a grenade.

She was hysterical. She'd completely fallen apart on the drive home, pulling over to await the inevitable each time headlights flashed in her rearview mirror. And now this!

"WELLINGTON FUMBLES ON THE ONE YARD LINE!" she screamed.

He came flying out of his slumber, reaching frantically in all directions for the ball.

"Did I lose the game?" He sat up and looked around, confused.

"For chrissake, get up! We're about to be murdered! MURDERED, understand?"

"What? Murdered because I fumbled?" He seemed under water.

"What's wrong with you? We're being hunted down like animals and you talk football."

***

When he stepped into the rectangular room the morning after his return from Cleveland, Shiller was met with applause from his disciples. He showed no emotion as he took his seat in the thirteenth chair.

"Your applause," he said, "is misplaced. No one, including myself, should be singled out for praise. This has been a group effort from the beginning, and it will remain a group effort going forward.

"You've had four days to revel in past success. That chapter is now closed. As we move to the next stage, our attention will focus exclusively

152

on the future. Why? Because infatuation with the past can easily morph into future complacency. We can't let that happen. If we fail now, everything has been for naught.

"Let's go over where we stand. We know the outcome of the presidential election. We are on track to have a veto-proof majority in both Houses of Congress. Thanks to upcoming resignations, we'll have a Supreme Court that rubber-stamps rather than obstructs. We've positioned ourselves to carry out the long-overdue transformation of America. Positioned ourselves only. The transformation is yet to be realized.

"We won't meet again until January 21. Today, I'm going to assign the role each of you will initially play in our administration. We'll then have an open forum on how best to seamlessly merge those roles into a political juggernaut powerful enough to effect the changes we want. Comments before I continue?"

One of the disciples stood. "General, Sir, what about Talladega?"

"Talladega has become unnecessary. We're not going to take additional risks, no matter how small."

"Understood, Sir. But does this mean there will be no further operations?"

"No further operations of scale."

"Which leaves open the possibility of smaller operations?"

"I'll get to that. Our real work begins in January. This means that each of you will have ample time to prepare for the assignment you receive today. But prepare with this in mind: once I'm in the Oval Office, we're going to move at a dizzying pace. There will be no 'first hundred days' in the Shiller administration. Historians will have to content themselves writing about the first hundred hours. We're only going to have a small window for instituting the reforms our country needs. When we begin our work, some will object. Others will interpret our actions as a military putsch. There will be an outcry from abroad. Our first priority is, therefore, to act before the skeptics and nay-sayers have time to coalesce into a serious opposition.

"Now to your question about smaller operations. There will be one. Lieutenant Hollis, better known these days as *Mr.* Hollis, my spokesman in tailored suits . . . "

The General was interrupted by subdued laughter. One of the disciples blurted out, "He had some good coaching, Jake did. On TV he actually sounds like he went to Harvard."

"Knock it off," Hollis grumbled, his nerves still raw from days of non-

153

stop badgering from the press. "I not only went to Harvard. I have a doctorate in Political Science from Harvard."

"All of you," Shiller said, "that's enough. Hollis, you did an excellent job executing the thankless task I assigned you. You will continue to do an excellent job during and after the campaign."

"You're going to keep me on as press secretary?"

Shiller smiled for the first time that bright July morning. "I most certainly am. The media people have come to know you. Two or three might even like you."

Laughter.

"You'll have to point them out to me, Sir. I hadn't noticed."

Again, laughter.

"I'll do that, Jake. First, though, you will carry out a mission in your original field of expertise."

"He has one?" cracked the man beside him.

Irritation flashed across Shiller's handsome face. "That will do. We had our moment of levity, the last we'll have today." His cold gray eyes went the length of the table and back, stopping to await a "Yes, Sir" from each disciple.

"Good. The operation involves my running mate. I want him eliminated. He's been attempting to dig too deeply into my past, and even indicated in Cleveland that he didn't think I won the nomination fairly. As far as the public knows I chose him to show my willingness to reach out to politicians not in total agreement with me. But that was not the reason. Making him my subordinate allows me to control him. Though he doesn't know it yet, he'll be traveling to Mexico, ostensibly to apologize to top government and law enforcement officials for the demeaning remarks he made about Mexican immigrants during the primaries.

"Hollis, you'll have his itinerary soon. It will be best if he doesn't return. However, you won't have a spotter and will only take one shot, and only if it is from 2,000 yards or more. You did it with El Lobo. I hope it wasn't luck."

"It wasn't luck, Sir. And I don't need a spotter. Just give me the when and where."

"Of course. Now to the assignment of roles. Hollis, you have yours. That means twelve remaining. Yes, that's right, I'm not going to just sit in my swivel chair while the rest of you work. We have three men capable of organizing three separate rapid-intervention forces, each with attributes I'll spell out shortly. You know who you are. You'll be working with

154

active commanders in the Army, Navy and Air Force with whom I have excellent relationships. We don't have the capacity to deploy as rapidly as we must, so you'll have your hands full. I've revised my early projections: each force will be made up of three to five divisions; each will consist of roughly 50,000 soldiers. We need them in battle as soon as possible. Successful military actions in the Middle East will draw public attention away from the White House.

"We have two videographers. Your roles will be critical. Each time God's Wrath commits an act of aggression against the West – or any civilized group – they will be encircled by a far superior force before they know what hit them. Military annihilation is our final, but not our only, objective. America has been hammered by these people. The public wants revenge. Better said, they want to *see* their enemy humiliated. This is an area in which you two are going to have to collaborate effectively with our intervention forces.

"We will eventually annihilate each group we encircle. First, however, we need visuals. There are two reasons for this: one is to slake the public's thirst for revenge; the other is to stop the recruitment of our people. To this end, we're going to apply the following rule of thumb. For each person – American, European or other innocent – who is beheaded, we will behead 100 of their fighters – on camera using the same means that they use.

"This has been part of my agenda from day one. The public has apparently accepted a brief period in which Hammurabi decides the nature of a 'proportionate response.' During this period, we want to get maximum mileage out of our captives. We want to think of ourselves initially as a big cat playing with a mouse, a mouse that has entertainment value only as long as he is alive.

"To this end, we're going to get medieval – but only with techniques God's Wrath has employed. A captive in a cage would be one example. He will be approached with a flame thrower, approached until his toes begin to smoke. Then he will be taken out of the cage, put on his knees while the flames lap at his body, asked for his last testament – during which we will make sure he is in agony – and then beheaded with one of their own crescent swords.

"That's the camerawork. The audio will be more impactful. When you two return from a battle, which I don't expect to last very long, you will craft as many short YouTube videos and social media posts from raw footage as you can. Our language expert will supply the subtext, both in

English and in Arabic. The theme will be: can these guys take what they give out? Their screams will be the answer.

"Our three female soldiers, our cyber wizards positioned in different states, will find every God's Wrath recruiting video, with emphasis on the boastful ones and those couched in seemingly reasonable online magazines – and redirect them to one of our thousands of sites. The potential recruit will see only cowardice and death among those he or she had considered joining. You will, of course, do the same with all forms of social media. This is an enormous undertaking, I know. If anyone can do it, you three can.

"Allen, I'm placing you in charge of the recruitment program of all young Americans into obligatory national service. You'll of course have the help of tens of thousands of government employees from various agencies. Your duties will include the distribution of manpower needed to fully populate the Armed Forces and to modernize the nation's infrastructure.

"Finally, Jim, your job will be to ferret out anyone who violates the social compact our voters have accepted. An executive order in a time of emergency will declare breaking that contract treasonous. Any hint of culture warring, whether waged by an individual or a group, will be punishable by death. However, the justice system will not be involved. I want you to come to me each week with your report. Hollis will take a short vacation from work, when needed, to deal with high-profile individuals. These are going to be numerous in the media, in universities, in places of worship and among judges. If a group is involved, I'll take care of it from this end.

"So that, soldiers, is the tip of the iceberg, the component of the great transformation the public will see first. As for me, apart from the performance of normal executive tasks, I'll be working with committee chairmen in both Houses to write the legal underpinnings of a new America – and the laws needed to sustain it."

Shiller glanced at his watch. "We'll break now for lunch in the regular dining room. I've requested that Jesús and Manuela prepare something novel but light."

As everyone stood, Jim moved closer to Shiller. "Sir, may I speak with you alone before we eat?"

"No. We're a group. What you cannot say in the company of your colleagues should not be said."

CHAPTER TWENTY-THREE

When Nellie had calmed down enough to listen to him, Beau convinced her that it would be a mistake to run. She understood that any interruption in their normal routine would be tantamount to announcing that she knew Shiller's darkest secrets. She was still hopeful they didn't know she had heard them, still scared to death that they knew – and still without a plan. The uncertainty became unbearable. Nellie decided Monday night to seek her boss's counsel, and Beau agreed to accompany her.

H. L.'s residence wasn't exactly an elegant Victorian Mansion like the Historical Society's. It was a ramshackle cabin several miles down the Roaring Fork River. Beau tripped over the uneven threshold and nearly went down. He knew she never locked the door: Nellie had told him. Only now he knew why. A thief would think he'd been trapped in a labyrinth of junk . . . and die of a heart attack on the spot.

"H. L." Nellie cried, trying without success to fight back the hysteria that again swept over her. "H. L., wake up! Please wake up!"

"I'm always awake," sounded a voice in another room. The lights came on. Art pieces, probably worth millions, hung over the chaos. Talk about strange, Beau thought. He'd seen some weird stuff since he left home, but this was a clear winner. The paintings were in climate-controlled glass cases like you saw in museums. But they weren't in a museum. They were on the log walls of this dump where rusty picks and farm implements should have hung.

H. L. limped into the dusty light, wearing a tattered gray shawl. Outside her unwashed windows, the moon shone over the peaks, and the river danced cheerily.

"Nellie, dear, there's an unopened bottle of Johnnie Walker in the cabinet above the stove. Go get it, and wash two glasses. I've got mine in the room over there. While you're up, spare me a painful trip."

"H. L., not now. We need your advice, not your medicine. We've just learned something that will get us killed – for a start. Us and probably you."

"They'd be doing me a favor, so let's focus on you."

"I'd better get the medicine," Beau said. "Nellie, start filling her in."

* * *

Beau watched in disbelief. After hearing of evil in its raw form and all the danger it posed for her, for them, for the universe, H. L. didn't look any different than she did when she was denying a permit to a Los Angeles real-estate developer. Her voice, however, told another story.

"This is serious. Are you sure, Nellie, that these two guys know you overheard them?"

"Not totally. But I'd say it's 90 percent certain. Like I told you, I was in the cool room and – "

"Like you told me. You don't need to tell me again. You trusted a Republican and a military man – and you expected something good to come of it. When's this genocidal freak due back in Aspen?"

"He's here right now. He left Cleveland after the Convention."

"And the guys who *believe* that you know . . . if they have the slightest doubt, which they do, they aren't going to say a word to their boss. Step into their shoes. Suppose you *didn't* hear anything and they tell the General you did. In that case, they'll have dug their own graves when they didn't need to."

"This is helpful," Beau said. "I mean, I'm getting a better perspective on where we stand."

Nellie said, "You maybe. Not me."

"I want to hear her out."

H. L. refilled her glass, neat of course. "Thank you, Mr. Beauregard. If the men come to believe *with absolute certainty* that Nellie overheard them, we're dead. We're not going to waste time on a given. But let me repeat: if they're uncertain, they won't want that their boss to know they *might have* let the cat out of the bag."

"You seem to know a lot about this stuff," Beau said.

"Well, Honey Child, I wasn't born with a career in historical preservation. I had another life before either of you pushed your way into the world. Beauregard is right. I do know 'a lot about this stuff.'"

"But H. L. – "

"Not now. Let me continue. Any sign of panic on your parts – especially yours, Nellie – means disaster. You'll be confirming their suspicions. If your friend panics, it's okay. With that slow-talking drawl, no one will notice. But you, Nellie, you're going to have to get yourself under control. You're going to have to project an air of calm. So you both continue to work for the General as if nothing has happened, which it might not have. Just go about your business as usual, writing the same right-wing garbage you've been writing, delivering the same food you've been delivering. Be warm, but not too warm; friendly, but not too friendly.

"Remember: these two talkative men are in the same boat you are. They're not 100 percent certain you overheard them. They're going to do everything in their power to change that. How? Let me tell you what will happen – soon. Your offices at the Historical Society *and* your carriage house will be gone over with a fine-toothed comb. I want you to delete all the stuff on your hard drives that might make you look bad, then copy what's harmless onto new hard disks. I'll get that little tech weasel to meet you over at the Society. Wellington, you have the keys. He'll bring new disks. He can then go over to the carriage house. Put him to work on things you're not able to do, like changing drives on laptops. And for the love of God, don't forget about smartphones and typed or handwritten material. Also notes, emails, everything like that. It's possible that the redacted information on the computers could redound to your advantage."

"H. L., come on," Nellie complained. "That's a waste of time. We don't have anything that could make anyone suspicious of us. We liked Shiller, I'm ashamed to say. We both thought he was the real thing."

"You'll find incriminating material where you least expect it. If you don't, they will."

"We don't have incriminating material *anywhere*. Let's explore other possibilities."

"You don't have incriminating material? Then, Nellie, we'll find nothing if you dump your purse out on the coffee table."

"Nothing."

"Then dump. Dixie, bring a floor lamp over here. Help me move closer to the table and pour me a proper measure of medicine."

***

H. L. had sorted through less than a third of the frightful pile when she came across six business cards. They seemed to pique her interest. She took out her magnifying glass and studied them.

159

"Six business cards, five belonging to the same agent. These would get you killed."

"What are they?" Beau asked.

"You tell me." She slid them toward him with her cane.

"Oh, yeah. Those FBI guys Nellie got to know bartending. I met them too."

"Where?"

"At the cop place over breakfast. Shiller knows them. They're supporters."

"They wouldn't be if we briefed them on what Nellie heard. Let's have a look at your wallet. Men don't get special treatment here."

H. L. pulled out two business cards, one belonging to Kenneth Hatcher, the other to Randall Connor. "Bigshots," she said. "Deputy Directors of the Los Angeles Field Office. Shiller obviously knows this. You can be sure his people are monitoring your phones. If you or I call these agents on a tapped line, you will have exposed yourselves."

"Jesus," Beau said. "Nellie was right to come to you."

H. L. drained her glass, snared the bottle with the handle of her cane and slid it closer. "We need to contact these guys. I'll memorize the names and numbers on those cards. Then I'll burn them. I'll also do the calling – from a public phone. There's one at the corner store. Help me get there. Remember what you said, little lamb. You don't have that kind of stuff anywhere. You have it, you have more of it than you realize. Scott will meet you at the Historical Society in twenty minutes.

"You, Son of the South, pull your truck up as close as you can to the porch. Nellie and I will finish with her purse pile . . . then I'll make the call to your agent friends from the corner store."

"But H. L.," Nellie said, "we still don't have a plan for dealing with Shiller."

"Say you."

"Well, what is it?"

"We're going to kill him."

CHAPTER TWENTY-FOUR

"WHAT?" Conner shouted at his young Latin assistant. She looked just like the girl at The James who brought him breakfast, and the one who delivered his raw fish.

"Tell me it's not true. TELL ME!"

"Sir, perhaps I should bring you your morning coffee?"

"Casa de Maxwell stays in the pot and I stay coffee-less mad until you tell me what happened."

"Nothing happened, Sir."

"Nothing? NOTHING? You get a lead on the biggest catastrophe in American history and you blow it off?"

"Sir, I did not get a lead. I just answer phones. When I got the call, it was for you and you hadn't come in yet. So I transferred the call to Special Agent Jenner."

"Jenner? JENNER? Jesus Christ, why Jenner, of all people?"

"Special Agent Jenner stayed two hours past the end of her shift because you weren't here. She was helping out."

"Send her in here this second."

"I'm sorry, Special Agent Connor, but she has gone home."

Connor put his face in both hands, elbows on the desk. "Okay. Look. I'm sorry for being a jerk. Bring me my coffee. We'll talk behind closed doors when you come back."

She seemed uncomfortable with the 'closed doors' remark. No wonder. He watched her go out through the bars of his finger jail. Goddammit, these young Latin girls all looked the same. That wasn't a bad thing. They all had world-class derrieres.

He stopped in mid-fantasy. How in the hell could he be examining the fine points of female anatomy when his country was hurtling toward the abyss? Jesus, he needed Kristýna back.

***

"Please sit down, Ms. Velázquez. No, over here. Right here at the desk. I don't bite, even if I sound like it." He sipped his coffee, and was changed man. "You are from where? I never asked."

"Monterey, Agent Connor."

"Monterrey. A nice place. My wife and I always used to stop there when we went to Mexico."

"Monterey, California, Sir."

"I see. Now let's go over what happened. From the start, please."

"Yes, but I won't be able to tell you much."

"You might be surprised. So the first call came in around two a.m.? From Aspen, Colorado?

"Yes. That is correct. Then I put the call through to Special Agent Jenner."

"Melanie Jenner? Not the guy."

"That is correct."

"And you said the person calling asked for me and sounded old. Was it a woman?"

"I couldn't tell, Sir. I think so, but I can't say for sure."

"Then what happened?"

"She telephoned again and, like before, I put the call through to Special Agent Jenner."

"And you overheard part of the conversation?"

"Her door was open, but it wasn't really a conversation."

"You mean Agent Jenner didn't talk?"

"No, Sir. I didn't mean that. She talked. But only for a few seconds. Then she banged down the phone and mumbled something."

"Something? You must have heard what the 'something' was, no?"

"Yes, but you will be angry again if I tell you. The something wasn't really anything."

"But I will be angry? That's probably true, Ms. Velázquez. But who will I be angry at?"

"Me, Sir. You always are."

"Oh, come on. I just seem that way. If I'm angry, it'll either be at Melanie or the world."

"Special Agent Jenner said it was someone *you* had made angry when you worked in Aspen."

"Her exact words, please. Those were here EXACT words?"

"No, Sir. But that's what she meant."

"I asked you to tell me EXACTLY what she said."

162

"It's hard for me to repeat, Sir. We are a very Christian family.

"I'm waiting."

"I didn't say it, but . . . well, *she* said . . . she said it was 'probably someone that fucking son-of-a-bitch Connor had pissed off.' God forgive me."

"Okay. Thank you. Sometimes irreverent speech can be spiritually calming. I'm sure God knows this and forgives. You should keep that in mind, Ms. Velázquez. And then? What happened next?"

"She kept on calling back. Maybe twenty times. Finally Special Agent Jenner told her she'd have to speak with you if she wanted to see you, but that you were late for work."

"Because of the traffic, I hope she added."

"Maybe. I'm not sure. But the person did say he or she wanted to see you."

"And you at least have the number this person called from."

"Yes, Sir. We traced it per protocol. It was a gas station corner store, a place like that."

"All right. Thank you. You've been most helpful. Now I would like you to send Special Agent Hatcher over here. And bring me another mug of coffee. Full this time, please."

"Yes, Sir." He watched her walk out the door, though he tried not to.

***

Connor was pacing, disheveled and frustrated, when Hatch strolled in. Jesus, did he always have to look like that? Slim, hair perfect, tie perfect, suit perfect, shoes polished like a mirror and one of those shirts he must pick up at the cleaner's twice a day. This man he considered his best friend always made him feel like he hadn't showered.

"Hatch, I called Melanie at home, pissed her off, I think. But I've got a pretty good idea who that caller was."

Hatch sat in a straight-backed chair, not the leather lounger in the corner. "And who is that?"

"Remember the old gray woman at the History place, the one that sexy blonde girl worked for?"

"H. L. Gibbons? Everyone who's ever met her remembers her. What about you? Remember who the cute girl's boyfriend was?"

"Yeah, the son of a bitch who sank The Big Orange. SBW Three. Nice guy, actually. He should have gone pro and made a few hundred million."

"Yeah, well, he's probably got those millions now – without suffering

163

ten concussions to get them. Do you have any idea what his Victorian houses are worth?"

"Victorian houses. That's it! That's the connection! These kids and H. W. all have an interest in those things. Then there was the General who had them renovated and is now going to be president."

"H. L., Randall, not H. W. And 'the General' is General Schiller. The girl working nights at the Jerome bar when we first got there was your cute blonde. Her name was Nellie, wasn't it?"

"I don't know. All I know is we drank too much Scotch."

"*You* drank too much Scotch. You gave her your card. Four, maybe five times. She was polite and always thanked you. You know, sort of like you hadn't given it to her already."

"Get to the point."

"What point? You're the one who pissed off Melanie. All I know is that she got an earful of calls from a person we think was H. L. Gibbons. I suppose you know what they were about."

Connor dropped into the armchair, making it yelp like a beaten dog. "Not enough. Not yet, anyway. The number on that card – "

"Those cards."

"For Christ's sake, I only remember one. What difference does it make if there were fifty? What I was saying is that the number, the telephone number, wasn't the one for out here. It was for someone at Hooverville who always knew where we were. Aspen, Crested Butte, New York, D.C. We were all over the place. That was the one number we could be reached through."

"And this was important?"

"You better believe it. H. L. called Washington first. Some sleepy secretary gave her the number to my Los Angeles office. Hatch, she was desperate to get hold of me. We're talking about an old crippled lady in the middle of the night. Calling from a goddamn gas station. Thank you, Melanie, for blowing her off. Now I'm piecing a few things together. She wanted to talk to me but didn't want me to call her at the History Society or anywhere else she has a number. She obviously suspected bugged lines, and for once I don't believe we're the ones who bugged them. She told Melanie she'd found out what we've been up against. The whole enchilada. Not some Islamic group, either. She said she had information from a couple of kids."

"Kids?"

"I'm guessing the blonde girl and SBW Three. She said it was information we *had* to have. She wouldn't say any more. So Melanie fucks up again and decides it's a quack call. Well, I've got a pretty strong feeling it wasn't.

"I want you to go there, Hatch. To Aspen. You don't stand out in a crowd. People tell me I do. No idea why, but that's what they say. Not good if it's true, so why take a chance? We'll set you up as a real-estate person or something. You know, someone who's interested in buying up a bunch of Victorian houses. H. L. didn't strike me as the type who'd make a big deal over nothing. I want to know exactly what she knows."

"Sure, Brother. Get me the order from Forsythe."

Connor was already reaching for the phone.

***

"Well what?" Connor was grumpy, his usual state in the long hour before lunch.

"Well, have you come up with an idea for my Aspen disguise? I'm not a big fan of wigs and paste-on moustaches."

"I'm still thinking on it. You?"

"I'm drawing a blank, Randall."

"Really? You don't shoot blanks. You shouldn't draw them."

They were walking along the outdoor promenades of the enormous Westfield-Century City Mall, a short distance from the Los Angeles Field Office. Waiters were setting up outdoor tables, coffee shops on flower-rich patios overflowed with latte-drinking, smartphone-scrolling, tablet-toting Yuppies. From time to time, the silence of this lobotomized multitude was shattered by nearby sirens; or boastful claims blared into Bluetooth headsets.

This, thought Connor, was like crossing the desert. You couldn't get a decent cup of coffee in one of these trendy places, and couldn't salvage a moment to think if you smuggled in your own thermos. You were trapped between God and the Devil, between the eerie silence of zombies and involuntary participation in one-way conversations of loud mouths. To add insult to deprivation, you couldn't eat lunch because it wasn't 11:00 yet. He thought of Duff at the cop place in Aspen. None of this bullshit, even though the same didn't apply to the rest of the town. At Duff's, he could get whatever he wanted whenever he wanted it, and find silence if he needed to think by sitting next to one of the bacon-starved vegans in the corner.

No, he thought, Hatch wouldn't be able to play the zombie any better

165

than the blaring business jerk on his Bluetooth. This was important: what Hatch could and could not do would narrow their decision on how his partner should disguise himself. Connor was just as concerned about Hatch's safety as he was about Hatch's success, though he wouldn't have told anyone.

A winning idea came to him just as they took their seats at B. J.'s Brew House. Because of the healthy ambience, no doubt. It was 11:01 and the place looked deserted. Connor asked for a table where it wouldn't get too noisy. The waiter couldn't guarantee silence: at noon, when most people ate, the place got a little rowdy.

No problem, Connor assured him. They'd be out of here by noon. He sat, reaching for the menu on the way down. "Have some fish, Hatch. It may not be from the health food store, but it's healthy. Also expensive. That's how you're gonna have to order in Aspen. Bran muffins and tofu won't fit with your disguise."

"My disguise? You said you didn't have any ideas."

"I had an epiphany when we landed in here. Hatch, don't be offended by this. The fact is, people who have seen you and see you again aren't sure it's you. You're everyman to everyman, which if you follow me is the same as being invisible. *You're going to go as Hatch.* We'll arm you with another name and a wardrobe of informal California clothes. I promise, you'll be a complete stranger in town."

"I don't like it," Hatch said, scraping the sauce off his fish. "Some people are bound to recognize me."

Connor washed down a big bite of his burger with a swallow of the house ale. "Some people. Could be. What we'll do is think hard and fast on this one. Like, where have you been and who have you seen repeatedly? You just avoid those places and people. Give me a list and I'll add anything I think's missing."

Connor hoped Hatch would think long enough for him to take a major dive into his fries. They were the fat kind, done just right so they weren't soggy. And the burger! If an image of Betty hadn't come into his field of vision every time he picked it up, he'd have to rank it in the top ten of all burgers he had eaten in a lifetime. For Special Agent Connor, that was no small thing.

"Still thinking?" he mumbled, shoving in another mouthful of fries. Betty hovered all over the place to harass him. She pointed at the salad he had shoved to the edge of the table. Fuck this, he thought in a sudden burst of fury. His life had been miserable enough lately. Those moments of pleasure were sacred. The bitch could do what she wanted. She was an image. She no longer controlled him. For the first time, he thought he might be able to banish her irritating ghost once and for all.

"Still thinking," Hatch said. "Could be our boys who specialize in this can come up with something better."

"Listen, partner, you're not going to top my idea. But you have to sign off on it. So here's the deal I'm proposing. We'll stop at that place we passed on the way over here. Josh Something – "

"JoS A. Banks. Not on your life."

"Goddammit, Hatch. Not on whose life? It's *your* life we're talking about and I have a way to make you invisible. You know, someone who can't get hurt because he can't be seen. Will you at least hear me out?"

"Lousy salad forks in this place," Hatch said. "Lousy salads for that matter. You can tell the greens aren't organic. Okay, I'm listening."

"We go into Josh's, buy you a complete wardrobe of stuff you've never had on."

"Randall, I only shop at Brooks Brothers. I may be cheap but I make an annual pilgrimage to their shop on Rodeo Drive. I made a vow as a poor college kid that if I could ever afford . . . "

"Come on Hatch. You came down the birth canal wearing Brooks Brothers. You couldn't afford the stuff then and it didn't stop you. I just want you to give it a try. One wardrobe on the Bureau card. One trip to the Field Office cafeteria. You know you're known in there. If we dress you up in the disguise I'm picturing you in, I'm putting my money on no one recognizing you."

"You're talking nonsense again."

"Wrong, Hatch. When I get a certain kind of vision, I'm always right. Just give it a try. How about tomorrow noon?"

"You want me to wear some Halloween costume to work?"

"Not to work. I'll have a change of clothes waiting for you in the locked bathroom. You slip in and change at 11:00 – "

"I eat at 12:30."

"Whatever," said Connor, trying not to show his aggravation. "You go in there just before lunch and change. I'll have shiny wooden hangers waiting for your Brooks Brothers stuff. No one's in our part of the office at 12:30, so that actually makes your habit a good one. You go down to the cafeteria and eat. If you end up eating alone, you'll wear my disguise to Aspen. If you have unsolicited company, we'll let our people dress you up. Sound reasonable?"

167

"Depends. What do you want me to wear?"

"Think California, man. Think of a dude who buys and sells stuff like currency. Or real estate. Get the picture? Nice knit shirt, creased trousers like the kind you'd see on a country club golf course – or in the board room of a start-up. Expensive sunglasses that never come off. Socks that don't look like industrial tubing. Casual shoes. Wear your Brooks Brothers drawers if you want, but the wife beater has to go. It'll look like an empty bra under your knit shirt. So, do we have a deal?"

"We've got a deal, Randall. But you should know one thing. I'm only doing this to please you."

"I can't think of a better reason. Thank you, partner."

CHAPTER TWENTY-FIVE

Mexicans, thought Hollis, paid closer attention than he realized to what politicians in the States said about them. From his perch atop the Hospital Star Médica he watched in the gathering dusk as protesters blocked the main routes leading to the Hotel Casino Morelia. Through his scope he focused in on the ugly cartoon-like heads of Vice Presidential Nominee Caskey, held on sticks above the crowds. They reminded him of the real thing, of real heads on spikes being paraded through a medieval town.

Well, he'd make them happy if his aim was good. And he'd have no one to blame but himself if it wasn't. A stillness hung over the town that conjured God above holding His breath. He loved an evening breeze in summer – most of the time. But he would gladly go with God this evening. Wind, even the tiniest breath of wind, could warp the trajectory of a bullet that had to travel over a mile to reach its target. Not by much, just enough to cause an otherwise perfect shot to miss. Sure, you could guess and measure all you wanted. You could get a reading on wind speed and direction to the fifth decimal point where you lay in wait with your rifle. But in an urban environment, with its tall buildings and narrow streets, that reading wasn't worth shit. The movement of air along the bullet's trajectory, blocked by all sorts of edifices and squeezed down narrow alleys like a stream in a gorge, was not a variable you could reduce to a constant.

So far so good. Caskey, unlike Shiller, had opted for government protection. Hollis, dressed in an authentic US Secret Service uniform worn by the CAT division of super-snipers, had attracted hisses and catcalls as he walked right through the center of town with his gun tote. They took him for what he appeared to be, these Caskey-haters, rather than for what he was. His entry into the hospital had raised eyebrows, sure. But the eyes behind those raised lids telegraphed anger at the inevitable: the bully nation sending security into *their* country to protect *its* man. And there wasn't a damn thing they could do about it. A deal would have been worked out with local and national authorities to permit their cooperative presence in Morelia. If they refused . . . well he didn't know exactly what would happen but it wouldn't be good for Mexico. So, when even the government couldn't say no to this intrusion, about all that was left was protest. To be honest, he couldn't blame them.

Up he had gone, up the service elevator to the roof, disguised perfectly by what looked like a lack of disguise. His only precaution was a little of the black stuff NFL players smear under their eyes, just in case one of these protesters had seen him on American TV.

His thoughts wandered back to his rifle. In the old days, you travelled in pairs; the sniper always had a spotter with him. That might still be the case in the military, but his new prototype scope had made the spotter a piece of unneeded baggage. Apart from wind speed and direction, which you still had to input manually, the scope did the rest. It measured range with laser technology, the bullet's drop, which would be over 100 feet from the distance he would fire, the Magnus effect, spindrift, the Coriolis effect which took into account the rotation of the earth, direction, cant, inclination, pressure, temperature, humidity, muzzle velocity, barrel length and twist, lock time, drag coefficient and other stuff he used to know but couldn't remember. That was the spotter's job, and the world's best spotter couldn't compete with the Linux computer system of this amazing device. Besides, the scope had fifth generation infrared, making long night shots a real possibility. It wasn't as satisfying to chalk up a kill with all this new-fangled stuff, but he had a hard time arguing with the results.

Morelia happened to be a favorite vacation spot of the Mexican President. Not touristy, magnificent in its historical aspect, elegant yet old, modern without looking it. Shiller, smart as usual, had been able to set the meeting in one of the President's preferred hotel restaurants, a magnificent building near the historic Morelia Cathedral. The town was 6,000 feet above sea level, the climate was perfect; low eighties on a normal July day, dropping to a nice temperature for late *al fresco* dining.

He liked the outdoor restaurant the dignitaries had chosen. There were cozy linen-bedecked tables under giant porticos that ran the length of the hotel-casino. And the hotel itself! Each suite had a balcony that gave onto the old town center. If Caskey didn't present himself for a clear shot at dinner, he would almost certainly step out on to his balcony before turning in. Or before breakfast. The mission was important to Shiller for reasons he didn't entirely understand, so Hollis would wait until morning if need be.

Presently, Mexican security forces were creating a large semi-circular zone around the hotel and its restaurant, driving the most determined protesters back with shields, cudgels and rubber bullets. The police, often thought to be corrupt, didn't seem that way. They checked every protester who remained in the streets, patting them down for weapons. Most protesters, however, went home: a 200 yard perimeter in the town center denied them the chance of having their antics seen by anyone but themselves.

The President and his entourage arrived from the local airport in a convoy of bullet-proof limos and quickly ducked into the hotel. Caskey showed up a few minutes later, surrounded by somber men in dark suits and a few snipers clad in Hollis's uniform. "Police" in stark letters adorned the backs of the CAT men, the hotshots of the Counter Assault Team.

Waiters had already set long tables that spanned three porticos. Caskey was going to have plenty of apologizing to do to ministers, police capos and newspaper editors. As for the regular press, they were treated like the protesters. Cameras and other media paraphernalia were great places to hide weapons. The recent death of El Lobo had led to several assassination attempts on the President by the dead boss's supporters, so the government wasn't taking chances. Hollis laughed to himself. Little did they know . . .

God was still holding His breath. The night was eerily calm as darkness fell. Around ten o'clock, the tables for the dignitaries began to fill up. Hors d'oeuvres and drinks were delivered on large silver trays. A microphone was placed down the table from Caskey's empty seat, examined by a technician and given a nod of approval. The few editors present would want a record of the night's talks. Hollis imagined they hoped for groveling apologies from the American. With resentment of the Big Boy up north running high, it would be a good story to pitch to the public, a small victory for a land that felt chronically abused. Hollis could understand. He liked these people. And not just because he'd had a hot Mexican girlfriend at Harvard.

Where the hell was Caskey? The government people had given up holding off on dinner and begun to sample wines and whatever those silver trays ferried from the kitchen. He was training his scope on an appetizer that always made him hungry – ceviche – when two Secret Service

171

agents in dark suits came to the table. They walked over to a man Hollis took to be head of the National Police and asked him something that caused him to swallow hard. They examined the microphone, carefully surveyed the table, checked the cordon of police officers on the street out front and went back inside.

Caskey finally emerged. All of the Mexicans stood to shake his hand, though Hollis didn't have a clue why they would bother. "No ceviche," thought the sniper, "you don't deserve it." Still calm, still no wind. The crosshairs were aligned by computer, nothing to dial in. This was the point at which most snipers paused, froze up, became uncertain, went over everything again. Not Hollis.

He increased the magnification of his scope to the max and gently pulled the trigger. He then waited four seconds for the bullet to pierce Caskey's forehead – four seconds that seemed like four minutes while the bullet hurtled above 2,100 yards of cityscape – and watched with a smile as Caskey's first taste of ceviche splatted uneaten to the table. Time to go. He ran down the hospital stairs. When a janitor tried to detain him, he pulled out his I.D., waved it under the man's fat moustache and shoved him out of the way. "The American Vice President's been shot," he shouted in good Spanish as he burst out the hospital's great glass doors and vanished into the night.

***

"You look familiar," the Hertz agent at Denver International Airport said to Hatch.

"Where do you know me from?"

"I'm wracking my brain, Mr. Wilson. The rental was prepaid by Edward James Investments out in L. A. It couldn't be there because I've never been to L. A. Hang on . . . hang on. Got it! Wells Fargo in Topeka, the branch in the West Ridge Mall."

"Nope," said Hatch, who was traveling under the name of Charles Wilson. "Couldn't be there. I've never been to Kansas."

"But I could have sworn – "

"You think about it. We'll talk some more when I bring back the car."

"But I could have sworn – "

"Sorry, gotta hurry."

"Your voice is even familiar. This is driving me crazy." The agent looked at Hatch's rental papers again. "Charles Wilson, Wealth Management Division, Edward Jones. So where did you work before that? Maybe it'll give me a clue."

"Listen, I really have to get on the road. Did my company specify the type of car?"

"Oh, yes. Lucky man. One of our dream machines. A Mercedes S550, darkened windows because so many movie stars want them. There it is, being brought around now. See it? The black shiny one. A real beaut, don't you think?"

"I do. Keep wracking your brain. Something's bound to occur to you."

Hatch put on his sunglasses, tucked the back of his knit shirt into his trousers and walked in "casual" shoes to the Mercedes. Now he knew exactly what Connor had been talking about: the poor rental guy was the face of acute anonymity.

In the dining room of the Field Office, just as bastard and best friend Randall Connor had predicted, Hatch had ended up eating lunch alone. However, he refused to believe it was anything but coincidence. Believe what he might, though, he couldn't escape the thought that Connor could have been right; maybe he was as unidentifiable as the man at the counter. Maybe, just maybe, others saw him as a Brooks Brothers suit stuffed with a featureless human form.

Enough, goddammit. He had serious work to do, and he'd have to do it in this plebian outfit because he'd lost a bet. But that was the whole of it. He, Hatch, had spent a long time in Aspen. He *would* be recognized, regardless of this voodoo scenario Connor had foisted upon him.

He stopped at a service station between Denver and the mountains, angry that he had let his keen rational mind sink into the gutter of superstition, and dialed up the Aspen Historical Society from a land line. Someone who would never have to worry about anonymity answered.

"Yes."

"Good day. With whom am I speaking."

"H. L. Gibbons. What can I avoid doing for you?"

"Avoid? Listen, I'm with – "

"A commercial real-estate company."

"Not exactly. I'm with Edward Jones Investments in Los Angeles, Wealth Management Division. We've been bringing our best . . . you know, our wealthiest . . . clients to Aspen for years. More and more now, these people are asking to stay in a real Victorian home – with all the modern amenities, of course. My company wants to be in a position to meet these requests, so we're in the market for such a place. If it's run down, we'll have it remodeled. We did our homework. We know about

173

the strict renovation codes. I was told to get in touch with the Historical Society first because . . . and I'm quoting our research department . . . 'Ms. H. L. Gibbons will steer you in the right direction.' I think I'm about four hours from Aspen, just the other side of Denver from the airport. That would give me an ETA of around one o'clock. Any chance we could meet and look at some properties?"

"I suppose so, Mr. –"

"Williams, Charles Williams. Wealth Management, Edward Jones Investments."

"Yes, Mr. Wilson, you've made your position clear. Are you driving over Independence Pass?"

"Independence Pass? No, not if I can help it. My GPS says to keep on the Interstate until I come to Highway 82."

"If you're not accustomed to mountain driving, that will be best. Stop at the Tourist Center on the outskirts of town and get a map. I'll be waiting for you at the Historical Society. We'll take your car if you don't mind. I'm not able to drive."

"Sure, no problem. I'm looking forward to meeting you."

H. L. cleared her throat and hung up.

***

Hatch breathed a sigh of relief. He was certain from their facial expressions that H. L. Gibbons and the cute blonde girl named Nellie recognized him. That meant they also knew why he was here, so he didn't have to write a long explanatory note on his tablet. Just a quick "SAY NOTHING – WE DON'T KNOW WHAT'S BUGGED" in 24 point bold. He placed the tablet on the center console, deleting the text when he was sure both passengers had read it. It was just a blurb, but deletion on an FBI device would scrub that blurb from all layers of the hard drive. In every other respect, it was a normal iPad. The tablet would henceforth be used for Hatch's notes and photos.

"Did you have a good flight, Mr. Williams?" Nellie asked.

"As flights go. I don't know if I could say the same if the company didn't send me first class."

"Take a right here," H. L. ordered. "The fourth house on the left is for sale."

"There's no sign up," Hatch said. "Are you sure?"

H. L. seemed irritated. "Look, Mr. Williams, I know this town. I know every home that's for sale, its condition and what will be required to restore it. Stop here and we'll have a look inside."

174

Hatch stood for a while at curbside, using the tablet as his note pad and camera. He captured the address, the number of trees out front and the peeling paint on the window frames. Then he strolled to both ends of the block to write down the cross streets.

"For Christ's sake," H. L. said as they prepared to examine the interior. "I'll give you a map with all of that information when we're finished. You can put your thing away."

"I'd just as soon keep a record of my own," Hatch said, snapping a few more pictures. "Nothing against your material. But I have bosses in L. A. who want a company profile of each home. The Edward Jones board is prepared to spend well over seven figures on its purchase and restoration, so I'm not going to argue."

"Very well. Here, give me a hand. I can't get around like I used to."

Nellie, who usually led the way, seemed glued to the sidewalk. The gray crew cab truck that had slowed out front drove around the block, returned and stopped. She hadn't been certain before, but this time she recognized both the truck and the man leaning toward the passenger window: one of Shiller's three beefy gatekeepers. She walked to the door, waited for the window to come down and smiled.

"How's it going at the ranch?" she asked.

He had something to say to her, nice words for a change, not the type of icy semi-silence that might have explained her pounding heart. He asked that ingredients for supper be brought to the outer perimeter of the Shiller's place and handed her a list. She smiled again when she saw what they wanted. No health foods. No weird energy concoctions. Just some steaks and a few bottles of red wine . . . and, he said, the trimmings Nellie could decide.

"Glad to. I have some ideas I think you'll like."

"Good. Around seven, please. Hey, whose car is that?"

"Which one?"

The man climbed out of his truck. "Which one? Jesus Christ, look at that thing. It must have cost a couple hundred grand." He walked over to it and, holding a hand against the sun, tried to peer though the darkened windows.

"I don't know what it cost," Nellie said. "It's a rental. That guy H. L. just went into the house with is from L. A. He flew in this morning. I guess he's got the bucks."

"Still, who rents out a car like this? I wouldn't."

"Me neither," Nellie said. "Not if it was mine."

The man dropped his keys. "Shit," he said, kneeling down to pick them up. He slipped on a patch of gravel. Fighting to keep his balance, he skidded again and kicked the keys under the car. It all looked real, but Nellie knew what was going on.

"Goddammit. I didn't use to be a klutz."

"You need steak, that's all," Nellie said good-naturedly.

"No doubt."

"You'd better do some stretches, old man."

He laughed, something new. She walked casually around the Mercedes as if she was worried he might ask her to crawl under the car, stopped on the grass strip between the street and sidewalk and examined the bark of an old Cottonwood tree. "No aphids," she announced to no one in particular. "At least not yet."

"There's a way of making sure you don't get them. I'll tell you about it when you bring the steaks." His voice sounded strained. She couldn't see him but knew he was prone, sliding close enough to the low car to fish for his keys – and place some kind of spy device on the frame, probably something for tracking where they went and maybe even listening to what they said.

"Got 'em," the man said, brushing off his clothes. "See you at seven."

"Hey, wait a second," she called over the hood. "Are you going to grill the meat, or should I have it done at the Jerome?"

"We'll take care of the cooking. You take care of finding us some good cuts."

"Will do."

As he closed the passenger window and sped away, she thought she glimpsed the end of a long-focus camera lens in the back seat poking out from under a work shirt. If that's what it was, he was still casing the Historical Society, carriage house and ranch for reporters. If Beau had insisted on going in there to beat up the chefs, Shiller would have found out.

Anyway they wouldn't only be listened to and followed all day; they would also be photographed. She couldn't say a word to H. L. or Hatch, and didn't know what she would have said if she had been able to talk. They were going to behave the same way regardless. She hoped they had both anticipated worst case scenarios; she sure as hell hadn't.

But she *did* know one thing: she had better look unperturbed, even cheerful, for the entire day. Someone might be spying on her from distant rooftops, from trees and bushes, from drones invisible at 80,000 feet.

These people were professionals, which translated for Nellie Vaughn into a very unpleasant afternoon.

***

Hatch's flight was scheduled to leave for LAX at 10:02 p.m. He was already on board, wondering what if anything his visit had accomplished, when his cell phone rang. It was the rental car agency letting him know that he had left his iPad in the Mercedes. It had, the agent said, apparently slid under the passenger seat.

"Dammit," Hatch replied. "I can't get off the plane. They've already shut the doors."

"Would you like us to overnight it to you? FedEx comes at nine o'clock tomorrow morning."

"That would be most appreciated."

"Very well, Sir. We have your firm's address on your rental papers."

Now, at last, he understood. When he put his carry-on bag and attaché case through airport security, Hatch was asked to take out his tablet. He had watched it disappear into the scanner and had picked it up on the other side. The tablet he now carried wasn't the same tablet he had brought with him!

Minutes later, he made yet another startling discovery. When he dug through his carry-on bag for his sweater, he found a light jacket he'd never seen before. Incredible, really. His hosts had prepared for his visit in a way he doubted the Bureau's best could have topped. Seconds ago, he had doubted the merits of his trip; now he felt it might reveal the secrets that had eluded America's intelligence services for months.

CHAPTER TWENTY-SIX

Connor said, "I've come to the conclusion that the Caskey murder is part of the larger assault on the U. S. I want to go over a few things with you before we look into the tablet."

"Shoot."

They were on the 17th floor of the Los Angeles Field Office, Connor's most hated work space. You couldn't escape the goddamn Southern California glare, not even with the blinds closed. To make matters worse, someone in Maintenance had put plants in the corners and cheerful pictures on the walls. This was supposed to be a "growlery," a sacred place where serious men cracked serious crimes. Plants, pictures and sunshine were an insult to the purpose of the room.

A knock at the door. It was Connor's Latin assistant, asking to water the plants. Connor didn't pay her any mind until she was on her way out.

"Maybe she can help us," Hatch said. "I mean with translations, stuff like that."

"Who?"

"Who? The girl whose behind seems to be your top priority."

"That's a broad field, partner."

"Your Mexican assistant. You know damn well I was referring to her."

"She's not Mexican. She's from Monterey, *California*."

"Randall, you know Forsythe wants us in Mexico heading up one of the investigation teams. Your Spanish sucks, and mine isn't much better. I'm sure she speaks the language. We could take her along so you'd have something to stare at every time you send her out a door."

"Yes, we could – if we were going. But we're not. They've got enough people on Caskey and no one but us on whatever's in your Aspen iPad."

"You were going to fill me in on Caskey's murder."

"Until you sidetracked me. I take it you've at least read the preliminary reports."

"Sorry. I came directly to your office."

"The man was dropped from a distance of 2,000 yards by a single shot. Ring a bell? Our people found the bullet lodged in a table leg. Its depth of penetration into the oak is what we'd expect of a .338 Lapua Magnum military issue that's travelled over a mile – "

"What kind of table was it?"

"An old one with stubby legs."

"I hope we're not letting the cops down there dig out the slug. If they do, it's gonna look like a bald monk. I still think we should be on site."

"We'll let Forsythe make that decision after I've presented my case for staying put. As for careless extraction, there won't be any. I've ordered the entire leg with the bullet still in it sent to Washington. Feel better?"

"Much"

"You will recall, Hatch, that the longest confirmed sniper kill – two of them, to be exact – used the bullet we think is in that table leg. I've talked to the Brit who took those record distance shots. He's retired, home in the U. K. – all verified by our people over there. He isn't our man, but if the bullet shows the same rifling as the one that felled El Lo Bo, we know it came from one of the British rifles used by an elite sniper squad in Afghanistan. I'm going to call Forsythe and get permission to work on the Aspen material. Then we'll discuss how you got a tablet that wasn't yours, and what's in it. Let's reconvene in the SAC's office in twenty minutes. I like those big leather chairs, thick curtains, blank walls, plantless expanses – and the proximity of a coffee maker. That's how an FBI office should be. A shame Richards is too dense to make use of it."

"Dense or not, you can't just walk into the SAC's office. Not even if you're the notorious Randall."

"Look, the dumb ass took off for Mexico with a Mariachi band playing in his head as soon as the shooting became known. The office is vacant."

"I'm sure you've got all the stuff you need to get in."

"No comment." Connor glanced at his watch. "See you there in twenty."

***

"We've got a problem," Hatch said. He waited for Connor's wrecking ball of an ass to slap the leather seat of Richards' armchair. "I can tell you exactly where the second tablet came from, but I can't tell you its contents."

179

"What?"

"Let me explain, Randall."

"Please do."

"There's some kind of crazy app that erases the whole damn tablet, everything on it, if you enter the wrong code more than three times."

"That shouldn't be a problem for our people in Cyber."

"Shouldn't be? Wait till you hear this. It's an alpha numeric code sixty-four digits long."

"And you consider that an impediment?"

"You don't?"

"No, I don't. You have the code with you or you wouldn't have been given the tablet. Think where it might be."

"Well . . . here's about all I can come up with. When I left Hertz, this tablet was in my attaché case; the one I took with me was hidden under the seat of the car I'd just returned."

"Think hard. Where else could the code be?"

"There was a jacket under my briefcase I'd never seen before. My first thought was obviously that it was in there. But I turned the thing inside out, looked everywhere, added up any letters and numbers I found. Nothing even came close. Anyway, I dropped it off at Forensics."

"If it's there, Hatch, they'll find it. If they don't . . . we aren't finished brainstorming. You have the code somewhere in the stuff you brought home. I know you do even if you don't. While the jacket's down in Forensics, we'll have a look at the other stuff you were wearing and took off."

"Like what? My drawers?"

"How about your sunglasses? There's all that tiny writing on the inside of one of the arms. We'll put that together with what's written on anything else we can find. Your e-ticket, for example. Where did you carry it?"

"In my attaché case."

"You know someone was in that case because tablet number two got in there. You know how tickets are. All sorts of crap on them. Letter codes, ticket numbers, frequent flyer numbers, flight numbers. We're not done yet, buddy. Assemble your stuff right here on the big kahuna's desk. While Forensics chops up the jacket, I want to make sure we're not sitting on top of the thing we're looking for."

* * *

Hours passed. Connor felt sick as he looked at the list of 64 alpha

180

numeric combinations they'd put together, a list with twelve entries that could, simply by switching digits, grow to a million. Three chances in a million, worse odds than a rigged lottery. And if you didn't come up with the winning number, you lost more than a couple bucks. You lost the contents of the tablet because the thing would erase itself. He had taken a wrong turn, which Hatch had been telling him from the start.

"Well, partner, another dead end. Let's call it a day."

"No," Hatch said. "You were right before. The code is somewhere or they wouldn't have risked everything to give me the tablet. We've just gotta find it."

Connor pointed at the list. "In that jungle?"

"No, Randall. It has to be in the jacket. I'm calling Forensics. Let's see how they're doing."

No answer, just the machine.

"Dammit, they've gone home."

"They're on break. No one is taking off early these days."

At that moment, a crisp knock sounded at the door. Hatch stood and opened. The two forensics people he liked best stood there smiling. "May we come in? I think you'll like our findings."

"You're goddamn right you can come in," Connor said, hoisting himself to his feet. "You've found it? Please tell me you've found those diabolical 64 characters."

"I guess we won't know till we try them," the female half of the team said, smiling wryly.

"Lucky for us," the man added, "that Celia's mom made her take seamstress lessons when she was a teenage brat."

"Nothing I hated more. Nothing that's been more useful. Moms know best."

"Come in, please," Hatch said. "Show us the golden key."

Celia, gray-haired and getting on in years, carried the jacket on a wooden hanger. Connor helped her hang it on Richards' fancy coatrack. "So tell us."

"I'd rather show you. Come close." She passed Connor and Hatch two of the magnifying glasses she'd brought up from the lab, kept one for herself. "I want you both to closely examine every seam in the jacket. Tell me if you find irregularities."

"Oh, come on," Connor grumbled. "We can play games later. Just give us the code."

"I'm sorry, Special Agent. It's in the jacket."

181

"You mean, after all of that, you didn't find it?"

"We found it. Now it's your turn. You need to know the skills of your unnamed allies. They could come in handy later. In fact, they could be essential."

"Okay, okay. Hatch, get some better light over here, and not by opening the curtains.

"Use your pen light. You're looking at seams. Isn't that so, Celia?"

"It is."

Connor and Hatch surrendered in less than ten minutes. "Sorry," Hatch apologized. "From what I see, it's a normal jacket in every respect. Completely untampered with."

"Give me your light," Celia said. She pulled out a side pocket of the jacket and stretched the fabric to illuminate the stitches joining the wool body of the coat to its silk lining. "Agent Connor, care to have a look?"

"I'd rather have a drink." He moved the magnifying glass in and out to get the clearest view. "Nope, nothing."

"Stay there. When I pull a little harder, are you able to see a line of misshapen thread holes."

"Yeah, barely. That could easily be a result of keys or coins being carried in there."

"Which is precisely why this spot was used." Celia took out something that looked like a miniature scalpel and cut a row of threads with surgical care. She shook the two layers of material above her incision, first gently, then roughly. Out floated a scrap of feather-light cloth. It swirled about on tiny currents of air as it made a slow journey to the floor.

"Your code," she said.

CHAPTER TWENTY-SEVEN

When Shiller learned of the assassination of his running mate, he arranged for an early evening speech to the nation. After the television crews left, a courier passed through security to give him a piece of mail that looked like the envelope of a thank you note. Shiller retired to his office to read the encrypted message. It was from Jim, and it described what had happened in the kitchen Thursday night. Whether he and Allen had been overheard by Nellie Vaughn they didn't know. However, it was a possibility.

Shiller felt his blood turn to ice water. Words, no one's words, could describe what he felt. But he had been in crisis situations many times on the battlefield. He knew how to keep his cool, even in the face of death. This knowledge, this rare ability, had allowed him to survive where others would have perished. The crisis visited on him minutes ago was no different. He would make rational decisions at every juncture, and he would have both the courage and the ability to see them through. First, however, he must determine whether the crisis really was a crisis – or a false alarm.

Shiller called Kent, Kyle and Doug – his three gatekeepers – to the ranch, invited them to have a seat at a small kitchen table and assured them they were not in trouble. Here, he would reenact the scenario Jim described in his note.

If Nellie had overheard, it was possible that his men's stupidity could prevent the salvation of America. It might also transform *him* from a national hero into an American Hitler. Might, if his inaction allowed things to spin out of control.

Schiller said, "Doug, come with me into the cool room. We're going to leave the door open a crack while Kyle and Kent stroll casually around the kitchen, discussing what they found out photographing journalists.

"I want you to speak in voices that are sometimes soft but never loud. Doug and I will listen. If we can hear you, we'll come out and give you

183

a summary of what you said. You will be the jury. Did we get it right or were your words too muffled for us to understand? Let's move."

Ten minutes later, the verdict was in. Every word that Kyle and Kent exchanged had been audible, muffled but audible. Nellie knew, which meant that meant others knew. "You had some items you considered important. Now would be the time to present them."

"Yes, Sir," Kent said, laying out the photos he had taken the previous day.

"Well," Kyle asked, "do you know him?"

The General went through the photos again. "Yes."

Not good. The circle already encompassed Nellie, Wellington, H. L. and at least two FBI agents. All five of these people had been Shiller supporters. Now they would be conniving on how to block his road to the White House. And the circle of five might be significantly larger than five by now. It was possible that the entire Bureau, the CIA and other agencies had been informed.

Shiller held up a hand to silence the men, who were back at the table. He could not countenance the slightest distraction when his mind was working at peak capacity, sorting through all possible courses of action still open to him.

Not knowing exactly how large the circle of those who had been told was, it seemed evident that he would need to cut a link in the chain which had allowed the transmission of his deepest secrets. Cut a link so that hearsay would have passed through so many channels that its credibility would be in doubt. Then he would need to identify those who stood to profit from such hearsay. It would be a big job, deciding the optimum place in the chain to cut the link, doing it in a manner that would not arouse suspicion and making a solid case before the press and public on why and how the "rumor" and been spread.

A big job, the grisly part of which he would give the disciples who had caused the current disaster. His mind was made up: the apostates would be forgiven rather than punished, at least initially. They were good men who had gotten drunk and divulged the unthinkable – a potentially fatal mistake. In addition to sinking the entire mission, their blunder could deprive them of their own dreams and land them on death row. He would allow them a chance to redeem themselves. Given the alternative, their will to succeed would be fierce.

"My spokesman and two of my elite bodyguards will return shortly," he told the three men at the table. "You will not speculate on the reason.

Rather, you will put your own operation on the highest state of alert."

***

H. L. called it preparation; Beau called it a dress rehearsal for their next move. "I'm scared," Nellie began. "He might want to kill me."

H. L. looked at her incredulously in the pale light. "Might? He *does* want to kill you and he's going to try. Your foreign friend and I are in the same situation, as are Agent Hatcher and the big man who was with him earlier in Aspen."

"Jesus," Beau said. "We'd better get out of here tonight. All of us. We'll take my truck and head South. My aunt might be gone, but I'm sure her closet's still full of guns."

They were in a utility room of the Historical Society's basement, hidden by a rotten entry door and surrounded by sledge hammers, pick axes and shovels. The time, Beau guessed, was about noon, though in the bowels of this old Victorian mansion the hour was always midnight.

Beau had brought one of H. L.'s old wheel chairs down the long dark concrete staircase for the drill. He and Nellie made do with random stones and rotting pieces of wood. There was no electricity. They had flashlights and a camping lantern.

Cobwebs hung everywhere. The unsteady light from the lantern cast their trembling shadows onto ancient foundation walls. In normal circumstances, this would have been a place of nightmares; on this day, however, it was a refuge from surveillance.

Nellie began to sob, carrying the theater – if it was in fact theater – a bit too far. Beau, trying to act as he would next time they entered the basement, put his arm around her but resisted the very real urge to tell her everything would be fine. This was going to be the launching point for an action H. L. had not yet disclosed. Platitudes, he knew, would lead to his verbal beheading.

Beau said, "So, H. L., we can't sit here forever. I was serious before. I think we should take off for Lake Providence."

"Mr. Wellington, consider your words. These are people capable of shutting down the United States. Do you really believe there is anywhere on earth to hide from them? They will track you down and dispose of you *wherever* you go."

"Great, H. L. If we're going to die anyway, why don't we go over to the Jerome and have a drink?"

"I didn't say we were going to die. I said your idea of escape would not achieve the outcome you want. The simple truth is this: we are

185

doomed unless we kill Shiller. So let's kill him."

"Yeah, right. I'm going to use *your* logic. Can we really get to someone who can shut down the entire country? I'd rather take my chances in Lake Providence."

H. L. ignored him. "Rehearsal over," she said in a voice she used when she didn't want to be messed with. "It yielded nothing other than familiarizing you with this enclave. I'll take it from here." She glanced at her old-fashioned watch with the phosphorescent hands. "We have an hour, and I have a lot to say. When I finish, Mr. Beauregard, you will drive me to the airport."

But they'll be watching us leave," Nellie said.

"They will not. He, too, must plan his next move – and it won't be something he can implement without time and serious thought.

"Going forward, we will assume that the phone lines of the Historical Society are tapped. In one respect, this is advantageous. We will use those phones for normal business, giving the impression that we don't know anything about their plans"

"What plans?" Nellie asked.

"Those that involve our elimination."

"My God. How do you know such plans exist?"

"I know, even if their formulation is still in progress. No more questions on the subject."

"Okay," Nellie said meekly.

"The downside of tapped phone lines is that we can't use them for necessary communication. I had Scott bring me six prepaid cell phones, cheap ones. Certain texting apps, he tells me, are encrypted. That won't stop these people, but it will slow them down.

"Now my plan. I leave Aspen at 3:43 on a two-stop fight to the Mayo Clinic in Rochester, Minnesota. The second brief layover is important, but I don't have time to explain why. Fortunately I scheduled my appointment two months ago, meaning that it won't be suspect. I will arrive at the Kahler hotel around 8:40 p.m. The hotel is connected to the clinic by a heated passage. It's customary for patients to spend the night there if they have a morning appointment the next day, which I do. After checking in, I will retire to the hotel bar, appropriately named Martini's.

"Assuming my tablet is successfully opened and read by Agent Hatcher, he and his partner will be in Rochester before I am. I've directed them to wait for me at Martini's. This is a critical meeting; this is when we take decisions that determine who lives and who dies. Put your faith in my ability to convince a couple of prominent FBI agents to become criminals for a night.

"I think you'll agree we can't confront these Shiller people on their home turf. No explosives, no guns, no IEDs or ambushes. Any questions?"

"Just one," Beau interjected. "They're going to try to kill us, but they're going to need all three of us together to stage an accident that won't create suspicion. The Historical Society is the only place where we're all together on a regular basis. Once they have their plan, we've got to assume they will strike here, correct?

"Correct."

"So how in the hell are we going to get out of the Historical Society once they know we're all here? This cellar enclave, as I see it, doesn't have any advantages. They'll find us in a few minutes. If we leave, they'll see us. I'm sure they'll have an "accident" plan ready for that. So why are we here?"

Nellie shivered. "Why, H. L.? This damp cold can't be good for your back."

"Let me tell you a little story. I took over the Historical Society in 1979. Soon thereafter, in 1981, we had a break in. Dixie, pass me one of those flashlights."

H. L. shined it on a square of cinderblocks in the center of one of the brick foundations walls. "That's the spot of the break in. We didn't have the money to patch the hole using bricks from the Victorian Era, and it never became a priority. The blocks weren't cemented together when they were first used. My decision. I considered them temporary. I still do . . . but they're still here. The tunnel dug by the thieves, who were obviously miners, feeds into an underground web of passages connecting mines that have been defunct for a century or more.

"These mines led to the great silver deposits responsible for the birth of Aspen, and gold was present in lesser quantities. But you don't go into the maze of passages connecting the mines and hope to live. Some sections, I hear, are flooded with toxic liquids; some sections are without air; and other sections end abruptly where rock and timber ceilings have collapsed."

"You make it sound like an escape route," said Beau. "It sounds to me more like a self-burial."

Nellie threw up. H. L. paid her no mind.

"It would be if I didn't have a map to guide us out the same way it

187

guided the thieving miners in. I found it buried in the dirt after the cops left. Anyway, the intruders began their operation from a 19th century mining entrance roughly a half mile from here, not far from a remote half-collapsed shack. If we remove the cinderblocks and do some claustrophobic crawling in the passage dug by those idiots, we'll come to the network of tunnels abandoned when the mines closed. With my map and your youth, we'll make our way to the entrance turned exit. Dixie!"

Beau looked up from comforting Nellie. "I'm listening."

While I'm away, I want you to remove the cinderblocks and enlarge the passage dug by the thieves. Keep the dirt in a pile just outside the foundation wall. We might need it later to rebuild what we wreck."

"Yes, ma'am."

"But H. L.," Nellie stammered, "why did these thieves want into the Historical Society in the first place? It's not like we've got a stash of gold bars."

"But there was a rumor such a stash existed, and who knows. Maybe at one time it did. Anyway, that rumor caused our cretins to undertake their long dig from the old tunnel system into our cellar. We'll be paying tribute to their stupidity if we get out."

"Nellie, pull yourself together. Take your friend into the attic, find that stretcher you took up there after my surgery and have Johnny Reb bring it into the enclave."

"So I can haul you through those passages?"

"I don't see any other volunteers."

CHAPTER TWENTY-EIGHT

Connor wadded up a piece of paper and hurled it at an especially grotesque painting of J. Edgar Hoover. It ricocheted off the glass and sailed into a waste basket just as Hatch walked into his office.

"Nice shot, partner. Let's hope you don't go cold in the fourth quarter."

"Not a chance. What's the word on Caskey?"

"Randall, you're not going to believe this."

"Quit pacing. That's my job. Have a seat over there and calmly describe your triumph."

"Thanks, but I've been sitting for two hours. Here's the latest. The murder weapon was the same British rifle used on El Lobo. We suspected that, but we didn't have a theory on the motive. Now we do. I called at least a dozen people who were in the intelligence services when Albrecht was president. Several of them had been approached by Caskey's military advisors. It seems Caskey wasn't satisfied with the official explanations of Shiller's missing years. Gardner, who's still over at the NSA, agreed to reopen the inquiry. He's already found twelve crack Special Forces people who were in Afghanistan and went missing the same time the General did."

"That, my friend, is first-rate work."

"There's more. The old lady at the Historical Society, the one Nellie dumped her story on, wasn't just an old lady at the Historical Society. Get this. She signed what she wrote in the tablet as 'Harriet Gibbons, Retired Special Agent.' We should have guessed it from the way she hid the code."

"Incredible. You've checked her out?"

"Yep. Stationed at the Minneapolis Field Office from 1967 to 1978. She was no slacker, either. Her record includes one FBI Star for wounds

189

sustained in the line of duty and three Medals for Meritorious Achievement. Only praise in her file. Her premature departure was caused by the shootout that got her the Star. You should have seen the guy at the other end. He was number three on the FBI's most wanted list. I found pictures of him when they brought him in. He looked like Swiss cheese covered in ketchup. When the old girl writes us that the hearsay from Shiller's kitchen isn't hearsay, I think we should listen."

"Agreed. But we're still going to need hard evidence."

"She claims to have it."

"I guess we'll find out tonight if it's the real thing. If it is, you know what that means? We'll have a hot potato on our hands with no idea where to toss it. Speaking of potatoes, I could use some fries and a burger before our flight. How about you? I'm buying – as long as you let me buy in a kale-free zone."

***

While H. L., Connor and Hatch were in the air, Shiller got a welcome surprise. The two disciples he had ordered to come to the ranch showed up in record time. Shortly after their arrival, Hollis strolled in looking very much the presidential spokesman. His hair was razor-cut, probably by a Mexican barber. He wore a dark tailored suit, English bench-made shoes, a white dress shirt and a red paisley tie that added a bold dash of color to his subdued attire.

The men retired to Shiller's office for a briefing on the perilous situation. The General explained matter-of-factly how the indiscretions in the kitchen had set in motion a chain of events that could unravel a mission seven years in the making. He made no threats or innuendos, but was clear about his expectations. Hollis would continue to charm the press. If rumors arose, he would dismiss these as baseless slander from desperate opponents . . . and say no more.

Jim and Allen would have the most on their plate. Their redemption required that they cut off the flow of information at its source – and further up the chain if necessary. In this way, any accusation directed at Shiller would be hearsay twice removed, a fact that would cause the judicial system to grind to a halt.

This approach meant the immediate elimination of the girl, her boyfriend and the woman who ran the Historical Society. Only a perfectly executed accident taking out all three at once would remain beyond suspicion. It would be a trivial job, well within the capacity of the two apostates. Time, however, was of the essence.

When the primary source of the information was silenced, it would be necessary to determine how far up the ladder the rumors had spread. At very least, the agent who had been photographed with the woman from the Historical Society and his cohort would have to go. This would be a more difficult undertaking for which he ordered Hollis to stay on call.

When dinner time came, Shiller telephoned the culinary director of the Jerome. He asked if Nellie Vaughn was working that night. She was. He requested that she cater a hearty meal for four. The director agreed, though his kitchen was understaffed. You didn't turn down the future president of the United States.

***

"It's going to be a night of tough decisions," H. L. told Connor and Hatch.

The agents, two active and one retired, sat in a small private room attached to Martini's, the late-night bar at the Kahler hotel. An ice bucket and a bottle of Johnnie Walker were front and center on the round table; the flowers had been removed at Connor's request. All four walls were plastered with oil portraits of celebrated Mayo Clinic doctors. Connor would have preferred to get rid of these, too. They reminded him of bourgeois censors, eager to report anything they found improper. But he knew the censors would have to stay: asking that they be taken down would draw unwanted attention to the room.

"No ice," H. L. said when Hatch reached for the silver tongs.

"You don't drink?" Connor asked.

"Because I don't like my Scotch diluted with frozen water doesn't mean I don't drink. Get on with the pouring, Agent Hatcher. We have a lot of ground to cover."

Connor said, "Probably less than you think, Agent Gibbons."

"H. L., please. We're no longer acting in the name of the Bureau."

"What?"

"You'll understand soon enough. Any objections to first names?"

"None."

"Your given names would be?"

"He goes by Hatch. Me, by Connor."

"So, Hatch and Connor, you've had time to look at the material 'Mr. Wilson' delivered?"

"We have," Connor said. "You had no worries we wouldn't find it?"

"I'm familiar with Bureau forensics practices. Finding the code was step one. A baby step. A beginning. The real challenge starts now."

191

"Wait a sec. It starts if we decide to participate," Connor said.

"You will." H. L. reached for the bottle and poured herself a healthy measure. "Does my material square with your own findings?"

"Not only," Hatch said. "We've also filled in a couple more blanks. One of the sharpshooters who worked closely with Shiller in Afghanistan took out Caskey. Why? Because Caskey had convinced the intelligence services to reopen an inquiry into Shiller's 'missing years.' We've also learned that twelve elite Special Forces soldiers from all four branches of the military were pulled from their units at roughly the same time. The official reason was the same as the reason given for Shiller's disappearance: work on a secret mission. No one ever learned what that mission was."

"No one?" H. L. said. She lifted her bag onto the table, pulled out a thick black diary and tapped it with her free hand. "You have, I assume, looked into my past service. I doubt you've had time to delve into my personal life."

"What's in the book?" Connor rasped.

"A lot. However, it cannot be properly understood without the background I'm going to provide." H. L. switched the diary from her right to her left hand, took a long swallow of Scotch, then placed the black book on the table. "I would ask for your patience," she said.

"You've got it," Connor mumbled, fidgeting impatiently. "Shoot."

H. L. filled her glass. "When I was in undergraduate school at Ratcliff, I roomed with Janet Nielsen. We became friends and took an apartment together when we moved out of the dorm. I assume the name rings a bell."

"You assume wrong," Connor said.

"Wait," Hatch contradicted. "Wasn't that the maiden name of President Albrecht's wife?"

"Correct. Janet and I remained close friends after we graduated. Very close friends. Friends who shared aspects of their private lives as we had done as college roommates. Friends throughout her husband's presidency. My work after I separated from the Bureau dovetailed with her interest in historical preservation. It wasn't only my persistence that led to my contacts in Washington. Connor, would you please stop fidgeting. I'm telling you this for a reason."

"Then get to it."

H. L. went on as if he weren't in the room. "When Grant lost the 2012 presidential election, no one understood what moved him to destroy all

White House records of his administration. He was thought to be an honest man, a Carter rather than a Nixon. There were, as you will remember, countless investigations. These produced nothing and ceased altogether after his death in 2013. However, one item remained – the item you are looking at as we speak. I don't know where Janet hid the diary, but I do know that Shiller was among the investigators looking for it. He of course did so under a false name and false pretenses. He got nowhere. Even I still don't know where the diary was hidden.

"Janet and her husband were patrons of the Historical Society. I was able to get word to her recently through means I won't go into. I asked if she had any information regarding the attacks that have befallen our country. If she did I told her she would find me today at the Minneapolis Airport, awaiting the Delta evening flight to Rochester.

"She was there. We only met for seconds, unobtrusively in the ladies room. She scribbled that her husband had regretted one thing above all else about his time in the White House – and flushed the paper down the toilet. I would, she said, find further clarification in the pocket of my overcoat. I did. Now, gentleman, you may have a look."

***

An hour later, after they had perused relevant parts of diary, it was clear to Connor and Hatch what Albrecht regretted above all else: early in his term, he had given Shiller and his people the means to perfect in total secrecy terror attacks on the United States. These attacks were never meant to be carried out but, rather, to demonstrate in a shockingly incontrovertible manner the vulnerability of the country. President Grant Albrecht believed this was the only way to awaken Congress to the growing threat to the Homeland posed by God's Wrath.

From time to time, Shiller delivered progress reports. Among the attacks prepared by the team were all of those that had recently crippled the United States. Albrecht had not intended to lose the 2012 election, but when he did he destroyed the White House records of his administration to hide the existence of a plan whose wisdom he had come to doubt. He had not intended to die a few months later. But on his death bed, and probably before, he grasped the enormity of his blunder: he had left his old friend, General Gordon Shiller, with the potential to bring America to its knees. Did he trust Shiller to do the right thing and destroy that potential? Did he trust anyone after four years in the White House?

"Questions?" H. L. asked.

"Yeah," Connor said. "What now?"

193

"What would you do in Shiller's position?"

"Get rid of you, the girl and her football friend – for a start. Then maybe me and Hatch. We haven't told anyone higher up yet, which he might or might not know. That means any and all rumors are just that – rumors. If the courts or intelligence agencies decide to look for a basis in fact, they will need months or years. By then Shiller will be president and we will have gone overnight from the world's oldest democracy to the world's newest dictatorship. Those who speak out against it will receive the "Putin" treatment. This clearly can't be allowed to happen. Not to my country. It might appear that his election is the will of the electorate. That's because they don't have the information we do. If they did, the *Make America Great Again* candidate would be counting his votes on the fingers of one hand."

H. L. drained her glass, giving no hint mental or otherwise that she had just finished a half bottle of Johnnie Walker. "Okay, Connor, here's where the rubber hits the road. You've said three things, which I'll clarify. First, American intelligence, law enforcement and courts won't be able to prove the rumors are true soon enough to reverse the outcome of the election. Second, to bolster his inevitable "malicious gossip" response, Shiller must eliminate Nellie, her boyfriend, me and perhaps the two of you in ways that can be proven to be the result of accidents. Third, once Shiller is president the United States will become the newest casualty of democratic government. The attacks will stop. Americans will again feel secure. There will be no going back. Your plans to prevent this?"

"Got me," Hatch said.

"No," Connor growled. "No, Hatch, 'got me' is not an answer to the biggest threat this country has ever faced. We have no choice. We have to eliminate Shiller, the sooner the better."

"How, gentlemen? We're not going to succeed by traditional means. I'm afraid he has us outgunned in that area. And were we to succeed, we'd be lynched. The FBI knocking off a presidential candidate? I don't think so. Which is why I said earlier we are no longer working in the name of the Bureau."

"So what do *you* propose?" Hatch asked, sure she didn't have an idea. He was wrong.

***

"Bear with me," H. L. said. "Do you now have the hard evidence you need to join me?"

Connor glanced at Hatch, whose color had gone from paltry gray to pasty white. "We have evidence that a presidential candidate has killed 65,000 Americans to get himself elected. We know from Albrecht's diary how he was able to pull off this seemingly impossible series of attacks. So, yes, I'm satisfied with the evidence. We all agree it's irrefutable.

"But this is America, at least for a few more months. He won't be convicted before he's elected. America lives in fear. A large majority of the population has put its hopes in him to return the country to the functioning and relatively safe place it was a year ago. You'd better accept that they'll initially cast their lot with his hearsay and forged handwriting defense – rather than with any rational proof we provide.

"Separating people from their last hope, even when the evidence is clear . . . well, that's not going to happen. So he'll be president and we'll be fucked. All of us, the entire goddamn country. I said he had to be eliminated. What I did *not* say, H. L., is that we agreed to join you. We haven't yet. We don't even know what your plan is."

"Will it make us murderers?" Hatch stuttered. "What good is it if me and Randall save the country but live out our lives in a maximum security prison? Who says I might not rather emigrate without having a criminal record? Denmark is sounding better all the time."

"Your job, Agent Hatcher, is to serve your country, not to worry about yourself."

"Hatch knows what his job is. He's having a panic attack, that's all. Does your plan, whatever the hell it is, make us felons?"

"It shouldn't matter," H. L. said. *"I do solemnly swear that I will support and defend the Constitution of the United States against all enemies, foreign and **domestic**; that I will bear true faith and allegiance to the same; that I take this obligation freely, without any mental reservation or purpose of evasion; and that I will well and faithfully discharge the duties of the office on which I am about to enter. So help me God.* "That's the oath you both took when you joined the Bureau, and it applies whether you're on duty or not. You'll be pleased to hear that I'm not asking you to commit murder. In fact, I doubt what I need from you gentlemen is even a third-degree misdemeanor."

The lights in the room dimmed three times, signaling the closure of the bar. "We'll have to hear the plan before we commit. Let's find another place to go over it."

"No," H. L. said. "Either you have confidence in me or you don't. I'm going to write down the address of my brother in Crested Butte. He's expecting you tomorrow evening by five o'clock. He has the coordinates of the place where you will pick me up. I've also faxed him a comprehensive list of things we'll need. I'll be with Nellie and your footballer between midnight and two a. m. – if all goes well. I should add that my brother knows nothing of the operation.

"Send your FBI plane to the East Coast in case you're being watched. You're smart men. Figure out the least obtrusive way to get back to Colorado."

H. L. drained her glass and walked out of the room.

CHAPTER TWENTY-NINE

Nellie met H. L. at the main entrance to the Historical Society and helped her up the steps. The heavy door closed behind them, confining them to a space they assumed to be bugged. The idea, Beau had told Nellie, was to avoid mention of anything that might alert a possible eavesdropper to their plans.

"Welcome back, H. L." Nellie said. "We've missed you."

"No one misses me."

"Well, you're just plain wrong about that. How did it go?"

"How did *what* go?"

"Your appointment at Mayo."

"It ended in the usual standoff. The surgeon ordered me to stop drinking. I told him I would when he properly repaired my back. Neither is going to happen. Where's Dixie?"

"Picking up sandwiches. He's bringing you a surprise."

"Fried chicken? Haven't I suffered enough in this lifetime?"

"H. L., try to be nice. I told him you would want a Reuben. He'll get it right this time, you'll see. I wrote down the instructions, just to be sure. You know what I think, H. L.? I think my friend is winning you over."

"Ole Greyback? I'm not sure he's my type."

"Well, you've won *him* over."

"His problem." H. L. limped into the parlor, stuck her cane in Aspen's only umbrella stand – a gift from Beau – and sat in her armchair. She looked fragile, but her voice was strong and steady.

"Did anything happen while I was away?"

"Nope, nothing unusual. The bookstore dropped off a box and a couple of guys from Atmos Energy showed up to check on something in the basement."

"The gas lines to the furnace, I imagine. Some of the older houses nearby had problems last winter. Did they find anything that needs to be replaced."

"Nothing that can't wait. They found a little corrosion on the iron pipes we're supposed to keep an eye on. I promised we'd have them checked every year."

***

The plan was in place. Beau had gotten the details yesterday on the drive to the airport, not verbally but in a few handwritten pages H. L. left in the truck, and he had perused them together with Nellie at least a half dozen times. When he arrived with the sandwiches, he instantly escorted Nellie to the door.

She gave him a quick kiss and walked toward the town center. They all understood how crucial it was that the three of them *not* be together at the Historical Society until they were ready to enter the tunnels. No reason to encourage a premature "accident."

"Mr. Beauregard, please carry that box from the library to my office."

"Office" was the code name for electronic eavesdroppers H. L. had given the dank basement storeroom in which they had met the previous day. Here, Beau could safely provide the update she had asked for when she returned to Aspen. He began immediately.

"Maybe Nellie has already filled you in. In case she hasn't, it was just like you predicted. Two men in uniform showed up at the front door with an entirely credible reason to come inside. They were down here in the cellar about a half hour doing something they called a 'precautionary check.' We stayed upstairs near the windows where we could be seen. If anyone was watching, they would have no reason to believe we suspected anything."

"Good."

"I'm dying to take a look around. God knows what I'll find."

"No. We have too much to do. There will be an explosion after Nellie gets back. The men were from the gas company, meaning we know what type of explosion it will be."

"Gas, right?"

"Natural gas. It's lighter than air and will rise to the upper levels. An explosive gas-air mixture won't be reached immediately, which is helpful to know."

"We'll also smell it in here when they throw the switch."

"We won't. If our friends plan to kill us in an accident, they're not going to provide an olfactory signal of their approach."

"But gas smells."

198

"Didn't they teach you anything but football at Ole Miss? You can't see or smell natural gas. When it's used commercially a harmless chemical called mercaptan is added. What's added can be removed and, in this case, it will be removed. Nellie's arrival is our cue to leave."

"How do you know all this stuff, H. L.?"

"Ask me later – if we're still alive. We've got work to do, and no slaves to help. How far down the tunnel dug by the thieves were you able to get?"

"A few feet. No slaves, no John Henry. Just a lazy Delta white boy with a spoon-sized shovel."

H. L. wasn't amused. "But you did practice arranging the cinder blocks? And you've got a large pile of earth behind the foundation wall?"

"Yes ma'am."

"Will you kindly stop calling me 'ma'am.'"

"I'll try, but it won't be easy. Can we get to the important stuff?"

"Take down the block wall, drag the box in there and drag me in behind it."

"*Drag* you in? What's that supposed to mean?"

"Take the wooden bars out of the stretcher, roll me up in the canvas and drag me in there. Some of the tunnels are barely two feet high. You and Nellie can crawl; I can't."

"Jesus. I hope some of the tunnels are bigger. Big enough for me to carry you."

"Thank you, Dixie. I appreciate your concern."

"H. L., what if something happens to you? I mean – "

"I know what you mean. We're both aware of the possibility. Nellie, on the other hand, has fairy-tale notions about miracles. Let's accept them for her sake. Smile, Dixie. We're going to make it."

Twenty minutes later Beau, H. L. in her canvas roll, and the box from the library were all inside the tunnel. Beau opened the box and found himself peering at leather-bound books. "What the hell are these?"

"Keep digging," H. L. ordered, pushing the canvas roll she inhabited away from her face.

"I'm digging. Any particular volume?"

"Don't be ridiculous. I told, Scott, the young man who cleaned up your computers, to research what
nutcases who explore abandoned mines take with them."

"So we could stop at the next mining store?"

"Drop the sarcasm. The nutcase accoutrements came to us with my

199

monthly library request."

"You sound like a spy."

"Would you quit throwing those books around. I don't care if you're on your deathbed. Books are to be respected."

"Calm down, H. L. There's something in here. I'll clean up the mess when I get it out."

A few seconds later he pulled up a tattered rucksack, put it aside and started repacking the books. Upstairs a door groaned on its hinges.

"Forget it," H. L. said. Nellie's here."

He glanced over at the old woman, lying flat on her back, wrapped like a salami in the canvas role. His relief over Nellie's arrival came with an unexpected sadness for H. L. It was a sadness she didn't seem to share – not for herself, not for anyone.

"Let's hope it's Nellie."

"Get going, Dixie. Let's see what's in that pack. Scott said he would leave a note."

"Yes ma'am. The note's here, along with a bunch of other stuff. Want me to read it?"

"Yes."

"Included is a small tank of oxygen with a mouthpiece, the kind divers use in emergencies. Also, three LED flashlights that can be turned on without triggering an explosion. The little thing that looks like a cell phone is a multi-gas detector. The device will beep at elevated levels of methane, oxygen, H2S and any other explosive gas. It is as indispensable as an LED light. The small rod is expandable to nine feet. It is used to measure the depth of pooled liquid. The bottle is optional."

"The bottle. It's a fifth of Johnnie Walker."

"I want you to listen carefully, Mr. Beauregard. You don't strike me as a technical wizard, but you are going to have to figure out how to work the meter and oxygen tank. You're in charge of keeping them with you at all times. We won't need either one until we reach an actual mining tunnel. Our first job is to get out of this gopher hole."

Before he could say anything else, Nellie stepped through gap in the foundation. "Yuck."

"Better than the alternative. Both of you, restack the cinder block. Dixie, shovel as much mud as you can in front of them, then stuff what's left into any cracks. Since we don't know when the gas leak will begin, let's assume the worst. LED flashlights only from now on, one at a time so we don't run out of juice. And Stonewall, watch you don't make a spark."

"A spark? I thought the new flashlights – "

"I'm talking about your shovel hitting a rock. Fast but careful. Nellie, dear, when you finish helping reconstruct the wall, work that silver rod and one of the flashlights into my canvas roll with me. There are three of them, one for you, one for your swamp fox. When Dixie finishes shoveling, we're off. Nellie first. Beauregard second, dragging the canvas. I'm going to be talking a lot, describing the plan to you. At this point, we should all know our objectives."

Nellie fought back tears. "No, that's not the reason. You're telling us in case you don't . . . "

"Nonsense. You believe in miracles. I don't, but I plan to prove you right. Hurry up with that wall."

"Give her some medicine," Beau said. "That cocoon's got to be uncomfortable."

"Not now, Nellie. We might need it for other purposes. Stonewall, do you have your map?"

"Shirt pocket," he said, piling the last shovel of mud against the cinder blocks.

"Nellie, your copy?"

"Jeans. Back pocket."

"Good. Keep them there for now. We know where we're going until we reach the labyrinth. After that we won't have a clue. Departure time."

Nellie went ahead on her hands and knees, her dread almost palpable. Beau lay down on his stomach and pushed himself feet first past H. L. Rolling onto his back, he grabbed the two straps hanging from the canvas roll and pulled. No problem, at least not while he was fresh: the roll slid over the mud until he and H. L. touched heads. He slid back until the straps were taught, then gave another powerful heave.

"Not like that," H. L. said. "Slow and steady. Save your strength."

"Okay."

After a few yards, the burrow seemed less treacherous. The ground was nearly dry; the ceiling and walls were braced by some sort of ingenious structure made of timber and Kevlar.

H. L. turned off her flashlight. Bad idea. The burrow went as dark as darkness gets. This would not do. Nellie would need light or she would panic. But she would follow orders: H. L. was the sole torch bearer until they reached the shaft.

How long did the batteries last? No idea, Scott wrote nothing on the subject. It didn't matter. Nellie was the weak link in a chain that had to hold.

Turn on the light. Set a series of small goals. Get to the mining tunnels and think no further.

In a nearly inaudible voice, she passed her thoughts to Beau. He sent them ahead to Nellie – with the addition of a small lie. Get to the mining tunnels and the worst will be over; the rest will be a cake walk.

"Good," H. L. whispered. "Good, Dixie."

CHAPTER THIRTY

"New moon," Connor said, his words jostled by the cracking and bouncing of their military Humvee over the rock-strewn jeep trail. "What new moon? You see any moon, Hatch?"

"No."

"No, huh. Then why don't the fucking books call it 'no moon.?'"

"Jesus, Randall, you're on a jeep trail cut into the side of a cliff. You've got headlights. You don't need the moon."

"Where's the top of this goddamn thing. Doesn't it have a summit?"

"It won't make any difference if you go off the edge playing word games."

"We're not going off the edge. We're staying in our lane. It's L. A. driving, just with cliffs instead of cars – and a few more bumps."

"You think we did the right thing?"

"Fuck if I know, Hatch. The brother seemed crazier that the old lady. Where'd he get this Marine Corps piece of shit?"

"You'd rather make this drive in a Bureau Suburban?"

"I'd rather not make it, period." Connor tightened his grip on the wheel. The rock trail bent into a series of switchbacks. His headlights swept across a valley 3,000 feet down as he fought to keep the military transporter under control.

Up ahead the trail narrowed even more. He slowed and crept forward. "We're not getting through there, partner. A cliff on one side, a friendly a vertical drop off on the other, loose rocks and a fat-ass jeep."

"It's gonna be tight. Stop and I'll do some measurements. Didn't that crazy brother say he had taken this thing to Aspen."

"Crazy fucker's the operative term. He didn't say he'd gone over Pearl Pass."

"Yeah, but this is the way he sent us. I checked the map. It's the best way over the top from Crested Butte to Aspen. He's still around so he must have made it."

"Must have? MUST HAVE? He probably drove on the highway. Hop out and measure while you can still open the door. Then get back in here. I want you with me when I go over the edge."

"You went over the edge a long time ago."

"Doesn't mean I can't do it again. The measurements please."

Hatch let himself down like he was getting off a ladder without a bottom rung, walked to where the road appeared most narrow and took out the tape measure the crazy brother had left on the seat. Nice of him.

The rock wall with tiny streams of water dribbling down its face was seven feet six inches from the other side of the road. Beyond was only night. "Any specs on this thing?" he asked when he climbed back inside.

"In that compartment. I was just looking at them."

Hatch flipped to the back of the fat manual. "Says here we've got a track width of 72 inches and a shipping width of 86 inches."

"How wide's the trail."

"Ninety inches. We can make it."

"Whoa. Not so fast, partner. The actual width seems to me more than 86 inches. You know, with armor and God knows what else they've added. Let's do the math. If we fuck up, this thing's in freefall."

"Want me to try another measurement?"

"Nope. The way we're shaped you'll be guessing. Let's guess from in here with big numbers."

"Okay. How much do you want to add to the shipping specs?"

"Let's say a foot of width on each side. That should give us plenty of leeway. Do the math. Where does that put the outer wheels?"

"If you're up against the cliff on the right?"

"Just do the math. We'll think about that later."

Hatch fished a pencil and scrap of paper from the compartment where he had found the vehicle specs, handed Connor the flashlight and began to scribble. "So here's what I get. We make it 24 inches wider, total. We start with the cliff side. You've got seven inches from the outside of the tire to the outside of the truck and another 12 inches we're adding on. That makes 19 inches from the tire to the widest part of the truck. Following?"

"No, but go ahead."

"We've got a track width of 72 inches. Add those together and you get 91 inches. That means one inch of the outer tire will be over the edge, but the rest will be on the path. That shouldn't be a problem. And remember, the calculations have some built in leeway."

"You forgot the part of the truck that goes from the outside wheel to the outside of my door . . . or wherever it's widest."

"I didn't forget, Randall. It sounds worse than it is."

"You didn't want to spook me?"

"Something like that."

"I don't spook. Part of the truck will be sticking out over the drop off."

"Doesn't matter. Most of the thing will be on solid rock."

"Solid? Give me a break. Big rocks and tons of shale don't make it solid."

"What do you want to do? Back down five miles you could hardly get up or call off the mission and walk?"

"Fuck it. I'm not backing up and I'm not walking. Get out and guide me. Let's get this over with."

Connor crept ahead while Hatch ran back and forth, signaling how close the Humvee was to the cliff and how far from the edge of the path. It didn't take long for him to notice the problem: the doors were not even close to factory specs. They had been reinforced by bullet-proof steel and outfitted with a protruding square window of bullet-proof glass. He was going to have to direct Connor so close to the cliff he would nearly scape it, and even so only half the width of the outer tires would be on the road. As for the widest part of the truck . . . well, it would be jutting at least two feet out over the edge of the drop off. If the trail bed was unstable, Connor's weight could be the straw that broke the camel's back.

Hatch climbed up on the hood. One of the panes of the front windshield opened outward. He could crawl inside and drive. Connor could stand on terra firma and do the guiding.

He tapped on the windshield that opened. "I'll drive," he shouted.

"Like hell you will." Connor revved the huge diesel engine. "Get the fuck down there and do your job. Or stay where you are and I'll plow ahead with my eyes closed."

No use trying to reason with him; no use bringing up the sensitive subject of his weight – not when he was in this kind of mood. They didn't teach you at Quantico to rely on luck. They also didn't teach you how to make a 12,000 pound troop carrier fly. Whatever they *did* teach you wasn't going to help now.

When his feet hit the ground, the beast was already inching forward. He heard the first rasping of metal on stone, smelled the distinct odor it created. "Okay," he yelled, looking at the front tire as it sent a cascade of shale and rock crashing over the edge. He pointed the beam of his flashlight toward the cliff as walked backwards. "Keep scraping! No leeway."

"Get on the hood," Connor yelled. "You heard me. Up on the hood. Enough of this shit. We're gonna blast through here."

Before Hatch could try to reason with him, Connor was coming. Rocks rained down the precipice, metal scraped the cliff. Jesus, he wasn't kidding. Up on the hood or flat on his stomach, those were his choices. He didn't know the clearance from ground to chassis so he jumped, caught the grill and hauled himself up. On the hood, he started to slide. Not forward, not backwards but sideways toward the drop off. He thrust his hands into the cooling slits his ribs had already cracked over, found handholds, good ones, as the trail started to collapse. He waited for his life to flash before his eyes. But his life was in his ears as Connor gave the mighty diesel one last chance. And then it was quiet, eerily quiet. He wasn't falling, why in the hell wasn't he? Could it be? Could the troop carrier have clawed its way back from disaster? Yes, miraculously it had. The Humvee, engine at idle, had stopped on a broad flat stretch of trail. Its headlights illuminated a makeshift wooden sign that read "Summit, 12,705 ft."

Luck, they didn't teach it at Quantico either. But Connor had learned – somehow, somewhere – how to use it. In 20 years, Hatch had seen enough to know that Connor's luck wasn't just "luck."

"Get in, partner. I've put the coordinates in the GPS. If we made it this far, we're gonna find out if gramma really has a plan."

CHAPTER THIRTY-ONE

When Nellie crawled out of the thieves' tunnel and turned on her flashlight, she imagined she had entered Notre Dame. All around her were stained-glass windows. There were velvet aisles leading to the altar, and a majestic dome reaching into the heavens. Only when she stood and steadied herself did her eyes surrender to reality. She was entombed in an abandoned mine. Her windows were jagged rock walls, the velvet aisles were rails to nowhere, and the dome was a granite ceiling braced by rotten timbers.

A wave of panic pressed the air from her lungs. Was she alone? Had something happened to the others? Yes, she was sure it had. Her image of Notre Dame was sent by God as a cruel reminder of the last rights she would be denied.

She hadn't heard Beau's soothing voice for what seemed an eternity, hadn't heard his straining to drag H. L. forward in her canvas sarcophagus. She fought to bring back her image of the cathedral. Instead, in the shadowy glow, she saw her grave.

Without warning came the rumble of distant thunder. The earth trembled. A shower of debris rained down from above. There was a deafening crack when an overhead beam split. The Historical Society had blown up like H. L. said it would, but she hadn't expected such a powerful explosion.

She forced herself to shine her light upward, deathly afraid of what it would expose. Fissures ran like insects across the rock ceiling, tiny fissures that quickly grew to gaping rifts. Tons of stone broke loose and fell, causing the ground to heave so fiercely it knocked her on her back and ripped the flashlight from her hands. She opened her eyes to blackness, patted around her, found nothing but rocks.

Little by little, the crashing noises ceased. In the silence, she heard the distant trickle of water.

207

She was disoriented. Where was the tunnel exit? It had been directly behind her. Frantically she searched in blackness until she found a cavern wall. She felt its cold chiseled surface with her palms, patted in all directions.

Nothing. Where was it? Where was she? Which way should she move?

She was sure Beau and H. L. had been buried alive. Maybe she could dig them out. Maybe. Every second counted, every second might hold a life – or extinguish it. She had to slow her breathing and try to think. She couldn't afford to crawl in the wrong direction. She strained to see something, anything. A blackness no eye would ever adjust to made her close her eyes. The pulsing red behind her lids wouldn't guide her, but at least it carried the warming touch of light.

Terrible images paraded through her awareness. The tons of rock that had come down had blocked the tunnel exit; the tunnel itself had collapsed, burying Beau and H. L. under tons of earth and stone. Think!

No eyes. Hands she had, but no way to tell them where to search.

An idea exploded in her mind. Stones. This cavern was full of stones. If she could throw them so they hit the wall at the right height and aim them so that they traced a moving line in one direction, then the other, she would be able to hear when she struck the mud opening.

Suddenly she remembered that the tunnel had only been mud for a few yards. After that it was held from collapsing by some kind of supports. The guys who had broken into the Historical Society were idiots, sure, but they knew something about tunnels. Then came the last stretch, how long she didn't know. It had been hacked, drilled or bored through solid rock, the same rock that surrounded her now. There was no way to find the opening – if an opening still existed. She didn't know how far behind her they had been . . . so maybe, maybe. She cried at the top of her lungs for Beau. And then she saw a faint glow The exit! They were alive! The Historical Society had blown up, but the tunnel had not collapsed. Its opening was not blocked by fallen stone!

The glow went out, taking her breath away. But it returned quickly before going out again. They would be trying to extend the life of the batteries . . .

She could rest, sitting on the rocky mine shaft floor with her back against the cold damp rock wall. She pulled her knees in close and wrapped her arms around them. Warmth ran through her veins and hot tears ran down her cheeks. They would be here soon.

"Goddammit," H. L. rasped, "get me out of this sausage skin. Hurry up, Dixie. One more minute in here and I'll go mad."

"H. L.," Nellie said, "H. L., we made it! I told you miracles happen. Just lie still. We've gotten this far. Beau and I aren't going to break your back trying to rush."

"Oh, be quiet. It wasn't a miracle. The survival of the Carlyle House might have qualified as one, had it happened. Not this."

"You're wrong, H. L. I can feel it. I know it was a miracle."

"Nonsense. It was your Southern slouch. He pulled me all this way. Now he will unwrap me at the fastest pace he can sustain. If you want to help, Nellie, reach in there and take out the measuring rod, flashlight and Johnnie Walker."

"The bottle didn't break?"

"No. Maybe that's your miracle. General Lee, if you don't mind, let's get started with the unwrapping. You seem to have fallen into a trance."

"I was looking at the sharp rocks around you," Beau said. "Unwrapping means rolling, and there's not going to be any rolling just now, not even Holy Rolling. Don't move. I'm going to cut you out."

"We might need the canvas."

"We'll keep a few strips. Sure you're okay?"

"Okay, splendid. Never thought I'd be indebted to a Southerner, but strange things do happen – not miracles, but inexplicable twists of fate. However, we've still got a long way to go. You needn't stop cutting while you cogitate. I don't understand why no one down there can multi-task."

The light wasn't good, the cavern was filled with dust from the cave in, but Beau could have sworn he saw H. L. smile. "Multi-tasking?" he said. "It sounds like something I should learn. Hold still while I start my apprenticeship." He slit through layers of canvas with his razor-sharp knife, making sure the last cut was from bottom to top. "There. You're free."

"Alright, children, our rest period is over. Help me up. We'll follow the rail tracks."

"I can carry you," Beau said.

"Help me up. It might not be necessary. I felt something in my spine when you dragged me over a bump. Something good."

Beau and Nellie hoisted the frail old woman to her feet and steadied her. "Let me go it alone," H. L. said. "Stay close, walk with me, but let me go."

"You're not limping!"

"Nellie, I might have to change my position on miracles. My back feels different, better than it's felt in years. If it stays like this, Stonewall has outperformed the bigshots at the Mayo Clinic."

"Me?"

"Yes, you. Come on. We'll check out the track together."

With each step H. L. moved more steadily, more confidently. She reached for Beau's arm once when her foot came down on the side of a stone, but her back remained strong.

They walked past ancient rusted mining equipment and stacks of milled timbers. Two tracks merged into one and the passage narrowed. Their view of the shaft ahead was blocked by a mining car on the rails.

H. L. studied the map while Beau looked on. "Okay, here's where the thieves went in and we came out. Here's where Nellie almost got buried. Here's the tunnel we're in now. Can you read what's written along the side, Mr. Wellington?"

"It looks like these jerks were pretty precise. The shaft, from the point where the tracks merge to where it ends, is 900 yards long. It says here there's a seven percent grade. I guess the original miners used some kind of pulley system to get the ore cars up the slope."

"The tracks on the map just end?" H. L. asked.

"Yep. They've drawn a square where you'd expect them to continue."

"Anything written?"

"Beside the square it says 'winze.' I guess that's mine terminology for something."

H. L. still stood without difficulty, but she looked chilled. Nellie put her arm around her shoulders, and H. L. did not object. She said, "A winze is a vertical shaft leading to a mine below. It all makes sense. A pulley system like the one that pulled the train cars up the slope brought buckets of ore up to the trains. I was reading about abandoned mines yesterday. Most winzes are filled with water, rust-colored from the contaminants leached out of the earth. Anyway, that's for later. First we have to cover 900 yards to reach the winze. Look at the width of the tunnel. There's not enough room between the side walls and the ore car for a person to squeeze through. There might be a hundred ore cars between us and the winze. How we tackle this is going to require some serious thought."

"I'll get up on the car and look."

"Don't drop the light," Nellie cautioned. "We'll be down to one if you do."

210

"Two," corrected H. L.

"One. Remember? Mine got crushed."

Beau took off, jogging toward the mining car. He hopped up on the coupling, slipped down into the hold and came up at the other end. Nellie was about to call to him when he disappeared from view.

"Another car," H. L. said. "If there are more than a few, you're going to have to leave me."

"No! That's not going to happen. Beau and I would both rather stay here and die with you – or die trying to get *all* of us out."

CHAPTER THIRTY-TWO

"Where the fuck are we now?" boomed Connor over the hoarse growl of the diesel. "Did you put me on the wrong path back there?"

"Shhh. From now on we're supposed to tread softly."

"Come on, Hatch. You're delirious. How do you tread softly when you're driving a bulldozer?"

"Calm down, Randall. In fact, stop. I think we're here. I'll read you the GPS coordinates she gave me. Check them against yours in the system."

Connor stopped the Humvee with a jolt. "Go! Read! My numbers are right here in front of me."

"Alright. Take it easy, would you? North 39.192299; West 106.824473"

"Read 'em again and I'll read 'em back. No one told me we were going halfway to Canada."

"We're not," Hatch said after the triple check. "In fact, we *are* here."

"I'll be damned." Connor's tone softened. "Nice night, isn't it? No moon, just stars. You don't see skies like this in New York or L. A. All we're missing is a coffee shop."

"Surprise," Hatch said. He dug a thermos from one of the Humvee's many side compartments. "Okay, I'll admit the brother was a little strange. But he knew what was important. And you'll be happy to know it's not Starbucks."

"Right now I'd settle. Thanks for putting up with me, Hatch."

"I've done it for 20 years. No reason to stop now."

"Wise guy. Ready for my next question? Is it – "

"No, Randall. It's not Maxwell House. It's something even cheaper. You'll love it."

Connor sipped from the metal thermos cup, sat back and sighed. "What now?"

"We wait. If they aren't here by 2:00 a.m., we go looking for them. But I have a feeling they'll show up soon. Just a feeling, Randall. Ever get those?"

"Nope."

***

"I can't believe we didn't think of this before?" Beau put his arm around Nellie, who snuggled in closely.

"Care to be more specific?" H. L. said.

"Those guys who broke into the foundation back in seventy-one – "

"Eighty-one, Dixie."

"Jesus, H. L., do you always have to be so nitpicky?"

"It's why you're alive, Mr. Beauregard. What about those guys?"

"They were miners, right?"

"Former miners from Leadville."

"Whatever. Anyone who knows about mining isn't going to make the trip we just made every day to dig a few more inches of tunnel. We should have asked ourselves what they did to go back and forth – because if we had, we could have quit worrying about the rest of the way out. There was an electric line hooked up to a motor!"

"Stonewall, there's no electricity within two miles of here."

"But there *is* something called a generator. It doesn't make any difference how they got their current. My point is, they had an entire system rigged up to move that one car back and forth from the swimming pool on your map to where they dug the tunnel. You can see the wires all over the place on the other side of the car. They rode it up like a trolley, shoveled in all the mud and rocks from digging the tunnel, then rode it back down to the edge of the water. The car's still full of the stuff they piled into it, plus a couple of busted electric lamps and a bunch of tools. Once we get around the car, it really is a cakewalk down to the water. There's a foot bridge across the pool and, as far as I could see with my light, nothing else in our way."

"That *is* good news," H. L. said. "But let's not celebrate yet. Two of the most common deadly gasses in these old mines are heavier than air. Worse, H2S comes up from winzes. Foot bridge or not, we'll have to survive it. This means using oxygen whenever the multi-gas meter goes off. We've got three people and one tank, so we'll have to improvise intelligently. By the way, Dixie, how far down the shaft toward the winze did you go?"

"Pretty much all the way."

213

"Did the meter beep."

"I'm not sure. Maybe just a little."

H. L. shook her head in disbelief. "You forgot the meter, didn't you?"

"I must've buried it there at the foundation."

"The oxygen too?"

"Sorry," he said without much contrition.

"Sorry? That's all you can say?"

"Hey, H. L., lighten up. I went almost to the winze and I feel great. There's no gas down there and no need for oxygen. You rest while Nellie and I build a ramp over the car. Then you're going to get the kind of piggyback ride they don't give up North."

"God help me."

Nellie said, "H. L., don't forget. This is a day of miracles."

"Tell me that at my funeral."

***

It wasn't long until they were at the exit. It was dark outside, but not dark enough to blind them to the welded rebar gate blocking their way out. Beau put H. L. down, her protestations still ringing in his ears, then grabbed hold of the gate and tried to loosen it. "Great. We're still in jail. The thing is anchored in concrete."

"Start thinking, Johnny Reb," H. L. commanded. "Parks and Recreation must have put it there after the tunnel incident. They don't know much about parks but they know how to pour concrete."

"I'd say it's your turn to think."

"Quiet, you two," Nellie said. "Do we still have that bottle of whiskey?"

"If we do, I'm drinking it."

"No you're not, Beau. It might be our ticket out of here. Those guys, H. L. – you know, your friends. Do you think they're close?"

"Shine your light on my watch, Nellie."

"I don't have a light, remember?"

"I'll do it," Beau said. "Jesus, this thing's getting dim. Son-of-a-bitch. It just died."

"Did you get a look at the watch before it went out."

"I think so. Five after one."

"They should be here by now," H. L. said. "How far depends on how exact my coordinates were."

"Give me your flashlight, H. L. The batteries should still be good. I'll stick an arm through the gate and signal them."

The old woman patted her torn, muddy clothes. "Beauregard, look in my pack."

"Gone," he said after a thorough search produced only a bottle of Johnnie Walker. "It must've fallen out during your ride."

Nellie had found a dry patch of undergarment, ripped it loose and wound it around the tip of their extendable pole. "We'll douse this thing in whiskey. Who has something to light it with?"

CHAPTER THIRTY-THREE

Connor was sleeping, snoring loudly. Hatch elbowed him in the ribs. "Randall, what's that?"

"Nothing."

"Goddammit, wake up. You didn't even look."

"You see someone?"

"I think so," Hatch said, pointing.

Conner squinted into the night. It wasn't long until he spotted a tiny orange dot moving back and forth near the remains of the mine shack. "Okay, pal. I see it. Let's go."

The signal vanished but they knew where it had come from. After almost driving over the grate, they jumped down, hooked a winch cable to it and yanked it up.

Through a garble of words, they helped the bedraggled escapees out of their prison and into the troop carrier – Beau and Nellie in the canvas-covered truck bed, H.L. in the cab between Connor and Hatch.

Hatch shook his head. "Agent Gibbons, I'm not going to ask you how old you are, but what you just did most of our young hotshots at the Bureau couldn't do."

"H. L., please. I appreciate the compliment, but it belongs to my cohorts. They literally dragged and carried me the entire way. Connor and Hatch, if memory serves."

"Connor and Hatch, that's right."

"I'm glad you men made it over the pass. My brother, Robert, said it would be tight near the summit. I asked him to leave a tape measure on the seat."

"It helped," Connor said. "What now?"

"You'll need to enter a fresh set of coordinates. Tell me when you're ready."

"Go."

216

Connor programed the system with the eight-digit numbers H. L. had committed to memory, then read them back. Two mistakes, which he attributed to bad lighting. He made the changes and hit the accelerator. They headed back in the direction from which they had come.

Connor drove off-road over holes and stones. "Tough jeep, this thing."

"Now that Robert has outfitted it with a proper skin," H. L. added

"Yeah," Hatch said. "I heard these things had some weak spots when we first went into Iraq."

"Cheapskates in Washington," H. L. volunteered. "They're accomplished at cutting the wrong budgets. I'm sure you men are aware of that."

"Damn right," Connor said. Following the directions of the military GPS, he took a hard left onto a dirt path. "Where the hell are we going?"

"To fetch a mountain lion."

"WHAT?"

"Perhaps you know it by another name. Panther, cougar, puma."

"I hope you're not serious."

"You'll know when I'm not serious, Agent Connor. It does happen, but rarely."

"Jesus Christ!" Connor roared. "Why didn't you mention this in Rochester?"

"One step at a time, gentlemen. The first step was getting you here."

Connor shook his head. "Yeah, well you might not be keeping us. Let's hear about step two *in detail*. My butt's sore. If I don't like your plan, I'm taking a limo to the airport."

"You'll like it. Even if you don't, I hope you're not the type to bail at the last moment."

"I might be. Now kindly tell us why we're picking up a mountain lion. I've done lots of crazy stuff in my career but . . . this lion shit is over the top."

"When Connor says over the top," Hatch chimed in, "he means *really* over the top."

"Gentlemen, I've just crawled out from under a mountain. The least you could do is evaluate my plan before rejecting it. Now please listen – if not for me, then for the country you've sworn to protect."

"Okay," Connor said. "But talk fast. You need to start making sense."

"And you, Agent Connor, need to learn a little patience. You seem to be thinking more about yourself
than about helping me stop a man who has killed tens of thousands of Americans."

The inside of the Humvee filled with sounds of the road as all conversation momentarily ceased.

"Allow me to continue," H. L. finally said. "A married couple who has given liberally to the Historical Society is going to help us."

"Generous of them," Hatch said. "I assume they know what they're helping us with?"

"Unlikely. They're in France."

"WHAT?" Connor shouted again. "I don't like the sound of this. Let's have the details, Gibbons."

"Wait," Hatch said, "Before you begin, you should tell us how much the kids in the back know about any of this. You agree, right Randall?"

"It wouldn't hurt . . . H. L.?"

"Nellie and Dixie don't know anything about anything. As for the diary, they don't even know it exists. They have faith in my judgment."

"Who the hell is Dixie?" Connor rasped.

"The footballer from Ole Miss."

Another sharp left, and they drove toward the foothills on a well-maintained gravel road.

"Back to where I left off," Connor said. "Let's hear it. Your crackpot plan. And I mean every little detail."

"Which you would have heard by now if you'd foregone your tantrum. The couple I mentioned found a puma cub in the woods behind their house several years ago. It wasn't more than a few days old. The mother was either dead or had abandoned it. They took the cub home and kept it as long as possible. By the time it reached 30 pounds, they had to make a decision: give it to Animal Services or build a fenced shelter no one would be likely to discover. They chose the latter, and it has turned out to be a workable arrangement. They have a caretaker who comes by each week with food – usually a deer."

"Dead or alive?"

"Dead. The boy hunts year-round with a crossbow. I've watched the feeding from a golf cart. In the wild these animals look ferocious – if you're lucky enough to see one. But they're shy and solitary. Sightings are rare, attacks on humans are few. The cat we're on our way to visit was raised by people and is essentially tame. The boy places a deer in the same spot within the compound once a week. During it's natural hunting time – night, dawn or dusk – the cat slinks out of the woods and drags off the dead animal. We have a deer in the back of the Humvee, compliments of my brother. We also have several tranquilizer darts and the guns to

218

shoot them."

Hatch gestured out the window. "That palace we're passing, is that the lion king's house?"

"Yes."

"So how far from here is the compound?"

"A couple of miles."

"Okay," Connor said. "We're hearing a few random details but nothing I can make sense of. We drag a dead deer in there, shoot the lion with a tranquilizer gun and toss it into the jeep. Why? To keep your friends company? What does any of this have to do with Shiller?"

"I'm coming to that."

"Then for Christ's sake, hurry up."

"I'm giving you the information you'll need. In detail, as you requested. My brother hunts the beasts, which is legal in season. But he uses techniques that aren't. Females become sexually active during what's called their estrus period. They give off a distinct odor, which Robert and a chemist friend have managed to reproduce. Hence his hunting success.

"Now to Shiller. When he's in Aspen, he takes a predawn hike up the same trail, stops at the same spot to think about whatever he thinks about, then heads back down. Dixie writes for him and has accompanied him several mornings. The hike goes through the territory of a male mountain lion about the size of the cat we're going to tranquilize. Shiller, according to Dixie, is usually able to coax the cat out onto the trail with a large piece of meat."

Connor said, "Shiller is *usually* able. There's not a chance in hell anything involving unpredictable animal behavior is going to work."

"I would agree, Agent Connor. However, we are not counting on unpredictable animal behavior. Our lion, and perhaps the other one, will play a role in the *cover-up*, not the killing. All I ask is that you help me tranquilize the cat and load him into the Humvee. If you pass out at that point, Dixie will take over the driving. We'll drop you off near the highway. You can walk to your greasy spoon and have breakfast with the sheriff. By the time you've finished eating, Shiller will be dead."

"Yeah, right," Connor said. "How do you fantasize this will happen?"

"You don't need to know if you're not going to participate."

"I might change my mind. Not likely but possible."

"We arrive early at the summit of the trail where Shiller stops to rest. As you know, he has declined Secret Service protection. He'll be alone.

Two of the tranquilizer darts I mentioned are loaded with fatal doses of ketamine. Dixie hides where he knows the General walks and darts him when he comes into view. He dies. One of us removes the dart, douses the body in my brother's estrus scent and, if needed, rolls the body onto the meat Shiller always brings with him. We drive back to town and park the Humvee behind my abode where Robert will be waiting to drive it back to Crested Butte.

"Two male lions, ours awake and agitated by now, find themselves in a single territory. Both the meat and the scent will eventually draw them to Shiller's corpse. If the lions arrive at the same time, they will fight. The vanquished will flee, the victor will ravage Shiller's corpse – first to get to the meat then, in all likelihood, to continue his feast with human flesh. And if the lions don't arrive at the same time, its first come first serve. Whatever happens, the cause of death will seem obvious. Questions?"

"Lots of them," Connor said. "From what I know, animal tranquilizers take time to work. Shiller will be armed. All of you will die. Have you thought about this? Second, how will you set up your too-small-to-succeed ambush without leaving Humvee tracks on the trail Shiller hikes? He's a military man. I guarantee you he'll notice them, no matter how dry the ground is. Third – "

"That's quite enough," H. L. said. "The enclosure is close so I'll be brief. You will have heard, perhaps in relation to surgery, of pentothal. The darts meant for the lion we're about to free, as well as those for Shiller, contain a pentothal derivative. The drug is fast-acting. Shiller will be out within seconds, giving the ketamine mixture time to act. In any case, we won't be in the area by then."

"I don't think so. You'll all be dead. You've got two amateurs with you."

"You could, of course, change that. I know breakfast is important, however . . . "

"Don't piss me off. I'm considering if we should help."

CHAPTER THIRTY-FOUR

Hours earlier, Shiller had signed off on the plan of his Delta Force apostates: they would blow up the Carlyle House with the three people he needed to eliminate inside. The accident would be staged so that investigators could not help but conclude a gas leak had been to blame, and nothing in the crater would suggest otherwise. In light of these findings any proceeding against him, legal or otherwise, would rest on hearsay. The indiscretions of his men would perhaps cause a small bump on the road to the White House, nothing more. All factual evidence pointed to success. And yet . . . the prospect of impending failure dominated his thoughts.

Why was this so? He could find no rational answer. Just after dark, he had watched a blinding flash above the hills between his ranch and Aspen. He could tell from years in the field that it had been a devastating explosion, similar to what you saw when a 500 pound bomb found its mark. Even now, an hour later, the sky glowed incandescent orange. It was clear that the intense fire still raged out of control. Yet Shiller, who took pride in his keen rational mind, continued to feel something akin to superstition.

Could his targets have escaped? Could blame for the explosion be pinned on him? No, they couldn't. But something beyond the world of reason called to him like a whisper in the dark, warning him of disaster.

Not comfortable with this unfamiliar assault of premonition, he retired to his study to look for a reason that would allow him to disregard it. After a lengthy Internet search, he found an article in the archives of the *Aspen Times* that provided a bit of clarity. In 1981, miners in search of a reputed gold stash had busted into the Historical Society's headquarters. It was hardly a normal intrusion. They had tunneled 200 yards through rock and earth to reach the basement wall of the Carlyle House. The ingenuity required to pull off such a feat, the *Times* reported, was rivaled only by the intruders' stupidity in believing they would find the mythical gold stash –

a bit of folklore conclusively debunked during Teddy Roosevelt's days. The Director of the Historical Society since the late Seventies, Harriet Gibbons, had held the two thugs at gunpoint until the police arrived. Her skill in avoiding pickax and shovel attacks she attributed to her previous career, that of an FBI Special Agent – a career she never dreamed would be of use in her new role of preserving Victorian Aspen.

A quick search of government records, to which Shiller had easy access, verified Gibbons' credentials and established both her competence and bravery on the job. Shiller felt better. A world without reason was a world whose existence he had long ago dismissed. He hadn't fallen victim to a premonition. Rather, it was the voice of reason shouting at him to wake up. They, his three targets, might have escaped into the labyrinth of abandoned mines and shafts. Whether they would get much further if they had was a legitimate question. He doubted it, but he had to be sure. Shiller was a cautious man.

The maps! When he had retired from the military and bought his ranch, he had studied every aspect of the town's history. Along the way, he had come across archival records of the silver mining claims staked in the days of Aspen's prosperity – and promptly archived photocopies of them in a little-used office. He located the oversized sheets of paper in a file cabinet. One by one, he unfolded the claims maps and spread them out across an architecture and drafting desk.

On the second map, he located the only spot at which the gold diggers of 1981 could have begun their tunnel: the boundary of the Redmond Claim alone passed near the Carlyle House. If the intended victims of tonight's explosion *had* escaped, this was the only exit they could have used.

Could have, thought Shiller. It was of course unlikely that they had managed to get out; but unlikely was not impossible. This he had learned more often than he cared to remember on the battlefield. Shiller next downloaded a topographical map of the area. Most of the Redmond Claim covered land along the relatively level base of a mountain. He foraged through articles written at the time of the break in. Access into the mine was at a spot he might be able to see from his reading room. When he searched "Redmond," a photograph of the collapsed wooden shack abutting the mine entrance showed up on his screen.

He had the information he needed; the only remaining question was whether he would have to drive to higher ground to see the shack. He hoped not: his years of military service had schooled him in the boredom and discomfort of nighttime vigils.

After a final look through the claims for another mine entrance that might be of use, he walked to his "museum," a collection of small military devices that had served him well over the years. He selected a pair of ITT Ellis Dual Sensor Night Vision Goggles recently sent to him by the company for evaluation. He then proceeded to his reading room. Along the way, he stopped at one of several wet bars to pour himself a glass of his oldest and best Scotch. Fill it up for the long wait, he thought. Or better yet, take the entire bottle. Once he had the shack in his sights, whether he was inside or outside, he wasn't going to abandon his post.

***

The Scotch was good, the night vision goggles better. By midnight, the General had located the mine entrance. He doubted anyone would emerge, but if they did he would personally deal with the situation. This meant eliminating the three before news of their survival became known. His mind sifted through the options at his disposable. There were many, and none of them struck him as unpleasant. On the contrary, the prospect of completing the job his men had botched presented him with the type of hands-on challenge he loved.

That challenge presented itself sooner than he expected. A fortified military transporter plowed into the field of his night vision and stopped near the mine. An hour later, a small flame signaled to the Humvee. The jeep then drove over a stretch of rocky terrain to the mine opening. He watched, stunned, as one of the men got out of the transporter and hooked a winch cable to some kind of a grate. If he wasn't mistaken, that man was the smaller of the two FBI Special Agents who had been stationed in Aspen. At the wheel would be the larger agent.

Wellington, the old woman from the Historical Society and Nellie Vaughn, the girl who had overheard his men, were helped by both agents out of the mine shaft and into the Humvee. Shiller got a better view of the FBI men: his suppositions had been correct. He watched the transporter drive across open terrain until it disappeared behind a rise.

His mind shifted into high gear. An attempt on his life was sure to follow while his escapees were still presumed dead. But when and where? He carefully went through the possibilities until he had ruled out all but one. Wellington and Vaughn knew the trail on which he took his morning walks. It was remote, and he followed the same daily schedule. If they had any sense, they would be waiting in ambush for him. Two kids weren't a threat, but the presence of FBI agents – two in their prime, one ancient but smart – transformed it into one. He had to get there ahead of them.

At the front gate, Doug kept watch while the other two slept. Shiller jumped out of his Land Rover. "Listen carefully. There's going to be an attempt on my life. You know where I hike. I want you and your boys at the trailhead in an hour. Make a round of the old barns before you leave. We'll need chains, coyote traps – you get the picture. Wait for me in absolute silence. I have to make a stop before I join you."

Shiller hit the gas and disappeared down the long gravel road.

***

Hollis had just ordered the $495 truffle tasting menu at Element 47, the restaurant in his Aspen hotel, when the blast went off. He stood and gasped along with the other diners as the tall windows shook and waves of thunder echoed in his ears. But his shocked response was an act. He knew exactly what had happened.

After waiting for reassurance from the restaurant staff that a residential gas explosion in a nearby home was to blame, Hollis sat down and sipped his Pernod. He shook his head with disdain as many of the diners filed out. It was ridiculous, this pervasive fear. Everyone had seen him come in wearing one of his trademark Italian suits. Everyone knew he was the spokesman of the presidential candidate who vowed to destroy God's Wrath. Everyone could also see through the floor-to-ceiling windows that the explanation of the restaurant staff had been honest. Stuff happened all the time – fires, explosions. To assume terrorism was the cause of all bad things struck him as ridiculous. Yet he knew a little more about terrorism than the man in the street. He wondered, had he been that man, if he would have had the same knee-jerk reaction each time a fire cracker went off. Oh well, he thought, that was their thing. He should rejoice over their fear. After all, if things worked out, it was his ticket to Washington. In time he'd reflect on where the mission stood; for the moment, he just wanted to relax.

***

And relax he did. Much later he was comfortably ensconced in the lounge of the hotel bar. The blast had been music to his ears; it had also thinned out the usual bar crowd. A welcome late-night calm enveloped him. This was good. He needed to think without distractions.

Hollis's liberal expense account had led him into the more esoteric realms of drink. Among his after-dinner favorites was Tequila, and Element 47's bar had a Tequila selection second to none. He ordered another

224

$70 shot of *Casa Dragones Joven* and settled a little deeper into the soft leather cushions of his armchair. Here he would realistically assess Shiller's situation and, more importantly, what it augured for his own future.

Jim and Allen succeeded in razing the Historical Society; about that there could be no question. Shiller had ordered the men not to stage their "accident" until they could eliminate all three of his targets at once. The men followed orders. This meant the girl, her boyfriend and the Society's director were dead.

So what could have happened *before* the hit to jeopardize the mission? One of the FBI agents who had earlier been stationed in Aspen returned to town shortly after the incident in the kitchen. He had been seen with the girl and the director of the Historical Society. He and his agency partner clearly knew the girl's story.

But who else in the intelligence community knew? Shiller was right if he assumed that these two agents would be hesitant to reveal their findings until they had hard evidence. The very idea that the terrorist attacks attributed to God's Wrath had been carried out by the Republican presidential nominee seemed far-fetched, if not downright ridiculous. It was not something professionals *without proof* would try to sell to their superiors.

Still, this was an assumption. Even if unlikely, it was possible that the entire intelligence community was aware of the girl's story. And there was another scenario that couldn't be ruled out. The agents might be more inclined to go up the ladder with their suspicions if they did not believe an accident had destroyed the Historical Society – even if forensic evidence contradicted them. If this were the case, they would pass on their information as quickly as possible, knowing they could be next on Shiller's list.

Hollis would begin by reflecting on the worst-case assumption – that intelligence and law enforcement at all levels had been, or would soon be, briefed on the possibility that Shiller was behind the attacks on America. What, if anything, did that change? He thought for some time about his own question and concluded that it would change nothing.

Hollis was surprised by the result of his reasoning, but in retrospect it seemed obvious. Even if the agents who knew the truth did not share their suspicions with their superiors, they would anonymously stir up curiosity in the media. This, in turn, would alert every player in the legal system and intelligence community to the existence of a new, if yet unproven, hypothesis. Investigations were sure to follow.

So what? All accusations against Shiller would still rest on the shaky foundation of hearsay; all media publicity could be painted by Shiller's staff as propaganda coming from the other end of the political spectrum. In the event of a trial, which there would not be unless new evidence surfaced, the General could drag out the early proceedings until he was sworn into office. Once he became president, any issues still alive could easily be suppressed.

The bartender came around for last call. Hollis charged the bill to his room, but not before he had put in an order for another Tequila. He returned to his thoughts.

What was yet to analyze? Three things, one obvious. Shiller would have realized this by now, but the elimination of the FBI agents in possession of the truth could not but increase any suspicion of foul play. He imagined himself in the morning mentioning this to his boss and being brushed aside like a dimwitted servant.

Now to less obvious areas of concern. Could there possibly be any record of the original mission that had survived the Albrecht Administration? He didn't think so. Dozens of investigations had turned up exactly nothing.

Finally, could there be any evidence regarding the terrorist attacks that could later be traced back to the group? Some said the technology required to carry out the attacks seemed beyond the capacity of God's Wrath. This ensured that increasingly sophisticated investigations were on the horizon. But time was on their side. Once Shiller became president, the investigations would be declared fruitless and called off.

So that, really, was it. A little stalling would be necessary, but Shiller's answer to America's need for change and security had by now become an entrenched part of the political landscape. It could not be dislodged in time to stop the mission.

His Tequila arrived at the same time as the General. "Come with me," Shiller ordered. "We need to change the issues you will and will not address at Thursday's press conference. What about your drink. Have you paid for it?"

"I have." Hollis was already on his feet. He walked with Shiller through the lobby to the General's Land Rover, which was idling under the watchful eye of a hotel attendant.

Shiller drove to an empty spot in the parking lot and stopped. "Jake, I've received intelligence from a source I trust. There's going to be an attempt to assassinate me. My informers suspect it will be this morning on my usual hiking path. You went up there with me once if I'm not mistaken."

"Yes, Sir. Twice to be exact."

"Do you remember the summit of the trail with the large boulders and rock formations?"

"Yes. We sat down on one of those boulders."

"That's precisely where I will be shot. However, I won't be hiking. With the information I have, we'll be able to set up an ambush well before dawn. I've enlisted my men at the front gate for ground support. I'd like you to find a spot with a good view of the area, a spot from which you could hit multiple targets in rapid succession. Don't shoot unless absolutely necessary. And no attempt at distance records. Five-hundred yards or less. One more thing. I would like you to leave immediately."

CHAPTER THIRTY-FIVE

"She didn't tell us it was a country mile up to the lion's table."

"Don't complain, Randall. It's a nice night, one like we won't see again for a long time. The stars, the smell of pines, the – "

"Be quiet. I don't know why we agreed to this in the first place. She had me convinced for a minute. Now I'm back where I started. The old bitch might be tough, but she's out of her mind."

"Excuse me," Nellie said. "She's the most remarkable person I've ever met. If it wasn't for her, Aspen would look like a strip mall. Who do *you* know who is 74 years old and could escape an explosion by crawling half the night through abandoned mines?"

"He knows who couldn't," Hatch said. "You're listening to him right now. A forty-six-year-old male who's having trouble walking across a meadow. I'm telling you, Randall. You need to lose weight and get in shape. This is as good a place as any to start. You should thank the old lady for the initial push."

Connor remained uncharacteristically calm. "Maybe you're right, Hatch. Not about 'thanking the old lady' but about losing weight and getting in shape. I haven't told you this and I shouldn't be telling you now. Kristýna has invited me to Prague for Christmas. If I don't stop eating, I'll have to make a stop in Memphis to find trousers that fit."

"Kristýna?" Nellie said. "Who is Kristýna?"

"My UNICEF kid."

"Agent Connor, I can't believe it! You have a secret lover overseas!"

"And you're as nuts as your boss."

"Agent Connor," Beau said, "we all know Nellie's mental state. But you don't really believe H. L. is nuts, do you?" Beau carried the dead deer from the Humvee effortlessly as he spoke. Connor struggled to catch his breath.

"Look," he rasped, "I go by what I see. So, yes, nuts would be the right word."

"Well, she's not. I thought the same thing when I met her. She's really different from how she seems at first."

"You were SBW Three when you met her. Now you're Dixie" Connor said. "That's what happens to people who fall under the spell of old witches."

"You shouldn't say stuff like that. About her, I mean. You can say whatever you like about me, but Nellie and I care a lot about H. L."

"Look, I'm sorry. Fact is, people change. She was a hell of an agent when she was young. Then she took a mean shot from a nine millimeter and, pow, her career was over. That was 40 years ago. Maybe it's the wound, maybe it's dementia, hell if I know. I told you my opinion of her sanity. Just because you couldn't kill her with a baseball bat doesn't make her sane."

"Hell of an *agent*?" Nellie said. "What's that supposed to mean?"

Hatch, who knew Nellie better than Connor from his day in Aspen, jumped into the conversation. "She never told you she was with the Bureau?"

"The FBI?"

"The FBI. It was a long time ago, like Connor says, back before you guys were born. We checked her out before we agreed to meet. Nothing but praise in her files."

"So *that's* how she knows all this spy stuff," Beau exclaimed. "It's been a huge mystery, at least for me. When Nellie told her the things she'd heard Shiller's men talking about, H. L. turned into someone we didn't know. I mean, right there, on the spot."

"It's true," Nellie said. "I've worked for her almost two years. I know she mentioned she had another life before she got involved with Victorian houses, but I wouldn't have guessed in a hundred lifetimes she'd been an FBI agent."

"We'd better stop talking," Hatch warned. "There's that tree we're supposed to be watching for. You can just make it out up ahead. She said the lion's table isn't too far past it."

"I don't get it," Connor said. "If this man eater is tame, why can't he come to the gate for his dinner. Even jail birds do that."

"Maybe he's not tame anymore," Hatch said. "What difference does it make? He's going to be sedated anyway."

Fifteen minutes later they found the stone slab where H. L. had told them to leave the deer. There were trees and bushes all around, plenty of things to serve as cover.

It must have been a while since the beast had eaten, because it appeared almost immediately.

"Jesus," whispered Connor. "That's one hell of a cat. You call that thing tame?"

The animal heard him and briefly looked up. Then, ignoring Connor, it locked it's fangs into the deer's neck and started to drag it toward the woods. Connor stood up as quietly as he could and aimed the tranquilizer gun. Bullseye to the hind quarters. H. L. was right. The stuff was good. The lion slowed down after a few seconds, dropped the deer and collapsed.

Nellie, who was carrying a hammock from the back of the jeep, stepped out from behind a nearby bush. "I'm glad that wasn't a bullet."

Connor shook his head. "You won't be if this thing wakes up while you're taking him for a ride. I'm guessing you don't know how long he'll be out."

"According to H. L., around 45 minutes. We can stick him with another one of those green darts if we have to."

"Okay. Let's get this guy into the hammock and haul him down the hill. Who carries first?"

"I'm in," Hatch said. "What about you, Sir Beau Wellington Three?"

"He's not SBW Three anymore," Connor grumbled. "Remember? He's been demoted to Dixie. No telling what *you'll* be demoted to if you fall under her spell."

"Agent Connor," Nellie said, "what's wrong with you? I hope you gave her a blanket before we left."

"She got her own. She'll be warm. She'll also be out cold when we get to the jeep."

***

H. L. wasn't out cold but she was clearly feeling the aftershock of all she had been through. Her back was out again, her legs cramped when she moved, chills racked her slight frame. Her voice, however, was strong. "Everything in place in the truck bed?"

"Yep," Connor said. "Lions, darts, footballers, tarts. By the way, your cat wasn't tame."

"You apparently haven't seen a wild one. Let's go. We're late as it is and Dixie might not be the best off-road driver. Three miles to the highway and you two can get out – with my sincere thanks for bringing the jeep over the pass."

Connor grunted as he fumbled around for the rotary start switch. "Lights? Do you mind?"

"I mind," H. L. said. "We're going 'black.'"

As the Humvee began to roll, she closed her eyes and willed herself into a sort of trance. She needed a better image of what lay ahead, and hoped distant memories would provide it . . .

***

The path Shiller hiked was known to her; she'd been up it a couple of times years ago with her former husband, Johnston, and had found the panoramic views at the summit spectacular. But there the path ended, closed by boulders and rock formations. Some you could climb, some were too high or too smooth. She and her long-deceased husband had once taken a high trail above and made their way down to the other side of the boulders. The path, rockier and less scenic, wasn't one they wanted to tackle on foot, but Johnston had been curious where it came out. No one seemed to know, but he finally found a jeep enthusiast who did. Hard to find, hard to navigate, he'd told Johnston. Not recommended, not even for jeeps. The trailhead could be reached through an unobtrusive gap in the foliage behind a defunct gas station. On the drive from Basalt along the Frying Pan River the road passed directly in front of the place. That's how you got there, and that's how you cracked an oil pan, blew a tire and destroyed your suspension. Have a look, but don't try to drive it . . .

***

Going black, thought Connor. No interior lights, no parking lights, no brake lights. He could see okay. The night was black, but the stars shone brightly. His eyes had adjusted. He'd been on the gravel road for a long time. No problem with vision. Which didn't mean there was no problem. His ex-wife, Betty, though officially banished from his conscious and un-conscious mind, had found a way to weasel in through some rodent hole in his psyche he'd left unplugged. There she was, just her face, bigger and more disdainful than ever. "Breakfast, you son of a bitch. You're going to have your beloved heap of body-bloating cholesterol while an old lady and two wonderful youngsters get themselves killed by the man about to become an American Hitler. Disgusting. Cowardly. Something the old Connor would never have done. No wonder Kristýna Sondheim left your fat ass. You heard me, Randall. Disgusting and cowardly."

"Shut up, you miserable bitch!" Connor shouted into the blackness. H. L. made an instantaneous return to the present.

"Excuse me?"

231

"Nothing," Connor said. "I mean, it's personal. I was formally addressing my goddamn ex-wife."

H. L. almost smiled. "It's alright, Randall. You'll be amused to know that I was also thinking about my ex. Not the same way, though. In friendly terms."

"You were asleep."

"My memory wasn't. He pointed me in a direction I hadn't thought about, the right direction. You're coming to the highway. Stop! I'll leave the kids in back. If you could help me with the driver's seat before you leave, it would be kind. As high and as close as you can get it. When you reach the highway, take a right. It's not far to town."

"Look," Connor said, "we aren't going to leave you. Crazy or not, we're in this to the end. I just hope you know what you're doing. So forget about the seat adjustments. Hatch, go tell those kids in back that the cab is occupied."

H. L. didn't seem surprised, and Connor knew why. *She* had sent Betty to shame him. In fact, *she* had started the shaming a long time ago with her talk about breakfast. But he had to admit. As obnoxious as they were, which was pretty damned obnoxious, the bitches were both right. Yep, both of them. This old lady beside him and the ex-wife who'd just visited him. You couldn't enjoy your sausage when a man who had killed 65,000 Americans was about to add three more to his list. Connor was in. And he was done thinking of H. L. as an old bitch. She was a former special agent of the FBI. She deserved respect, his respect. Besides, she had worked hard to earn his cooperation, even if the mountain lion bullshit was off the wall. So they'd go kill Shiller with darts and *then* have breakfast. The coffee would taste better. The bacon too.

"Stay dark," H. L. said, her voice even stronger than before. "Take a left onto the highway, then a right when you come to Basalt. You'll have a stretch of easy driving . . . and then a shot at the impossible. You can do it. My husband said you can't, but you can. We put a man on the moon. Putting this Humvee a few miles up a hill will be a joke."

"Say you."

***

"I know he smells," Nellie said, "but I still think he's cute. Look at his tail. It wraps all the way around him. And that perfect black nose. Maybe we could raise one ourselves."

They were stretched out in the covered back of the jeep with the drugged mountain lion between them. The ride was smooth, good for

232

administering the second dose of tranquilizer. Without word of warning, Beau jabbed the beast in the buttocks with a green syringe.

"Beau! It wasn't time yet."

"The hell it wasn't. I saw him twitch an ear. Let's keep him in pet mode a little longer."

She stroked the beast's back. "Tell me before you drug him again. I'm serious. You might kill him with an overdose if you're not careful."

"I love you," Beau said. "I'd kiss you if this guy's giant ass wasn't in the way. If you like him so much, why don't I buy you a Maine Coon kitten. They get almost as big as panthers."

Before they could continue their discussion, the jeep slowed, plowed through bushes they could hear scraping the canvass roof and began to bump wildly about. "Next stop, Shiller," Beau said. "We'll have to help your cat out of the jeep when we get there – if he hasn't eaten us yet."

CHAPTER THIRTY-SIX

"Jesus Christ," Kent said, "this thing is heavy. What would you say to a break, Sir?"

"We don't have time for a break."

"I just thought – "

"Don't think," Shiller said. "Walk. You guys lift weights. What's the problem with a few bear traps?"

"Sir," Kyle whispered. "Sir, it's not the traps. It's this goddamn chain."

"Deal with it. You're the one who decided what to bring. And watch your step. Night vision distorts your depth perception."

"Tell me about it," groaned Doug, who had already hit the deck more than once. "The General's right about depth perception. You go down wearing 200 pounds of metal, you feel like staying down."

"Quiet," Shiller said. "We're almost there and I don't have an ETA for God's Wrath."

Onward and upward they marched until the trail became broad and level. Through gaps between large boulders, they could see the lights of Aspen, those still on at 3:00 a.m. Also visible near the base of the mountains was another light, the ember-strewn crater left by the explosion.

"Okay," Shiller announced, "we're here first or we'd already be dead. How many traps are attached to that chain?"

"Seven, Sir. That farmer you got the ranch from was . . . "

"Finish your sentence," Shiller ordered.

"Loaded for bear, Sir."

"Not funny. Stretch out the chain alongside the path. Set the traps. Find a spot where you'll be hidden from anyone who comes for me. *Then* you can rest. But stay alert and *stay quiet*. I don't know when or if the attack will come – or what it will look like if it does. You might have to improvise. Take prisoners if you're able. Since you've brought these

234

goddamn traps, we might as well use them."

"General, respectfully," Kent said. "Why would we fuck around with prisoners if we get a clear shot?"

"That's the last question you're going to ask, any of you. If we're lucky enough to capture the bastards, we'll let them star in our first video. Take up your posts. And remember: surprise is our best defense."

***

Hollis was as comfortable as he could get up here, perched on a sawed-off tree trunk 700 yards away. He had watched what he could see of the strange procession up the trail. It was almost as if Jesus had hired Sherpas to carry his cross. Shiller led the way, both hands free. He still wore the same business suit that made his appearance at the Element 47 Bar seem like . . . well, like business. People were weird. It seemed he could have tossed the hiking boots and photographer's jacket he usually wore up here into the trunk. But Hollis had learned years ago that Shiller always had a reason for what he did. If he was wearing a business suit, it meant something. Just what it meant up in the mountains at three in the morning, he didn't have a clue. A strange guy, Shiller. Maybe that's how *all* men with balls the size of planets and enough gray matter to fill oceans were. He couldn't say for sure. Hollis had only met one such man in his life, the man he was presently looking at through his scope.

***

"Goddammit, H. L.," Connor barked, throwing the Humvee into reverse. "How the hell are we going to get through this rock field? Your idea of driving dark sucks."

"Is that so?"

"Yes, it is so. You're not driving. Some of these things are the size of tanks. I need light or we're gonna bust something. How far to the top?"

"A ways yet," H. L. said. "I don't know this trail."

"You don't know it? Really? I'd say we've gone as far as we're gonna get. You stay here with Nellie and the lion while the men walk up."

"No. We'll need to get out of here fast when the job is done."

"You wanna drive?"

"No. But I do have an idea. Send Hatch out there with his pen light. He'll walk ahead and signal you when he's found a clear path. I might not know this trail, Connor, but I know these mountains. Around here, a boulder field below the timber line doesn't go on forever."

"Hatch, you heard the lady. Find me a way forward."

"Calm down, Randall, or you'll blow a gasket before the jeep. We've come at least two miles. If we can get through these rocks, we might find something drivable."

"Hurry up. I want to get this over with."

While Connor waited, H. L. appeared to fall asleep. He notice that chills were racking her body. They seemed to get more violent the longer they went on. Not good. If she conked out, they would be lost.

A pin prick of light shone up ahead. Connor drove slowly toward it, scraping a few trees and stones but hitting nothing head-on. Five more mini-advances and he drove onto a roadbed of shale and stone. He knew this stuff from the pass. He could handle it if he didn't smash into anything. He would drive slowly, as slowly as a Sunday driver in Shreveport.

Hatch climbed in and slammed the door, banging H. L. out of her semi-conscious state. "Looks good for a ways, Randall. It must be getting lighter because I can see trees up head. The gods are with us."

"Yeah, well the gods have a way of going deaf when you need them. Let's keep Heaven out of this."

"I didn't say 'God.' I said 'the gods.' They don't live in Heaven. How's she doing?"

"Not great. Check behind your seat for blankets, a tarp, anything. She's shaking like crazy and passing out."

"I'm fine," H. L. said. "I'll worry about me. You worry about driving."

An hour and two boulder fields later, they came to the giant stone barricade H. L. vaguely remembered from her hikes 40 years ago.

"What now," Connor said. "What's the plan, H. L.? We're not getting over or around this thing."

"No, we're not. This is the end of the line. If you notice, you are starting to see even better. Dawn is close; so is Shiller. Turn this thing around and shut it off. Get Beau and the lion out of the back. Bring Nellie in here. She can stay with me. While you're doing that, I'll load two pistols with the death punch. Hurry."

***

"How much time 'till this thing wakes up," Connor asked.

"I'm not sure," Beau said. "We gave him another shot while you were stopped."

"Okay, let's get him out. We'll put him over there onto the side of the hill. Dixie, you'll be making a trail of drops with the smelly stuff. Hatch and I will do the shooting. Nellie, you're staying here with H. L."

"No way. H. L. will be fine." She dug her nails into Connor's arm.

236

"I'm not leaving Beau."

"You are, and please shut up. Shiller will be here any minute."

She kicked him in the shin. Connor flinched. He knew she was going to give him trouble, Betty-style. He decided it would easier and faster if he let her do what she wanted.

"Kindly take your claws out of my arm," he whispered. "Keep your voice down. Come if you want, but not a sound. Hatch, Beau. No more talking."

They unloaded the sleeping lion and tossed the hammock back into the jeep. While Hatch and Connor returned to the cab for the pistols H. L. had loaded, Nellie and Beau moved toward the cliff and looked for an opening. Beau directed traffic when the agents caught up, sending Connor through a level zigzagging gap and Hatch up an easy climb. Beau followed Connor into the clearing where Shiller liked to entice Rommel out of the forest, pointed the agents toward the other side of the trail and pulled Nellie in the opposite direction. They hid behind the boulder Shiller always sat on to rest and reflect when he had finished his climb.

A pink sliver of dawn stretched along the eastern horizon. It wouldn't be long until they heard his footsteps.

CHAPTER THIRTY-SEVEN

Dawn had begun to break.

"Beau," Nellie whispered, "Beau, what's that thing?"

"Shhh."

"No. You have to see it." She nodded at a tiny gap between the boulders. "Out there. On the path."

He pretended to look, shrugged his shoulders, pulled her toward him to make sure she was hidden.

"Beau, please. Please!"

He put a finger to his lips and leaned toward the gap. She could feel him tense. Maybe he knew.

The thing was a rusty metal ring a couple feet across with curved teeth all around it. The teeth looked sharp. Thank God, she thought. Thank God they hadn't stepped on it.

Beau wasn't going to let her have a second look, so Nellie tried to conjure in her mind's eye an image of what she had seen. It looked like some medieval torture device. A chain, also rusty, snaked toward the edge of the trail. Where did it go? Did it just end like a snake's tail? No! It was attached to a fatter chain. A fatter chain running down a miniature gulley made by runoff when it rained. She tried to pull Beau toward her, but he yanked his arm away and took a step toward the opening. In the dim light, she watched him shake his head. When she pulled his arm the second time, he came closer and pushed her against the huge rock that hid them.

"They're animal traps," he whispered.

"There's more than one?"

"Yes. My uncle uses them at home to keep bears out of the garbage."

"Dear God."

She pulled free of Beau and ventured another glance. This time it wasn't traps that caught her attention. Two of Shiller's gatekeepers were violently shoving Hatch and Connor out on the trail. They held guns to the agents' heads. The dart pistols lay on the ground.

Before she could warn Beau, the third gatekeeper came out of nowhere and knocked him to the ground with the butt of a pistol. While she looked on, frozen with horror, she felt cold metal against her nape. She started to turn around when someone grabbed her hair and pulled her viciously upward.

"Little Nellie," Shiller said, his voice unmistakable even now. He pushed the pistol into the side of her neck until it wouldn't go any further. "Walk. Don't fight me or I'll shoot."

She knew he meant what he said. Their ambush had been ambushed. They were going to die. "Beau!" she called out, feeling as if she would faint.

"Not another word," Shiller said. "If I give the order, Kyle shoots. A messy ending to your affair. Not interesting but graphic. Walk. Look down. Don't step on a trap. They're for later."

In what seemed the blink of an eye, all four of them were in the clearing, the three men with a gun to their heads, Nellie with a gun to her throat and a powerful hand gripping her hair.

"Relax Nellie," Shiller said. "If no one moves, not your friend, not the FBI, if no one moves, you might live. So men, don't make me do it. I always liked her, but if any of you so much as twitches, you'll force me to pull the trigger. *You'll* force me, understand. Whoever moves will be the killer. I will merely be delivering the message."

***

H. L. knew something had gone wrong when she heard voices through her partly opened window, voices not belonging to anyone in her group. She knew she had to do something, but what? Both of the pistols with lethal darts were with the FBI agents. The animal tranquilizer guns and leftover darts would be in the back of the jeep. If she could get to them, she might be able to come up with a plan. But she was still shaking badly and almost totally incapacitated from the mine tunnel escape.

She managed to push open the side door. Fortunately the Humvee was pointing downhill. The door, weighted with armor, stayed open. Gravity was her friend – until it suddenly turned on her. Looking down, she saw there was no running board, no step, nothing for her to put her foot on. Getting in she'd had help. She must have assumed she'd have help getting out.

Given the jeep's high clearance, she estimated the distance from her seat to the rock-hard ground to be around four feet. Maybe she should get down on the Humvee floor and hang her legs out. Would that make any difference? Maybe, maybe not. From four feet she would crack an ankle, shatter a hip, break a leg – of that she was certain. From three feet the results would probably be the same. Still, three feet was better than four.

She couldn't sit here forever hoping for a tire to go flat. She laid down and stretched out on the seat, legs facing the exit, and tried to lower herself with the help of the seat belt. No luck. Her arms were shot. She crashed onto the jeep floor so hard it almost knocked the wind out of her. Move! Still gasping for breath, she rolled onto her stomach and shoved herself backwards, a little at a time, until her legs were hanging out the open door. She still couldn't touch the ground. She would have to let herself drop – how far she couldn't tell. But there was a chance she could slow her fall if she grabbed the raised metal along the bottom of the door opening on her way down.

Don't think! What's going to happen is going to happen whether you go now or next year. She pushed and shoved until she dropped, feet first. Her hands caught the raised metal but they were too weak to make a difference. Her heels hit first, she lost her balance and fell backwards. Her head whacked the ground. Not pleasant but there were no sharp pains, no broken bones. Could she get to her feet? If so, it would take a lot of willpower; her body couldn't do the job alone.

She recognized a voice, Shiller's. He seemed to be holding court, giving some kind of a sick lecture. It filled her with disgust; it also gave her hope. If he was talking, someone was listening. She had heard no shots; her people must be alive. But how long would they stay alive? The thought jolted her into action. She managed to roll over and get to her knees. No strength, none. She reached for the metal rise beneath the Humvee's open door. It had done nothing to break her fall, but it was going to help her now. With both hands inside the door and her knees screaming for strength that wasn't there, she stood. Exhausted, she leaned against the jeep and tried to think.

The spare tranquilizer darts and gun to shoot them were in the back where Beau and Nellie had been. She had to get them, but how? It would be impossible to pull herself up to the bed, let alone to get down again. She'd have to worry about that later. Right now she needed to get to the back of the Humvee and look inside.

Still leaning against the jeep, she took a small sideways step. The pain that hadn't been there after her fall returned, worse than ever. Her back was a body-length nerve without bone. Her hips, knees, ankles and feet felt as if someone had driven nails into them. But she was moving, faster each time Shiller raised his voice. The physical pain of a lifetime seemed compressed into one critical moment. She ignored it and continued to shimmy sideways until she reached the end of the jeep.

She could see inside. They had brought the hammock back after unloading the lion. Did it cover the box with the darts? What about the gun?

She spotted the box, scarcely visible in the murky light. It was in a far corner, at least eight feet from where she stood.

Shiller began pontificating more loudly, disrupting her ability to think. And the mountain lion! It was waking up. She heard a clawing as weak as her own in the dirt, heard strange noises accompanying Shiller's sermon. Think!

Beau had never handled the pistol. He had been in back with tranquilizer syringes to make sure the lion stayed calm. The pistol. Where was it? Connor had used it to tranquilize the lion. He hadn't brought it back into the cab with him.

Then she noticed a length of fabric holster strap hanging from a closed compartment she could reach. Luck, good luck. The compartment was not locked, the gun was still in the holster, two tranquilizer darts were still in their pockets.

In minutes, she was wearing the high-riding holster, not that much different from the gun holsters she had worn 40 years ago. She shortened the long hoop over her neck and attached the belt that kept the holster in place between her waist and arms. She was ready. Her eyes were on the opening where Beau had directed Connor to pass through the rock formation. She had some hundred yards to cross until she could support herself on the rock wall. There was a stout branch up ahead she could use as a walking stick. She tried to pick it up but couldn't lean over far enough.

A hundred yards. She would have to make it to the rock formation without support, would have to get there fast. If she fell and didn't break anything, she would crawl. No time for hypotheticals. She would get there, period. She stood for a moment without the support of the jeep. Still shaky, still unsteady, she took her first step toward the rock formation.

***

Hollis, watching through his scope, decreased the magnification, widening his field of vision to take in the entire scene. What was he to make of it? He was high enough to see the Humvee and the old lady who had

241

taken a hard fall, then pulled herself up and managed to find a pistol and holster. What kind of pistol? It looked real, but the fabric holster told him it wasn't. He kept his scope trained on her until she disappeared behind the outcropping. A little thought and he realized who she was: the woman from the Historical Society. Good that she was here. If she made it through the rock formation onto Shiller's side of the path, she wasn't going to do any damage. Shiller would see to that. But she *was* going to give the General the opportunity to eliminate the five people closest to the leak.

He studied the bear traps, all attached to a fat chain looped at either end around a tree trunk. Seven traps, five prisoners. Confusing, yes, but at least he could hook the old lady to his trotline. Was he waiting for others or were the extra traps superfluous? Hell if he knew, but Shiller's leisurely approach to his victims suggested that he was waiting. And if he wasn't, it made no difference.

Hollis had hoped Shiller would leave the two FBI agents in peace. He feared that their disappearance at the same time as the Carlyle House explosion would seem more than coincidence. Shiller, he was sure, had come to the same conclusion. The agents must have shown up with the others, giving him no choice. So it goes. You always have to deal with the unexpected.

The plan, from what he could tell, was to shoot the five who were already down there . . . and the other two he appeared to be waiting for. He would then use the bear traps to keep the bodies together. But why did he need to worry about keeping corpses together. They weren't going anywhere.

Then it hit him: the chains were to weight the bodies. This meant he planned to dump them in a deep body of water. That's where he imagined the Humvee was going too.

One of the big guys, keeping his gun trained on the smaller agent's head, stooped down and picked up a fat branch. He shoved the agent toward a trap at the far end of the line and brought the branch down on the trip plate. With awesome power, the trap snapped shut. It's teeth nearly chopped the end off the branch. The big guy twisted it until it broke, then shoved the agent to the next trap and conducted the same demonstration. No fun to watch if you were destined for one of those things, Hollis thought. But the man's antics answered one of his outstanding questions. Shiller was not waiting on anyone. He needed five traps, and five traps remained set.

Another question was why the General, who still held the blonde girl by the hair with his gun to her neck, was bothering to talk. It seemed crazy. The sun was about to rise; day was about to break. Why didn't he just get it over with? Well, Hollis mused, Shiller would have his reasons. He always did.

***

"Where's Gibbons?" Shiller asked.

"Coming for you," Beau said, believing she was still in the jeep.

"Good. It will save me an extra trip."

"If you're planning to make us an offer," Connor said, "the answer is no."

Shiller had wrapped Nellie's hair like a rope around one hand. He jerked her head, pressed his pistol into her neck until she let out a muffled cry, then he yanked her in Connor's direction. "I'm sorry you won't have right of first refusal. I have nothing to offer other than an explanation of what you, perhaps unknowingly, have done. A man or woman being put to death deserves as much. Don't you agree?"

"Show some mercy," Hatch said. "Shoot us now so we don't have to listen to you."

"There will perhaps be mercy, but of a different sort. You've seen the bear traps and what they can do. Mr. Wellington keeps looking at them, imagining Nellie's leg being snapped at the tibia, imagining the crack, imagining her screams. I don't believe any of you will have to endure that fate. It's too much work.

"The traps will keep you together in death. They will make certain a body does not flee your cohort and float to the winze surface of the Lucky Bore mine. If you're not familiar with the Lucky Bore mine, it's entrance is halfway up the mountain. It was abandoned in 1894, a year after the Sherman Silver Act. However, the entrance is still accessible by jeep.

"The first shaft is angled at 45 degrees and is large enough to drive a train into. The shaft ends at the top of a vertical winze almost one half mile deep that is now filled with toxic water. You and your military vehicle will sink to the bottom of that winze, where you will enjoy a wet, cold and very silent grave.

"Now, Agent Hatcher, I have explained the mercy you will receive. But you will have to listen to me a bit longer. And I don't want a sound out of any of you. One peep and I will let Ms. Vaughn experience what a bear feels when he steps on a trap. It is, I imagine, like having your leg ripped off by a shark.

"Death is the penalty for treason, which you have committed. I am determined to make America great again, both here and abroad. We cannot attain my goal with our present system of government. I don't deny the truth of what you all know. However, certain truths are easy to misinterpret. This is such a truth."

A light breeze rippled through the pines. Shiller ventured a hint of a smile as he drew in a deep breath. "What I and my men have done would have happened anyway. God's Wrath has managed to recruit a large number of top scientists from the West and elsewhere. The group will have the capacity to replicate and go beyond our own work in a matter of years. And our country, as I have shown, is entirely incapable of defending itself."

Connor started to say something. Shiller nearly pulled Nellie off her feet as he quickly fired his gun into the air. He returned it to her neck. "I haven't finished. I want you to hear what I tell my people when the issue of killing Americans arises. We are at war. War requires sacrifice. Those who have given their lives on our soil have given their lives for America. Their sacrifice has made my rise to the presidency possible. They have contributed to the salvation of the United States.

"Had they died on foreign soil defending our country, they would be considered heroes. Heroes, even though they fought to maintain a political system that is allowing our once great country to sink into the muck of mediocrity. Think about it. The present sacrifice of 65,000 of our compatriots will save millions in the next few years. And it will accomplish so much more.

"I am a patriot of the highest order, as are those who serve with me. I'm afraid the existing political and legal systems would take a different view. By spreading word of the means I have selected to awaken the country we all love, word that could never be interpreted correctly, you have interfered with a sacred mission.

"I'm glad I could stop you at this point. Perhaps, Agents Connor and Hatcher, you're not aware of the diversity of allegiances with the Bureau. Some of your agents, for example, keep me exceedingly well-informed of developments on the West Coast. Friends in the intelligence community and Justice Department do the same in their jurisdictions. Your story is not known to others. It will die forever with – "

A frantic thrashing nearby startled everyone. Beau knew what it was. The drugged lion had awoken. With lightening reflexes, he spun and delivered a fist to the solar plexus of the man holding a gun to his head. The

244

man went down. His gun skittered away. When he lunged for his pistol, Beau caught him with a foot to the side of the head. The man seemed dazed, paralyzed, scarcely able to move. Beau kicked his pistol away and came down hard on his back.

Connor and Hatch used the distraction to turn the table on the men behind them. In seconds their guns were in the hands of the agents, jammed into their backs so that a shot would exit through the heart.

"Wellington, watch," Shiller shouted. "Watch!" Slowly he slid his pistol up Nellie's neck to her ear.

***

"Over here," screamed H. L., who had made her way to the rock formation and beyond. She had the General's flank in her sights and fired. Nellie saw the dart sticking out of his side and instinctively grabbed his arm. It felt like an iron bar. His gun didn't move from her ear. She closed her eyes. The end had come.

***

Hollis watched through his scope as a drama more intense than anything he had experienced in combat unfolded. The Ole Miss footballer turned on the huge guy with the gun and knocked him to the ground. Almost simultaneously, the FBI agents pulled some tricky Quantico moves on their unsuspecting captors.

By then he had already made his decision. The mission was over. Who could say if Shiller would be taken alive. You never knew how a person would behave in combat . . . or in captivity. He might give up the identities of his disciples. He had to go.

Hollis had squeezed the trigger of his sniper's rifle just as the old lady he had written off fired the dart gun. It wasn't a long shot, only 700 yards. It would take the bullet less than a second to travel that distance. Shiller was going to shoot the girl in the head . . . or so thought Shiller. An instant before he assassinated her, Hollis's .338 Lapua Magnum slug shattered his skull. He watched Shiller fall as he fired. The bullet meant for Nellie, Shiller's bullet, struck him in his own hand.

The girl's hair, free at last, tumbled in every which direction. She yanked the dart from Shiller's flank and ran toward Ole Miss. Smart girl.

Hollis had no idea how much the gatekeepers knew. They might sing under duress if they had anything to say. He thought for a brief second about what he should do, then decided there was no reason to take risks. He would make a clean sweep of it before he got the hell out of here. He fired three carefully aimed shots before slipping quietly and swiftly through the pines.

"Let's move!" Connor shouted. "And don't worry about bullets. If they were targeting us, they'd still be firing. Beau, Nellie, help H. L. to the jeep while we wipe any fingerprints. Don't just stand there!"

"Agent Connor," Nellie said, remarkably composed after what she had been through. "We're not going anywhere until we spring those remaining traps."

"Give me a break. Let's go."

"Sorry. We brought a pet cat up here. He saved us all when he woke up and started his crazy thrashing. Then there's Rommel, the cat Shiller feeds. You might not like cats, but these two saved us. We're not letting them die a horrible death. So how do we spring the traps?" She and Beau started looking around for the kind of fat branch Kyle had used on traps six and seven. Nothing but rocks and pine needles.

"Jesus Christ!" Connor erupted. "Those are mountain lions. Who cares what happens to them?"

"I do. Beau does. H. L. has let out her friend's pet. And there's something else. The fake scent. Beau can pour what he has left of it over the bodies. You can forget about prints on everything but the guns. We've solved your problem. Now it's your turn to do us a favor."

"Jesus Christ!" Connor shouted again. "Jesus Holy Christ. Convicted because of animal lovers. That's how the papers will read." He saw an image of Betty holding her cat in one arm, her Shi Tzu in the other. It looked like he was on the losing side.

Beau and Hatch had, in the meantime, accepted reality. While Hatch wiped the dropped pistols, Beau dragged Shiller to one of the traps. He lifted his leg at the knee and, holding his upper tibia, drove his foot onto the trip plate. The medieval-looking ring with the rusty spikes slammed shut. A crack echoed off the rocks, the crack of a bone snapping like a twig. Connor joined in, springing two more traps with two of the gatekeepers. Beau took care of the third gatekeeper, then shoved Shiller's arm into the last loaded trap.

"The scent," Nellie cried. "Beau, shake it out on the bodies, the most on Shiller's. Then, Agent Connor, then we can go."

*   *   *

"Leave it idling," Robert told Connor, who had just pulled into the overgrown parking spot behind the cabin. "Sorry, H. L. I've got to be in Gunnison by noon."

"About the battle scars," Connor said. "Get 'em fixed and send H. L.

246

the bill. We'll take care of it."

"No bill," Robert said. "The thing looks better now than before."

When everyone was out of the jeep, including the bag of potential evidence, Robert drove between the towering cottonwood trees and onto the road along the river.

"Better than before?" Connor shook his head. "It looks like a giant bumper car to me."

"A bumper car you won't miss," Hatch said as the Humvee disappeared around a curve. "We'd better go inside and discuss what we do next."

"The back door is open," H. L. murmured. She was leaning on Beau for support. He picked her up without asking. Long after he deposited her in a chair, the words Stonewall, Robert E. Lee and Johnny Reb echoed in his ears.

Nellie hung back with Connor, who was ambling along at a leisurely pace. "I would never have believed it," she said, smiling. "Never."

"Believed what?" Connor seemed intent on knowing. "WHAT?"

"That you have a secret lover in Prague. I know who Kristýna Sondheim is."

"Goddammit. You THINK you know who she is. You don't. She's my UNICEF kid."

Nellie put her arm through his. "You're a good man, Agent Connor. Big trouble, but a good man."

***

The next afternoon, Hatch and Connor returned their rental car to the Hertz office at the Denver Airport. Hatch put the keys on the counter.

"Hey," the agent said, "don't I know you?"

"I believe we've been through this before."

"What? I just got transferred here yesterday. You work at Wells Fargo in Bismarck, right? Car loans."

Hatch turned to Connor. "Not a word," he said. "Not even a peep."

EPILOGUE

Several days later . . .

Contingency plans were numerous. No one doubted that an operation with so many moving parts was susceptible to catastrophic failure. C-19 was the only plan that did not include Shiller; the only plan he had not helped to design; the only plan of which he was unaware. Whether he would have objected to its existence was a question that accompanied him to the grave.

Contingency Plan 19 spelled out the actions members of the group were to take if Shiller was killed or captured, possibly putting them at risk. It called for immediate departure from North America, with access to at least four separate identities. Passports, clothes and other necessities were stored in the lockboxes of reputable banks – one identity near the pre-planned escape airports in the United States, three in equally secure locations around the globe. No one would leave from the same airport or land in the same country.

Only after the last leg of their journey, which was to Paris, would they meet again – as employees of an international vitamin supplement company whose papers had been legitimately filed in Jakarta. Whether the conference goers arrived at one of the city's two international airports, or by rail, they were to pick up their hotel assignments and itineraries at a travel agency on the Rue de Rivoli.

Ten of the original 12 disciples, lightly disguised, arrived at the Novotel Paris Gare Montparnasse as scheduled. The meeting began at three o'clock in the afternoon in a small but well-appointed conference room. After a short break, Hollis continued their exchange of ideas.

"I have described the events that convinced me to eliminate the General. We must now make a decision that won't be easy."

"Excuse me, Jake, but Jim and Allen are absent. Shouldn't they be in

248

on this?"

"Jim and Allen are dead. Shiller gave them a chance to repair the damage their leak had caused – or at least transform it into unreliable hearsay by eliminating those closest to it. They failed. When they found out the girl who had overheard them in the kitchen had survived their assassination attempt, they must have been consumed by an insane desire for revenge. When she returned to her home, they stole a bucket truck from the local phone company. Then, posing as telephone workers, they tried to shoot her through a window. Instead of killing her, they electrocuted themselves. They were found fried to a crisp, their rifles welded to the bucket. Anyway, we came painfully close to achieving our objective. Those of us here today worked brilliantly and discretely for long years, driven not by ego but by love of country. What now? Do we use our knowledge to help God's Wrath? Do we gamble on the prospect this will bring sanity to our nation's leadership? Or do we go our separate ways?"

The large window looked out onto the street. Rain had begun to fall. The heavy overcast obscured the tops of high buildings, and the wind shook the leaves of the London Plane trees lining the sidewalk.

After a long silence, the same woman spoke again. "Jake, we should take a while to think on this, several weeks or more. A rash decision could have unintended consequences."

"I fully agree," Hollis said. "How about Islamabad in a month? Objections?"

There were none.

Two weeks later . . .

Connor tried to wash down a bite of bran muffin with a drop of espresso, but his cup was dry. "Jesus," he grumbled. "I feel like I'm in prison."

"Come on, Randall. There's not a more beautiful place on earth."

It was Saturday. They sat in an outdoor café in Santa Monica under a large brightly colored umbrella. A light breeze wafted in from the Pacific, carrying off the heat of the South California sun. The potted plants lining the terrace gave off an alluring fragrance, and the azure sky stretched unbroken to the horizon. Hatch had brought Connor here to begin the second day of his diet and exercise program.

"I can't see beauty when I'm choking," Connor said. "Can't I get a pot of regular coffee? It hasn't got any calories."

"You can't, Randall, because they only serve upscale drinks here. How's the muffin?"

"Inedible without butter."

"Listen, my friend, you're going to have to change your attitude. You asked me to put you on a program that would have you looking great for Prague. You also asked me *not* to let you quit. You'll see when we get to the gym why you don't want a Sheriff Cousins breakfast sloshing around in your stomach."

"The gym? We have to do that too?"

Hatch tapped the shopping bags on the chair beside him. "You gave me 200 bucks to make sure you had the right work-out things. I picked them up for you yesterday afternoon."

"So I walk in there with shopping bags?"

"We'll get you a stylish sports tote on the way over. I'll take care of everything. Locker, head bands, membership, Fitbit, all of that. Anyway, what did you make of the preliminary report?"

"Garbage, as expected, but not their fault. Imagine the crime scene, Hatch. They find Shiller and his three bodyguards, or what was left of them after being gnawed to the bone by mountain lions, with bullet holes in their heads. Bullet holes made by the same rifle that downed El Lobo and that creep of a Veep candidate. And that's just the start. Shiller shot himself in the hand with his own pistol, and all four of these guys were stuck in bear traps, bones crushed, wounds licked dry of blood by lions."

"Also, Randall, forensics has confirmed the shots were fired from closer up and that the shooter had a downward trajectory. I think I know which peak he was on."

"Don't tell anyone, for Christ's sake, or they'll put us back on the investigation."

"Okay, partner. For once I agree. We can't let that happen. Enough is enough. Want to split another muffin?"

Connor stared at his empty espresso thimble. "Hatch, I've just changed my mind."

"Oh? On what?"

"I can't do this diet and work-out shit for more than a day. If she loves someone I'm not, someone who's miserable all the time, is that what *I* really want?"

"So you're not going to Prague in December?"

"Wrong, partner. I'm going. But I'm going as me. No disguises. She can take it or leave it."

"She'll probably leave it."

"I guess that's her call. Listen, Hatch. I noticed a real breakfast place up the hill. Care to drop me off on your way to the gym?"

Connor stood, picked up the bags of work-out stuff Hatch had gotten him and strolled to the nearest recycle bin. When he stuffed them into it, he gave another push to make sure they didn't resurface.

Hatch noticed something on his partner's face he hadn't seen before: joy, pure innocent joy, the joy of a happy kid.

One month later . . .

"The Aspen leaves are beginning to turn gold," Beau said. "It's amazing how they seem to dance in the sunlight. I didn't believe you. I didn't believe the cat had come home, either." He pulled tight and latched the last strap of the tarp covering his truck bed.

Nellie stood on tiptoes and kissed him. "He came home, that cat, but he forgot to close the gate." They laughed and kissed again.

H. L. was drinking a stiff morning pour of Johnnie Walker. She shifted in her chair, a $1000 Victorian beauty Beau had carelessly dragged outside and placed in the shade. "Do you kids need to be so intimate?" she asked, sounding mildly disgusted.

"H. L., we're in love!"

"I hadn't noticed."

"Well, that should do it," Beau said. "Will you be okay, H. L?"

"Of course."

"And you'll honor your promise to visit us in New Orleans?"

"Yes, when I've recovered. I didn't tell you, but I'm scheduled for surgery at Johns Hopkins end of next month. The film from Mayo convinced them that an experimental technique will work on my back."

"That's great," Beau said. "I hope it does."

"I'm sure you do, Dixie. Otherwise you'll have to drag me through another tunnel."

"I'll be waiting by the phone."

"Cut it out, you two," Nellie said. "We were serious, H. L. You can stay with us while you recover. We'll show you everything from The Big Easy to Lake Providence!"

"A dream come true." H. L. drained her glass. "Who knows? I might surprise you. I'm going to miss you terribly, Nellie. It won't be easy running the Historical Society alone from a real-estate office downtown."

"I thought the City had found the original plans for the Carlyle House."

"They have. But you know how they are. It's going to take forever to rebuild."

"H. L.," Beau said, "I have a deal to propose."

"Southerners always have deals to propose."

"You might like this one."

"Don't get your hopes up, Dixie."

"I want to donate this house, the Emma Claire, to the Historical Society. When the City manages to finish the Carlyle House, you can give it back to me, keep it, sell it, do whatever you want. You're the most incredible woman I've ever known . . . with the possible exception of my Aunt Lilly. It doesn't matter whether you like me or not. This is my gift to you."

"But Beau, you and Nellie were going to spend summers here."

"We still are. Don't forget. I own three other Victorian houses. Fully restored, thanks to your friend, General Shiller. I don't think we'll have a lodging problem."

"See, H. L.," Nellie said. "This guy is too good to be true."

The old woman managed to get to her feet. "I'm going to tell you both a secret," she said. "I've been of that opinion for months." She glanced over at Beau who, as usual, was wearing an Ole Miss T-Shirt and faded jeans. "If anyone had told me last year I would be doing this, I would have called Social Services. But life really is full of surprises. Come here, Dixie. I want to give you a hug."

♦ Books by Thomas Kirkwood ♦

The Quiet Assassin

Lacking Virtues

SAVE ITALY Forget the Rest
(Writing as Tommy Vilar)

The Svalbard Passage

The Trade

The Poppy Broker

FAITH A Secret Life
(Writing as Chub Yublinsky)